"I need to talk to you...."

Caleb insisted. "Can I stop by later and take you out to dinner?"

"I don't know—" Rae began.

"It concerns the case, Rae."

Though his words were gently spoken, she sensed a force of will behind them that more than matched her own. Oh, well. Why not get it over with? He wasn't asking for a date. He wanted information for his investigation.

"Six-thirty then." She sighed. "And just for dinner."

"Such enthusiasm for my company."

"I'm as enthusiastic as you are."

"Ah." Dancing lights sparked through his eyes. "In that case, it should be a very... interesting evening."

SARA MITCHELL

A popular and highly acclaimed author in the Christian market, her aim is "to depict the struggle between the challenges of everyday life and the values to which our faith would have us aspire." The author of seven contemporary and two historical suspense novels, her work has been published by many Inspirational book publishers.

Having lived in diverse locations from Georgia to California to Great Britain, her extensive travel experience helps her create authentic settings for her books. A lifelong music lover, Sara has also written several musical dramas and has long been active in the music ministries of the churches wherever she and her husband, a retired career air force officer, have lived. The parents of two daughters, Sara and her husband now live in Virginia.

Night Music

Sara Mitchell

Love Inspired

Published by Steeple Hill Books™

STEEPLE HILL BOOKS

Steeple
Hill™

ISBN 0-373-87013-2

NIGHT MUSIC

Copyright © 1998 by Sara Mitchell
Text revised for Love Inspired™ edition

Copyright © 1989 by Sara Mitchell
First published by Accent Publishing under the
title *Walk in Deep Shadows*

This edition published by arrangement with Steeple Hill Books.

® and TM are trademarks of Steeple Hill Books, used under license.
Trademarks indicated with ® are registered in the United States Patent
and Trademark Office, the Canadian Trade Marks Office and in other
countries.

Printed in U.S.A.

The Lord is my light and my salvation; whom shall I fear? The Lord is the strength of my life; of whom shall I be afraid?

—*Psalms* 27:1

With grateful thanks to Linda Phillips and
Dawn Dale-Bartow, for their cheerful assistance:
Linda, for functioning as a go-between;
Dawn, for lending her legal expertise
to bail me out of a plotting snarl.
Couldn't have done it without you both!

Prologue

Carnegie Hall, 1989

All eyes in the audience were riveted upon the second of three finalists in the prestigious Jeremy Lake Piano Competition—a young girl still in her teens. Anticipation mounted as the orchestra approached the tumultuous climax of Liszt's Piano Concerto no. 2 in A Major. At the front of the stage, an oblivious Rae Prescott waited, hands poised over the keyboard of the grand piano. Her heart swelled along with the music as she automatically counted. *Five more measures...three...steady. Don't rush it—now!*

The final crescendo poured from her fingers in a soaring burst of energy. Even after the music stopped, the last notes rang in the packed auditorium. Rae sat, head bowed, hands quiet while her spirit protested the descent into reality. It was over. The competition for which she had practiced and dreaded and anticipated for eleven months was over. The course of her future hovered somewhere between the first measure she'd played— and the decision of the blank-faced judges seated out front.

Then the wave of applause crashed over her. Slowly Rae straightened, lifted her head. Her stunned gaze focused first on Alexi Barinsky, the conductor. He was clapping. *Clapping.* For *her*. Even more incredible—he was *smiling*. Barinsky never smiled at the finalists. Never.

As if in a dream, Rae managed to stand and execute a graceful bow. Then she realized that the audience had also risen, to give her a thunderous standing ovation. A smile spread across her perspiration-streaked face, and she blinked back tears of joy and humility. The applause resounded in her ears, cascading into her bloodstream so that her pulse began to beat in rhythm with the clapping.

Poise wavered when her tear-bright gaze focused on the gaunt figure of Uncle Floyd, applauding so vigorously his thin face above the white Mark Twain mustache had turned the color of a ripe tomato. Everything Rae had accomplished in the last dozen years—from the tentative plunking of childish fingers to this present triumphant moment—was due to her uncle. The smile suddenly filled her face, and in a spontaneous rush of affection she blew him a kiss. Laughter and another storm of applause followed her as she floated gracefully into the wings.

"Miss Prescott?"

Still smiling, Rae turned to two sober-faced men in neat suits who had stepped forward, blocking her way. Behind them, the final contestant brushed by, walking onto the stage to fresh applause. "Yes?" Rae wondered fleetingly who the men could be and how they had circumvented security. She tucked loose strands of the slipping chignon behind her ears and smoothed tired hands down her long black skirt.

"I'm Agent Kevin Davis, and this is Agent John Landis." A shiny badge flashed briefly in front of her face. "We're sorry to intrude at a time like this...."

"You play beautifully," Agent Landis added. A band of red stained his cheeks and the bridge of his nose.

"Ms. Prescott—" Agent Davis paused, sweeping Rae in rapid, faintly regretful assessment "—this concerns your father."

"My father?" As though whisked into a dark soundproofed room, applause and movement ceased. The notes still dancing in her head died in a shattered instant. "I haven't seen or heard from my father since I was four." Her lips felt stiff, and she had to force the words past a constricted throat.

"Yes, well...he was arrested late last night, up in Michigan near the Canadian border, and I'm afraid we need to ask you and your uncle some questions."

Chapter One

Colorado Springs, Colorado
Present Day

It was late, a little before ten o'clock, when Rae finally pulled into the driveway of the red sandstone Victorian mansion, home for over twenty years now. With a faint exasperated mutter she turned off the engine and climbed out of her car, juggling a sack of groceries on one hip. The narrow walk leading to the back entrance to the kitchen was completely dark because once again she had forgotten to replace the burned-out lightbulb on the back porch light. *It only needed this.* With the way her day had gone, next she'd probably trip and break her ankle on the uneven sidewalk.

Thin streams of moonlight fought their way through wispy clouds, casting shadows on the driveway and over the lawn. The turrets and gables that made the Prescott mansion a city landmark at this moment loomed more as dark, subtly menacing shapes. Rae paid little attention. For her, the massive pile of bricks, as her older brother described the house, was *home*. Right now, all she wanted was a soothing mug of hot tea before she collapsed for the night.

Choir practice had run longer than usual, since Easter was only three weeks away. Unfortunately, the church choir still sounded less than triumphantly joyful, and Rae's feet dragged as she inched her way up the back steps. As keyboard accompanist for the church, she sympathized with the beleaguered choir director's frustrations, though she had learned to stifle her impatience as well as her training behind a smiling mask. Jerry knew she had trained at Juilliard, knew she had been on the way to the top as a concert pianist—but he didn't need to have his face rubbed in it. Besides, he had far more training than Rae at directing oftimes untrained all-volunteer choirs.

"All right...where *is* that key?" she grumbled, fumbling in her purse.

Off to the right, the untrimmed hedge of evergreen bushes stirred, rustling in the brisk night silence. That wretched mutt! Rae thought. She plopped the sack and her purse on the stoop, then peered beneath the shadow-dark bushes. For almost a week now, the stray dog had been wandering around the neighborhood, pilfering garbage and digging holes, eluding the Humane Society while ignoring annoyed residents who shooed him away. Rae had discreetly left meat scraps by the garage a couple of times, though she was careful not to share her softheartedness with the neighbors. Unfortunately, yesterday the animal had tried to bite old Elijah Mortenson, who lived two houses down from Rae.

"Scram, mutt," she called softly. "I'm too tired to be nice, and I'm out of scraps. Besides which, you've about outstayed your welcome around here." Mr. Mortenson might be irascible, but he didn't deserve to be bitten by a stray dog. And the DeVries family across the street had two small children.

There was no response, not even a growl or the sound of retreating paws. For a moment Rae listened, shivering in the cold black shadows of the lightless porch. "That's it," she finally announced. Stepping down, she groped along the edge of the walk until her fingers closed over a rock. "Scram!" she repeated, shooting the rock into the bushes.

Instead of a canine yelp, a rough, bitten-off curse split the night like the unexpected explosion of a shotgun. A dark amorphous figure erupted from the bushes, and a face smeared with black paint turned directly toward Rae. For a frozen second she stared in numb disbelief.

Then the figure took a step toward her. Rae whirled, stumbled up the two porch steps and clawed for her purse. The Mace. Where was the can of Mace she always kept in her purse? Clumsy with fright, her fingers closed over metal and she yanked it out, dropping the purse as she whipped around and aimed the can.

Just as she opened her mouth to scream, the man tore off across the lawn and disappeared around the corner of the house. A few seconds later Rae heard the faint scrunching sound of his footsteps fleeing across the street. The noise echoed loudly in her ears, pounding in rhythm with her stampeding pulse.

A long, trembling moment passed. Finally Rae lowered her arms, gathered her belongings and fumbled her way inside. Methodically she turned the lock, fastened the dead bolt and deposited the groceries on the kitchen counter. Then she forced herself to walk down the long hall to the music store, which now comprised the front rooms of the mansion. All clear. She checked the rooms at the back where she lived. As near as she could tell, the man hadn't broken into the house.

She called the police and made herself a cup of hot tea while she waited for them to arrive.

Officer Nash was a tall, hard-looking man with penetrating brown eyes. He walked through the entire house, including the unused levels. There was no evidence of a break-in, no evidence of even an *attempted* break-in. There was nothing to prove that a prowler existed, though the policeman did point out to Rae that searching the place by herself had been foolhardy.

"We'll keep a patrol check in the area for a while," he promised. "But that's about all we can do right now—hiding in your bushes is not considered a crime, since your yard isn't fenced in." One corner of his mouth lifted. "That foot-high stone wall doesn't count as a fence."

"You mean anybody can skulk around in my bushes, and I can't do anything about it?" Incensed, Rae shook her head, amazed and disconcerted when the world-weary police officer shrugged.

"'Fraid that's about the size of it, for now."

"What about trespassing?" She glared, trying to get a glimpse past the man's urbane facade. His casual acceptance of the world's unpleasantnesses sent shivers dancing down her spine.

Of course, his world and hers had about as much in common as hard metal rock and a Mozart sonata.

Light from the hallway streamed out the open back door, glinting off Officer Nash's badge and the butt of the revolver at his waist where one hand idly rested. He glanced at the burned-out light and frowned. "You ought to fix that," he observed mildly, thankfully ignoring Rae's rising temper. "Ms. Prescott, we'd like to promise safety to all the upright citizens living here, but anymore that's just not possible."

The hot words trembled on her lips. Rae prayed she would manage to keep her lips zipped and the words unspoken. It wasn't as though she'd asked the Springs Police Department for round-the-clock protection. But still...

"I've always liked this old place," Officer Nash commented, glancing down the angled hall with its golden oak walls and turn-of-the-century sconces. "I take it one of your ancestors built it, since your surname is Prescott."

"My great-grandfather."

"And you live alone?"

Her chin lifted. "Yes, I do."

"Well...just be careful." He started down the porch steps, then paused and looked back. "A prowler's a nebulous call—unless and until an actual crime is committed, there's not a lot we can do." He looked as if he'd like to say more, but he must have sensed Rae's tenuous control and contented himself with a polite farewell. "Call if you need us."

I did call, she felt like yelling. *And a fat lot of good it did.* Taking a deep breath, she forced herself to methodically bolt and chain the door. Why had she had to inherit the tempestuous side of her mother's nature, anyway? Every day Rae struggled against the lifelong fear of losing control. The image of her mother during that last nightmarish year loomed in her memory—the screaming frenzies and drug-induced temper tantrums that had terrified Rae and her older brother, Tyler.

All her life, Rae had vowed to be different from her mother. She would never be sweet and gullible—nor turn without warning to a screaming termagant. Never be weak. Never depend or anything or anyone. Except God, of course. It was acceptable to acknowledge God's sovereignty when you were a Christian. Whether a prowler leaped out of the bushes or a policeman patronized her, she was supposed to call on God's help to stay in control.

"I'm fine," she murmured, walking slowly to the tiny galley kitchen, where she stood staring sightlessly at the old-fashioned appliances, the wooden cabinets she had finally repainted last month. "Absolutely no reason to be afraid." Her cup of hot tea—stone cold now, of course—sat on the burnished maple parson's table. Rae very carefully emptied the mug, rinsed it and propped it in the drainer.

Her hands were trembling.

"I'm not afraid." She defiantly turned out the lights and marched down the hall to her bedroom. "I'm in control, and I'm not afraid."

But that night, for the first time since she was ten years old, Rae left a light burning all night long.

Chicago, Illinois

Caleb Myers sprawled bonelessly as a cat in Jackson Overstreet's office as the president of Polaris Corporation explained the reason behind his panicked call. Polaris specialized in space-tracking technologies and at present had a contract with the U.S. Air Force in Colorado Springs.

Two days earlier, the civilian contractor had called to warn Polaris that their system had been sabotaged.

"We're pretty sure it's a virus program," Overstreet said, his face bleak. "The OSI's working it from that end, along with the FBI, but I figured you'd still be the best behind-the-scenes man for the job." The corner of his mouth twitched briefly. "Fortunately, the FBI agreed, probably because of your reputation."

Caleb idly toyed with his watchband. "I'll do what I can, and of course since my contract's with Polaris, you'll have my first loyalty. Professional as well as personal. But you also know interagency cooperation is dicey at best, and an independent is seldom welcomed by any of them. I'll have to be careful and keep my end of things primarily to consulting." He sat back, keeping his uneasiness hidden. He was a private computer security consultant, and he and Jackson had been friends for years.

Both men had been around the block enough to know how the game was played, especially in the nation's capital.

But Jack also knew Caleb wouldn't turn down a friend in trouble, no matter how many other agencies were involved—or the personal inconvenience.

"There's not another man or woman on either coast who can sniff out computer fraud like you, Cal," Overstreet said, almost as though he could hear Caleb's thoughts.

With a deep sigh Caleb sat up straight in the chair and fixed a congenial but penetrating stare across the desk. "Then why didn't you call me eighteen months ago, when you lost that Navy contract? From what you've just told me, the circumstances that resulted in that debacle sound like the same sort of sabotage as the Starseeker case." He studied his friend, carefully wiping any censure from his expression and voice.

"You were in Europe at the time," Jackson answered. "Besides, my own security people are some of the best in the business. At the time we had no reason to suspect any problems beyond faulty technology."

"Until your canceled project with its faulty technology turned up six months later in a rival company—no longer faulty."

"Yeah," Jack agreed heavily. He exchanged a frustrated look with Caleb before turning to pick up a bulging accordian folder from his desk. He thrust it toward Caleb.

"I understand three of the people who worked on that Navy project are also out at Falcon now?" Caleb murmured, leafing through the folder.

"Right. Wilson, Forbes and Fisher." Abruptly the other man jerked upright and slammed his palms on the waxed mahogany desktop. "Cal, they've all been with Polaris five years or more! Not only are they required to update their security clearance regularly, but I pay them enough to keep them in a life-style an Arabian sheik would envy. It's *got* to be someone from the outside!"

"Take it easy, Jack." Caleb stood and strolled around to give his friend a commiserating slap on the shoulder. "Whoever it is, we'll find them. I'll fly down to the Springs tonight, all right? Whatever turns up, you don't want to lose another contract."

"You're mighty right about that. Thanks, man. I knew I could depend on you to keep a level head." Overstreet shook his head.

"Even after all these years, you never cease to amaze me, Cal—you and your infernal detachment. We used to place bets, back at the university, as to what it would take to rattle your cage."

Sometimes Caleb wondered the same thing. "Well, let's hope this won't be it." He tucked the folder under his arm. "I'll be in touch as soon as I can. In the meantime, try not to worry yourself into an early grave."

"Sorry about your vacation."

Caleb waved an indifferent hand. "The ocean'll still be there when I can get away, as will my boat. And my folks are used to me not showing up for the annual Easter reunion." He enjoyed going to the rambling old house on the Georgia coast whenever he could, because he knew how much it meant to the family. But this year, Jack's frantic call had been a relief. Sometimes his mother couldn't resist nagging him about his single status, much less his habitual isolation.

"You have the instincts of a caring pastor but the personality of a hermit," she'd complained the last time he flew home to visit. "Why couldn't you have gone to seminary, like your Dad and I wanted you to? At least maybe you'd be *married* by now, instead of chasing crooks all over the earth."

Caleb drove to his apartment with absentminded skill, so used to the maniacal Chicago traffic he could have been driving down a deserted country lane with the same unruffled calm. Three hours later he caught the last flight for Colorado Springs, settling back against the first-class seat with a serene smile for the flight attendant. Her professional aplomb crumbled into blushing promises of solicitude for the duration of the flight. Caleb found himself struggling with the inward battle against cynicism he'd been fighting for what seemed like years. Would the pretty flight attendant have promised the same good service had he been some balding, middle-aged and conspicuously married passenger in an economy seat?

Shaking his head, he forced his mind to the problem ahead of him and his attention to the three Polaris employees whose dossiers filled the accordian file folder—a lot more productive use of his time than fruitless mental conundrums. Human nature being what it was, he figured one or more of Overstreet's hand-picked associates—albeit unwillingly—would soon provide the key to the solution of the sabotaged Starseeker technology. *Sorry, Jack,* he whispered to his absent friend. *There's a Judas lurking on every street corner. And as always, the innocent suffer the most.*

Chapter Two

～

Heavy gray clouds rolling sluggishly over the tops of snow-sprinkled mountains greeted Rae the next morning. The thermometer on the outside of the kitchen window had plunged below the freezing mark. While water boiled for her tea she gloomily watched the clouds swallowing the foothills. There would doubtless be a snowstorm by afternoon.

The weather suited Rae's mood. She stood at the window, sipping tea, thinking of all the tasks facing her today that would have to be dealt with regardless of her mood or circumstances.

After tugging on corduroy slacks and a cowl-necked sweater, she hurriedly ate an English muffin and juice before opening the store. The darkened rooms were quiet, serene. Blessedly normal, as though the terror of the previous night had never occurred. She hoped enough customers would descend before the snow to keep her busy enough to forget last night's incident.

Joyful Noise, Rae's store, specialized in religious and classical sheet music, though she tried to stock a smattering of popular and seasonal songs, as well. She had converted the parlor, living room and a small sitting area to accommodate the store, while leaving enough rooms at the back for living quarters. To conserve heating costs she had closed the upstairs off after Uncle Floyd died. Between the store's income, her salary as the church accompanist and the piano students three afternoons a week, Rae was just able to keep the wolf from the door.

Her brother had finally quit nagging her to give it up and move to New York where he claimed opportunities abounded for an ex-classical pianist and winner of the prestigious Jeremy Lake Competition. "As if you'd know," Rae muttered as she flipped light switches around the rooms. Tyler Prescott might have elbowed his way up the financial ladder to become a successful stockbroker, but what he knew about musical careers wouldn't fill a demitasse cup.

Apparently the threat of bad weather had persuaded customers to run their errands early. When Rae crossed the huge parlor to flip the Open/Closed sign, she was startled to find a woman waiting outside the double oak doors.

"Good morning," Rae said, dragging open the heavy doors after she finally forced the stubborn, antiquated lock to release. "You must be trying to beat the weather."

"It's almost five past nine," the woman snapped, eschewing social pleasantries. A statuesque brunette who looked to be in her early forties, she brushed by Rae and hurried inside, darting a quick, inquisitive glance around the room. Sharpish brown eyes came to rest on Rae. "I don't know much about music—I'm just trying to do a favor for a friend. I need a copy of—" she whipped out a folded piece of paper and glared at it "—Schubert's 'Marche Militaire,' it looks like. Could you hurry? I'm late for an appointment."

"Certainly," Rae returned equably, though her insides always clenched when customers treated her as though she were a personal servant. "That will be in this room." She gestured to the large front room where she kept the classical music, and the woman followed her, hovering impatiently while Rae found the piece.

Rae managed to suppress a smile while she rang up the purchase, but after the customer left, a laugh escaped. The woman had looked at the music as if it was a scroll of Egyptian hieroglyphics.

A few minutes later a couple of music teachers Rae knew from guild meetings bustled in to poke and prod in the bins. Then a young man stopped by to look for some contemporary Christian rock songs he could adapt to guitar. Rae helped him find something with the cheerful efficiency she showed the majority of customers. She tried hard not to hover—the streak of possessiveness might be understandable, but it was misplaced in a retail store.

After three years she was doing better, but there was still that occasional lost sale because she hated letting people paw haphazardly through what Rae considered *her* music. It was a secret point of pride that she knew almost to the sheet where every piece of music was located. When there were no customers or piano students she filled the time by checking the circular displays and the bins to make sure everything was in its proper place.

The morning passed uneventfully, though Rae heaved a sigh of relief when, a little before lunch, the tinkling doorbell announced the departure of a mother with two preschoolers. A man held the door for them before entering. Rae, busily restoring the scattered music in the small popular section, glanced back and smiled.

"Be with you in a minute," she called.

"No hurry," the man returned in a pleasant baritone. "I just wanted to look around."

Rats, Rae thought. Another browser. On the other hand, when she managed to leave them alone, sometimes browsers turned into her best customers. Tyler liked to point out in his infrequent communications that she was an idealistic fool to struggle for every dollar in the unstable market of retailing, especially a market that depended exclusively on sheet music. Rae would quietly remind him that at least she had successfully saved the best part of their heritage, even if he was determined to deny they had one. Not, of course, that Rae blamed him.

In an almost eerie echo of that train of thought, the man walked to the small circular alcove and stopped, speaking over his shoulder. "This place is fantastic. Do you know anything about its history?" His gaze roamed appreciatively over the hand-carved San Domingo mahogany and golden oak woodwork. Finally he turned and strolled to Rae.

She straightened, wiping her hands on her hips as she studied this unusual customer who seemed more interested in the woodwork than her store wares. On the surface, he presented a very attractive male package. Rae's best friend Karen would have been drooling by now. Ginger-ale-colored eyes framed by uncommonly thick eyelashes smiled into Rae's. His hair, slightly wavy and unruly with a lock falling over his left eyebrow, was the color of nutmeg, a delicious blend of brown and blond and maybe a hint of auburn. In sunlight it would be stunning.

He was probably shy of six feet but powerful looking, with broad shoulders, long, lean legs and a certain self-assured manner that made Rae feel oddly dominated by his presence in the confining space. Casually she wandered around him and into the parlor area. "I'm very familiar with the history," she said with a smile. "I've lived here most of my life."

"Oh?" One thick eyebrow lifted and disappeared in the unruly lock of hair. "Was it difficult, turning it into a store?"

"Yes...and no," Rae answered slowly. "Opening a store was the only solution I could come up with to keep from selling the house."

He nodded, the warm gaze sympathetic. "I imagine the property taxes alone rival the national debt."

Rae shrugged, hiding a sudden spurt of uneasiness. Something about this man—perhaps his very casualness—warned her that the friendly interest disguised an undisclosed agenda. A distinct current radiated from him, filling the room. Rae found herself watching his hands as he unbuttoned his trench coat. Her initial suspicion that he was a house-hungry Realtor faded. Those hands were not the slender, pampered hands of a man who spent his day behind a desk or the wheel of a fancy car. The fingers were long and strong-looking, the blunt fingertips topped by neatly trimmed nails, and the hand was large enough to span at least an octave and a half. *I bet he'd play a mean Grieg concerto*, Rae mused distractedly.

Whoever he was, she didn't believe he had stopped to browse.

"'I washed m'face 'n 'ands before I come,'" he quoted in a surprisingly accurate Cockney accent. Then he grinned. "*My Fair Lady*, remember? You're staring at my hands like my mother used to when she inspected them before dinner."

Rae was annoyed to feel a blush heat her cheeks. "Sorry. As a pianist, I guess I notice hands. Ah...are you a fan of late Victorian architecture?"

There was the slightest of pauses before the man replied. "Amateur league only, though. That staircase is a masterpiece, isn't it?'' He ran his hand over one of the elaborately carved griffins guarding either side of the stairs, then glanced at the stained glass window on the landing. "Mind if I go up?"

"I've closed it off," Rae said, then bit her lip at the abrupt tone. She couldn't afford to tell the man to either make a purchase or leave—but the temptation hovered on the tip of her tongue. "It costs too much to maintain when I—" She stopped, unable to believe she had almost blurted out that she lived alone. Last night's prowler highlighted the need for caution, but the undercurrent of poised alertness emanating from this man was almost as alarming as the unexpected intruder.

Rae adopted what she hoped was an expression of professional blandness. "You're welcome to look around the store itself if you like," she said, subtly emphasizing the word *store*.

The bell jangled, and with craven relief she turned to the new customer, an older man who wanted to select a solo to sing at his church. Rae spent the next few moments helping him look, but the whole time she felt as though a peregrine falcon was hovering, waiting for just the right moment to swoop upon her to...to *what?* Out of the corner of her eye she marked the amber-eyed man's progress. He strolled about the rooms, hands thrust in the hip pockets of his worn, faded jeans, looking for all the world as if he was admiring the architecture.

When the soloist was paying for his selection, the man came and stood behind him at the counter, slightly back, gaze seemingly lost in the middle distance. But Rae felt the intensity of his interest, and her lips tightened.

She took her time ringing up the purchase, walked with the chatting soloist to the door, then returned to barricade herself behind the counter. "Was there something, ah, *musical* you wanted?" she finally asked, head lowered as she noted the sale in her log book.

Without warning the man leaned over, resting his elbows on the high wooden counter, and Rae suppressed the urge to scoot backward. "Not today." He spoke very gently, but his eyes scorched Rae in a sweeping perusal. "I just want to tell you how much I admire your family home. And—" his head tilted "—to remind you to be careful." He nodded toward the door with the sign stating Private—Keep Out. "You live here alone, don't you?"

The pen dropped to the hardwood floor, clattering loudly on the scarred surface. "Why do you want to know?" Almost unconsciously her fingers began to play a Liszt melody on the countertop.

Shrugging, the man straightened to his full height. "Just wondered. This is a big house, located on a side street. A lot can happen unnoticed—especially to a single woman." Suddenly he grinned, a wholesome, boyish grin that Rae found disarming. "Wipe the militant gleam from your eye. I was merely making an observation. You *are* a woman. If you do live alone, conforming to the Christian beliefs implied by the Bible verse on that plaque hanging over the fireplace, then you're a *single* woman." The teasing grin faded, and he gave her a somber, penetrating look that would haunt Rae for days. "And you need to...be careful."

Rae straightened and regarded him with stormy eyes. "It's none of your business, but I'm perfectly fine. And I'm always careful." Rae stared into the man's amused eyes.

He smiled, a smile so free of artifice and deceit Rae responded in spite of herself. "I'm not here to harm you, Rae Prescott," he murmured. "I've always liked that quote on your plaque myself, but you ought to consider that you might need someone besides angels guarding you in all your ways." There was an electric silence.

Before Rae could gather her scattered senses for an appropriate retort he was gone, the cheerful tinkling of the bell lightly bouncing behind him.

Caleb let himself into the run-down but clean motel room he was renting by the week. He shrugged out of his coat and tossed it on the bed with one hand while the other reached for the phone. After he finished the call, he retrieved a small black notebook from the pocket of his coat, then made himself comfortable on the sagging bed, propping both pillows against the headboard.

For several moments he reviewed his notes, a resigned scowl faintly wrinkling his forehead. Then he picked up a ballpoint pen and jotted an additional note. "Checked out mansion—actually music store. Owner a woman, mid to late twenties. Single. Nervous.'' The wary gray eyes had watched him even when she was waiting on another customer.

Caleb paused, tapping the end of his nose with the pen. He was irritated when his thoughts stayed on Rae Prescott instead of the Starseeker case. Her slim straight back, stiffening like a poker when he was prowling her store. The way strands of her straight brown hair kept slipping free of the loose chignon she had fashioned, and how she kept tucking them absentmindedly behind her ear with incredibly long, slender fingers. Those fingers should have looked delicate and feminine, but instead they looked graceful and powerful. She was not particularly beautiful, not in the usual sense of the word. But attractive. Maybe too attractive. She was slim and not very tall, but strength and character shone out of her face.

Caleb had never had trouble concentrating before. As Jackson had pointed out, his detachment and ability to focus were legendary. But something about that lady played over his mind like a record needle stuck in a groove.

Lady. *That's* what it was. She reminded him of...not a Victorian lady, but an Edwardian one. Genteel, refined but strong. With a temper she was having trouble controlling at the end. Caleb knew he had made her nervous, even intimidated her, but she hadn't backed down an inch. He liked that.

He did *not* like liking that, and with grim determination forced his thoughts to his notebook and the Starseeker case. He'd been blessed with a photographic memory and didn't need to write anything down, but going through the motions usually helped pull together the missing pieces in most of his cases. He flipped back a few pages and read notes he'd made several days before. His scowl deepened as he began to write again. *F. been twice. Innocent or planned? P.M. watch starting tonight.*

He hoped, for Ms. Prescott's sake, that the surveillance would turn out to be boringly routine. He found himself hoping, as well, that she had understood the reassurance he had offered when he paraphrased the verse from Psalms.

Unfortunately, he had a feeling she'd better understood his warning.

Chapter Three

The storm dumped a little over two inches of snow, just enough to turn the surroundings into a winter wonderland postcard. Early the next morning, Rae stood on the back steps gazing into the yard, where sculptured dollops of sparkling white icing coated the low brick wall, the tree branches.

The bushes where the prowler had hidden the other night.

Her smile faded. Then, shaking off the tension, Rae tightened her grip on the handle of the snow shovel and cleared off the steps and a path to the detached garage. She only had an hour before time to open the store. Dry and powdery, the snow flew in showers of sunlit powdered sugar, and the scrape of metal on the walk rang out in the frosty air. Across the street, Mr. DeVries emerged from his house, briefcase in hand, and they exchanged waves. Pausing for breath, Rae watched as his car backed out and drove cautiously down the plowed street. Her eye wandered over the pristine white blanket of her yard, as yet unmarred by footprints—

At first she couldn't believe it. Dropping the shovel, she took a hesitant step, then tugged off a mitten to rub her eyes. Breath escaping in sharp puffs of steam, she walked with the slow gait of a somnambulist toward the bushes, where a set of faint but definite footprints left a silent, terrifying trail in the snow. They followed the contours of the house and disappeared around the

jutting covered porch that used to be the front entrance. Rae
tracked them to the brick pathway leading down to the sidewalk
that bordered the street. At that point the prints disappeared at
the curb, obliterated by the snowplow.

She called the police. Then, oblivious to the cold, she sat on
the front steps, arms wrapped around her knees, eyes frozen on
the footprints, until the squad car pulled up.

"So I decided the store could wait a few minutes—I needed
some old-fashioned tea and sympathy to bolster my courage,
even if the tea is cider." Her hands around a stoneware mug,
Rae settled into an antique settee in Karen's upstairs apartment.
She lifted her gaze to her friend and had to smile.

Even at eight o'clock in the morning, Karen somehow managed to look like a model, in spite of the fact that she was only
an inch taller than Rae's five feet four inches. Now—thanks to
Rae—she looked more like a model for a murder mystery. Her
huge blue eyes were wide with astonishment, and her lithe, en-
ergetic body fairly strummed with dismay and indignation.
"They told you the same thing they did last time? That there
isn't a law against people poking and prying around your house
and just to continue to be careful?"

Drained, Rae nodded.

Karen's slow southern drawl was markedly absent. Her arms
flapped in a brightly colored caftan. "I think you better move in
with me at least for a while— Let me finish, now." She overrode
Rae's automatic denial. "I'm only two blocks down so it's not
like you'd be abandoning the place to that creep who's creeping
around."

Rae's answering laugh was hollow. "Karen, I willingly
dropped out of school. I renounced a very prestigious—and lu-
crative—award. I gave up a career as a concert pianist to keep
from selling the Prescott family home. Do you honestly think
I'm going to slink away and hide in a corner just because some
weirdo is trying to scare me?"

"*Trying*, honey?"

Rae's fingers began running furiously up and down the
glass-covered tabletop that stood beside the settee. "All right, so

I'm scared. But I'm not going to run." Her expression matched her voice—composed and determined.

With a frustrated sigh Karen capitulated. "She who runs away lives to run another day," she misquoted darkly. For a moment she studied Rae, her glance sliding finally to Rae's hands. "What are you playing?"

Rae's fingers clenched, and she slid them to her lap. "Bach," she confessed. Then, because Karen's blue eyes were starting to fill up with what looked like pity, she swiped the last crumbly Danish and waved it with a flourish. "Don't worry about me, Karen. 'I can do all things through Christ,'" she quoted with some of Karen's dramatic flair. "Oh, all right...stop looking at me like that."

She tossed the last of the Danish onto the plate and sat forward. "Seriously, Karen, I'm not trying to be stupid or heroic—I'm trying to be realistic. The police officer told me the guy could be anything from a prankster to a Peeping Tom to a careful cat burglar, since no attempt has been made to break into the house or the store. I've been pulling all my shades at night—always have—so if he's a Peeping Tom he ought to give up soon. If he's out to rob me and he's that determined, eventually he'll succeed, but I can't spend the rest of my life cowering somewhere while I wait for the worst to happen. I want to try and stay as—as normal as possible."

Her hand was back on the table, mindlessly playing a furious but soundless melody. "Maybe," she added flippantly, "God will dispense a few guardian angels to protect me from all those shadows and things that go bump in the night." Unbidden, there welled up in her the memory of a mysterious stranger who had obliquely quoted the Psalm, his voice mellow and warm as golden honey. He'd also told her to be careful.

She had not mentioned the incident to Karen, because in spite of a messy divorce two years previously, Karen was rapidly turning into a rapacious manhunter. "I like men," she cheerfully confessed. "Besides—what's the alternative?" Karen would be after a man like that curious stranger faster than snow melting on the radiator. She would also leap onto her second favorite hobbyhorse—psychoanalyzing her friend Rae.

Rae forcefully quelled all thoughts of the unnerving man. Instead she focused on the onerous task of braiding the tangled,

almost waist-length strands of her hair. She promised herself—
not for the first time—she was going to have this mess cut off
one of these days when she had the time and money. And courage. "The police want me to remove all of Uncle Floyd's and
Aunt Jeannine's keepsakes from the store," she confessed, gratefully accepting the bobby pins Karen dug out of a nearby drawer
for her. "Not to mention all of Uncle Floyd's birthday gifts to
me. I'm supposed to box everything up, put them in, uh, temporary storage." With jerky motions she secured the braid in a
scrunchie she dug out of her pocket. "Substitute 'permanent' for
'temporary.'"

"Well, I've warned you for years that it was asking for trouble, leaving them on display in the store," Karen retorted. She
shook her head.

"What good are they if people can't enjoy looking at them?
I've gotten lots of compliments, and it keeps the store from looking so...commercial." Rae sighed. "Besides, I always hated the
way Uncle Floyd hoarded everything away upstairs. Lladro and
Limoges didn't intend for their creations to be stuffed inside a
box. And the antique Roseville collection—"

"Would bring a thief or dope addict a pretty penny on the
black market. It's still a marvel to me that one of your customers
hasn't filched anything."

Rae shrugged. "I'm not going to worry about it. They're valuable, yes—but it's the house I really care about, Karen. It's the
only part of my past I can be proud of. Sometimes I wish—"
She stopped. Usually she kept the inadequacies and her lack of
self-esteem safely buttoned up, where not even Karen could
reach. The prowler and those footprints had shaken her more
than she realized. *Deal with it, Prescott.*

She had a criminal for a father and a mother whose weak-
nesses had proven greater than her love for her children. All the
wishing in the world could not undo reality. So what? Even if
her genes were predisposed to run amok, she still had a choice.
God had given human beings free will, hadn't He? She could
learn from the past, and she hoped God would show a little
mercy concerning the future. At least she and Tyler had had
Uncle Floyd. He'd done the best he could as a middle-aged wid-
ower, loving them as though they had been his own children.

"I'd better go." She stood up, flipping the braid over her

shoulder and reaching for her coat. "We both have businesses to run. Tell Sylvia the Danishes were scrumptious. Between the two of you, Gibson Girl is going to outshine every other restaurant in Old Colorado."

"What—not the entire city of Colorado Springs?" Karen wrapped her in a brief hug, but did not badger her any further. Rae was grateful, and after promising to call that evening, headed down the back stairs.

Outside, a small crowd had gathered, waiting to enter the restaurant for breakfast. Rae stepped off the curb to avoid them, accidentally bumping a broad-shouldered man wearing a blue and yellow ski jacket who leaned casually against the eighteen-nineties lamp pole.

Rae apologized but kept on walking, too intent on her thoughts to feel a pair of eyes burning a hole in her back.

Customers were sparse that day, even though the sun came out and melted most of the snow by late afternoon. A retired couple traveling through the area bought a collection of Chopin waltzes and a teacher's choice grouping of short classical works for their granddaughter. The balding, stoop-shouldered man who had been coming in regularly the past several months returned to query her about early editions of Beethoven's works. Apparently he collected old sheet music, though he didn't play himself. Rae found him a couple of Schirmer editions and he departed, pleased. Three giggling teenagers trooped in after school and rearranged almost all the popular music. Fortunately it was also a teaching day, and except for the three teens, her students for once enjoyed Rae's full attention. Most of it, anyway.

The large, sunny room behind the cash register had become Rae's studio. A local music store leased her the grand she used for teaching. The year before she had had folding doors installed, which could be closed whenever there were customers. Her students quickly learned not to waste time even when Rae had a customer. Her ear and training were so acute she could hear and correctly identify the note a chime was playing on a church bell six blocks away. The guilty student who fiddled around playing "Chopsticks" ended up practicing extra scales and arpeggios as penance.

It was a good thing her income was multifaceted, Rae mused late that afternoon after she flipped the sign to Closed. She had made only four sales the entire day. Oh, well. Low sales were part and parcel of retailing, and if you didn't learn to roll with those sporadic punches, you better find another business. Something less stressful—like stockbroking. Rae smiled while she put the store in order. By the time she finished cleaning it was dark outside, the bloodred sunset evaporating into a frigid, frosty evening with typical Colorado abruptness. Rae tucked the last piece of music in its proper place, then moved behind the counter to tally the meager receipts of the day, using only the floor lamp by the cash register for illumination. Its yellowish glow cast grotesque, jagged shadows over the dark room.

At first she didn't notice anything unusual, because the scraping, shuffling noise was faint. When the sound finally filtered through Rae's preoccupation, she froze where she was standing, fingers gripping the money bag holding the day's sparse takings. The sound came again, as though someone was outside in the bushes, underneath the portico window. If that prowler had returned...

Rae's hand shot out and yanked the lamp chain. The room was plunged into blackness. Frightened and furious—the Mace was inside her purse in her bedroom—Rae debated whether to call the police or wait until she knew for sure. Out in the street a car backfired, and loud barking erupted from beneath the window.

"Good grief." Rae smacked her palm to her head. "It's that wretched dog again!" She slammed the ancient cash register shut, bitterly aware that her angry response was far out of proportion. At the moment, she didn't care. Stomping and slamming doors released at least some of the tension. Besides, who was there to see? Defiantly, enjoying the loud bang, she slammed the door that separated Joyful Noise from the rest of the house. Yep, that felt real good.

After depositing the money in the hidden safe Uncle Floyd had installed almost forty years earlier, she stalked into her bedroom to change out of the ridiculously expensive six-year-old angora dress she'd worn for work that day. The fresh reminder of her uncle's thoughtless extravagance initiated another surge of irritation.

"Clothes make the man—or woman," he used to tell her, over and over. "If you plan to make something of yourself in the world, you need to dress the part. Making a statement with what you wear is important, so long as you convey the right message." Translated, that meant, *Don't ever dress like your mother used to.*

"But I don't need all these designer clothes," Rae protested. Uselessly. "Uncle Floyd, you know you don't have that kind of money. I promise not to dress like Mama used to."

She knew why he bought the clothes, knew the burden of shame he carried—and the guilt that haunted him for over two decades. It mirrored her own. "Daffodil" Prescott had died from a drug overdose when Rae was six. Rae knew her mother had displayed a pitiful courage when she showed up with two ragged, crying children on her brother-in-law's doorstep. At the very least, Rae should honor the memory of that courage. But she hadn't, not really.

"I loved my mother—but I don't want to be like her," she announced, hearing the pathetic admission drop with a dull thud into the oppressive silence of her bedroom.

God? Can You forgive me? I don't want to turn out like Mama....

As always, the flash flood of emotion eventually dribbled out, leaving behind a sludgelike exhaustion. Carefully Rae hung the angora dress in the crowded closet, thrust on faded jeans and a sweatshirt and padded down the hall to her private music room.

Control. She had to regain control of her emotions, and her life. That was the answer—and Rae knew of only one time-tested way to establish her equilibrium. Playing her piano. Wraithlike, she drifted to the ebony Steinway grand Uncle Floyd had given her for her high school graduation. It stood in solitary splendor in the middle of the room, welcoming and patient.

Rae sat down, opened the lid, adjusted the bench and began to play. This evening, it was a long time before the music worked its magic.

Chapter Four

Saturdays in the store were usually Rae's busiest days, even in winter when the tourist trade was down and most of her customers were locals. On this particular Saturday a cold drizzling rain splattered the windows all day long, but not even the dreary day dimmed her revived spirits.

It had been a quiet, uneventful week. No stray dogs, no break-ins, no prowlers. Rae's peaceful mood spilled over onto her customers, who bought more than usual. She hummed snatches of gospel songs and contemporary Christian rock while she alternately waited on people who needed assistance and smilingly retreated behind the counter when they wished to browse or seek momentary harbor from the weather.

Late in the afternoon a woman whose arms were wreathed in silver bangle bracelets entered the store, bracelets as well as the store's bell announcing her arrival. "I need a copy of Beethoven's Fifth," she told Rae. "You know—the one with 'Ode to Joy.'" She hummed the first few phrases of the chorus in a low contralto made raspy from too many cigarettes. "You know the tune, of course? It's always been one of my favorites."

Rae opened her mouth to correct the woman, then stopped, opting for discretion in keeping with the amicable atmosphere. Besides, there was something about this customer.... "Don't I know you?" she asked as she led her to the classical music.

"Something about you looks familiar." Tentatively Rae selected an easy version with "Ode to Joy" printed in large letters across the top, and smiled as she offered it to the woman. "I'm a whiz at memorizing music, but I'm terrible with faces, so if you've been in here before, I apologize. Ah, is this edition all right?"

The woman gave the music a cursory glance. "It's the 'Ode to Joy.' It's fine." She ignored Rae's friendly apology.

With a mental shrug Rae rang up the purchase. She didn't try to chat further. The woman tersely thanked her and left, leaving behind the acrid cigarette odor that had been clinging to her clothes. If the woman returned, Rae thought, maybe she could tactfully point out that "Ode to Joy" was the choral symphony from Beethoven's *Ninth*, not his Fifth.

After she closed the store Rae walked down the street to Gibson Girl, hoping for a chat and early supper with Karen before the dinner crowd descended. It had been five years since Karen converted the turn-of-the-century cottage to a cozy restaurant, and Rae was almost as proud of its success as Karen. She tried to eat there once a week, in spite of the expense. Karen would have gladly fed her breakfast, lunch and dinner daily, on the house, but Rae always refused her friend's hospitality. Decorated in the style of Charles Dana Gibson's "girl" drawings, the atmosphere was both cozy and chic. Copies of work from old issues of *Collier* and *Life* were framed and hung on the mauve-painted walls. Waiters and waitresses dressed in period clothes, and there was an old gramophone scratching out tinny turn-of-the-century tunes.

Rae opened the oval cut-glass door and deposited her dripping umbrella in a ceramic umbrella stand. Mouth-watering odors mingled with the pleasing sounds of voices and clinking silver on china. Sniffing appreciatively, Rae tugged off her gloves and greeted Cheryl, the supper hostess, then shivered when a cold draft blew around their ankles as the door opened behind them. The man who entered shrugged out of his bright blue and yellow ski jacket and hung it on the coatrack as Cheryl led Rae to a corner table for two.

"Looks like your day's been as busy as mine," Rae observed a few minutes later when Karen finally plopped down across from her for a hurried break. "It's only a little before six, and the place is already three-quarters full."

"Where would we small business owners be without Saturdays?" Karen added, glancing around with an assessing smile. "I'll probably have to leave before I finish, but I want to try Sylvia's split-pea soup—she's modified the recipe and this is the first night we've served it."

For several restful moments they chatted, catching up on each other's weeks while the drizzling rain accelerated to a downpour. Rae lingered at the table after Karen left, but when the restaurant filled she wandered upstairs to Karen's apartment, reluctant to return to her isolated house and the omnipresent chores she was too tired to address tonight. She watched a movie on cable TV—another luxury she denied herself. But when Karen dragged upstairs a little before eleven, Rae rose to leave. "You're exhausted, and I have to be at church early in the morning."

She hurried up the street, clutching her wrap coat, head down against the cold. A relentless wind blowing from the southwest had pushed the clouds onto the prairie, leaving behind a clear sky and rapidly dropping temperatures. Streetlights glowed a hazy yellow, shining on the icy puddles dotting the street and sidewalks.

Rae crossed the dark, quiet street in front of Joyful Noise and started up the brick path that led to the kitchen entrance. The towering Chinese elms flanking either side blocked much of the streetlight, and Rae lifted her head to scan her surroundings. Even though there had been no evidence of the prowler for over a week, she wasn't dumb enough to ignore the potential danger inherent in being alone. On the other hand, she refused to turn into a neurotic bundle of anxiety afraid to stick her nose outside without a bevy of bodyguards crowded around her.

Be careful. Unbidden, the quiet voice of the mysterious stranger whispered inside Rae's head. Shivering, she suppressed a twinge of uneasiness, although her gloved fingers searched inside her purse until they closed around the can of Mace. Over the past week she had convinced herself that the smooth-voiced customer was nothing more than a predatory male who got his kicks from trying to frighten vulnerable females. When Rae refused to be intimidated he'd given up.

On the other hand, the persistent little voice nagged, maybe he really *had* been trying to warn her. Her gaze moved around the yard, then focused on the front porch and the store.

On the dark shape drifting across the window in front of the religious section.

Someone was inside the store, moving with a soundless stealth that raised hairs on the back of Rae's neck. Her disbelieving eyes zeroed in on a thin beam of light playing over the room. She felt dry-mouthed, and her pulse leaped into a staccato gallop when the pencil-thin light played over the bins of music, paused, then moved across the hall toward the next room.

A wave of hot anger bubbled from the pit of Rae's stomach. She whipped out the can of Mace, her mind racing. If she wasted time running to Karen's to call the police, the intruder would escape. Her best hope lay in surprise—and noise. If she yelled loudly enough to rouse the neighbors—no. This time, she needed to document his presence, sneak close enough to establish visual contact so she could identify the person in a police lineup, if called upon to do so.

Outrage at the violation of her property drowned all warnings. Rae crept toward the front porch, armed with the Mace, eyes glued to the windows. *This* time, the police would not leave with nothing but a polite pat on the hand. If only she could have afforded to put in that alarm system....

Without warning a dark form leaped from the bushes at the corner of the mansion, hurtling toward her with the speed of a charging bull. Caught totally off guard, Rae fumbled to aim and press the button, but she wasn't fast enough. In a single violent swipe the Mace was knocked free, and a pair of brutal hands closed over her forearms. Malodorous fumes of alcohol, tobacco and sweat engulfed her as one of the hands shifted to cover her mouth.

Frightened but furious, Rae bit the encroaching hand, kicking at his legs, stomping on his feet. She twisted, struggling in maniacal fury, and finally managed to free herself. She staggered backward, her breath coming in tearing pants, then turned and ran. But the knee-length boots were awkward, and the assailant caught her before she reached the street.

This time the attacker's hand snagged her braid, yanking her head back so viciously bobby pins scattered and the braid came unwound. His other arm wrapped around her waist, lifting her completely off her feet. Rae felt as if her scalp was being torn off, her body squeezed in two.

"Let *go* of me!" She managed the beginnings of a healthy scream before his hand clamped around her windpipe and he began to choke her.

Rae dug her elbow into a mushy stomach, then reached backward to claw his face with her fingers. The hand choking her moved to her mouth. His fingers dug into her jaw and smashed her lips, crushing her face so she was unable to bite. Doggedly Rae refused to give in, regardless of the pain. A harsh grunt grated in her ear when her flailing hand struck a beard-roughened, fleshy cheekbone. But the vise around her middle squeezed harder, driving out the air in her lungs.

Rae squirmed and struggled, but she was weakening rapidly. Her blurring senses registered the sensation of movement off to her right—the prowler in the store, coming to the aid of his lookout! Rae renewed her struggles in a desperate burst of adrenaline. Red sparks whirled through encroaching waves of blackness. In a few more seconds she would lose consciousness.

"What the—" The guttural exclamation disappeared in a grunt of pain. The hands holding Rae slackened.

She staggered, her limbs feeling curiously weightless, yet weighed down with sandbags. In spite of her willpower her knees buckled, and she collapsed onto the chilly wet sidewalk. Breathing raggedly, head ringing, she sat watching the bizarre events unfold in a dazed state of semiconsciousness.

Two yards away a silent battle raged as Rae's attacker and another darkly clad man exchanged vicious blows. The dull thud of fists against flesh was gratingly obscene. The two men fought in silence except for the harsh sound of their labored breathing and the blows. Suddenly her attacker wrenched free, then turned and fled, his huge body surprisingly fast.

Dizzy, in pain, Rae nonetheless tried to rise, to run—because she at last had recognized the man who had attacked her. The rhythm of his fleeing footsteps, the hunched, shuffling flight, were identical to those of the prowler in her bushes ten days earlier.

Rae's rescuer gave chase, but stopped at the corner of her house and turned back. Rae managed to lurch to her feet, but they refused to obey the urgent order to escape. She stood, sway-

ing, and tried to summon enough air in her lungs to scream if
this man decided to turn on her and—

"It's all right. I'm not going to hurt you. Please don't
scream." The words were soothing, reassuring, the voice unnervingly familiar. He stopped several yards away. "It's all right,
Ms. Prescott," he repeated.

Fresh goose pimples raced over Rae's bruised, stinging skin.
"You?" she gasped in a painful croak. She recognized that mellow voice with its undertone of a drawl as surely as she had
recognized the fleeing man by the sound of his footsteps.

He approached slowly, holding out his hand. "Easy...I just
want to make sure you don't fall again."

Rae slapped the proffered hand away. "Who *are* you?" Her
throat was so raw it hurt to talk. She backed a step, almost falling
off the curb, then glared at the man when he started forward. He
went still, dropping his hands to his sides.

"My name is Caleb Myers," he said, an inflexible note warning Rae that he was restraining himself with an effort. "I'm a
private computer security consultant. If I'd had any idea something like this was going to happen, I would have introduced
myself the other day in your store. Ms. Prescott, I'm not going
to hurt you—but I *am* going to help you inside. You've had a
shock, and you need to get warm."

She hadn't realized until he commented on it that she was
shivering almost uncontrollably. "If you really wanted to help,
you should have come to my rescue before that—that disgusting
creep practically squeezed me in two." She lifted her hand to
her scalp. "And tried to pull my hair off."

Tossed by the wind, her long hair swirled over her face, neck
and shoulders. Rae held it aside with one hand. A corner of Caleb
Myers's mouth suddenly twitched upward. "I was on the second
story of the building across the street there," he commented
mildly, pointing to an abandoned hardware store. "I got here as
soon as I could—didn't even take time to call in reinforcements."

Reinforcements? Rae bit her lip. He sounded more amused
than irritated. But maybe it was because he was a...a consultant?
What was he doing in the old hardware building? It had been
vacant for years. Rae pressed frozen fingers against her aching
head, trying to think. Unfortunately, she hurt too bad to analyze

further. "Well..." She tried ineffectually to gather another hand-ful of hair from her face. "Thank you for, ah, coming to the rescue. You're a really great hero. What—"

A sudden gust of wind almost knocked her off her feet, and this time when Caleb Myers's hand shot out to steady her she didn't jerk free. "Maybe we better go inside. My purse—" She stopped, trying to remember what had happened to her purse. She stared toward the porch, and almost panicked. "There was another man. Inside the store." Her gaze swiveled to Myers. "How do I know it wasn't—"

"It wasn't me." The hand holding her arm squeezed, a gentle, reassuring squeeze. "Trust me, all right? You say there was an-other man? I'll go check. Perhaps if you stay here, under the streetlight—"

"I most certainly will not," Rae snapped unfairly, discon-certed by her response to the warmth and strength of Caleb Myers's firm hold—and the explosion of panic at the suggestion that she be left out here all alone. "How do I know there's not a third man hiding somewhere? And why should I trust you? What kind of proof can you produce to convince me that you're not in cahoots with them?" She was talking too fast. *Zip your lip, Prescott, before you really blow it.*

"I'm a private consultant," Caleb Myers repeated patiently. "But right now, I'm...lending a hand to the FBI. We've had your place under surveillance for almost two weeks. If you'll allow me to check the premises, we can go inside and I'll explain while we wait for the police."

Had her home under surveillance? Rae's chin lifted. "I want to see some identification."

There was a short pause.

The trembling intensified. She could not prevent her legs from quivering, and all the feeling had left her hands and feet some time ago. But she was *not* moving another step until this gen-tle-voiced, eagle-eyed man provided her with some proof of his identity, not to mention an explanation for his astounding reve-lation. She stared into his shadowed face, a little disconcerted because in the shrouded moonlight it looked as though Caleb Myers was *smiling.*

He reached into the back pocket of his jeans and tugged out a worn leather wallet that turned out to be his identification instead of a wallet. "Here." A small penlight appeared as if by magic and shone on an official-looking ID with a badge on one side and a grainy head photo on the other. It stated that he was indeed Caleb Andrew Myers, and a resident of Chicago, Illinois. He had brn. hair, lt. brn. eyes, was 5'11" and weighed 177 lbs.

"Your eyes aren't brown," Rae said. "And there's red in your hair—or at least under the street lamp there's red in your hair, and I saw some that day—in my store."

"The man typing out the information didn't have much imagination," Caleb Myers returned. He added very gently, "Ms. Prescott, I think you need to go inside. I need to check around a bit first, and I'm not going to risk your safety by taking you with me. So. You wait here—under the streetlight where I can keep an eye on you. I'll be back in a minute." He looked at her, and something in his face quashed the last of Rae's protests.

"Hurry."

"I will." He glanced around, his gaze seeming to penetrate even the blackest shadows, then turned to Rae. "Hang in there." He started to say something else, but ended up doing nothing more than giving her shoulder a last bracing squeeze before he ran soundlessly in a low crouch toward the porch.

Rae shuddered when another gust of wind tugged at her coat and bit her ears. She wondered what had happened to her gloves. She wondered what had happened to the can of Mace. Would have been nice, having that can about now. Oh, well...perhaps she should sing a song, try to divert her mind...hurt to think. Only song floating through her head was a sixties oldie talking about eyes....

She could lose herself in Caleb Myers's eyes. They were an unusual color. Of course, that might have been the streetlight. But the way those eyes looked as if he was smiling even when he wasn't... On the other hand, when he cavalierly ordered her to stay put, she'd felt positively immobilized by the stern warning he'd communicated in a single look. Most unfair, for a man to have eyes like that.

She shivered again, and her voice cracked. Maybe singing wasn't such a good idea.

Caleb Myers returned, cupping his hand under her elbow. "All clear outside. I found your purse, with some keys. Will one of these open the door to your store? I think it's best if we go in that way—the intruder's long gone.''

"Wait." Rae broke free and hurried stiffly across the grass, where the Mace lay in a patch of moonlit ground. She scooped it up and returned to Caleb, who watched with the untwitching patience of a cougar.

He ushered her up the steps and waited while Rae fumbled for the key. The patient expression did not alter when it took her three attempts to unfasten the door because she refused to let go of the Mace.

"It's a shame you weren't able to use that on your attacker," he commented easily. "Um...are you sure you don't want me to unlock the door? You can keep me covered, if you like."

Rae did not back down. "Very funny. You'll have to excuse me, Mr. Secret Agent Myers. This is my first brush with the underworld." The door finally gave way with a protesting groan, and she stood aside to let Caleb Myers enter first.

"I'm not a secret agent," he pointed out, sounding resigned.

"Fine. Then you won't mind if the first thing I do is call the police."

"If you hadn't, I would have."

His voice was much too agreeable, Rae thought as they entered the dark store. On the other hand, she was safe inside, and right now all she really cared about was checking on Joyful Noise. She walked across the floor on shaky legs, grateful to be out of the wind. She turned on the floor lamp by the cash register, immediately checking to see if she'd been robbed. Caleb Myers followed, shrugging out of a thick fleece-lined jean jacket.

In the more revealing light Rae studied him closely. The wind had blown his hair into thick, unruly waves all over the sculptured planes and angles of his face and head. It made him look tough, rakish and aggressively male. Then she belatedly realized that he was studying *her,* with such—such compassion pouring from the extraordinary eyes that a painful blush heated her frozen, chapped cheeks.

"Unless you think you need to use it on me, I think it's okay to put that down," he eventually observed, smiling as he nodded toward her hand.

"Oh." Rae's gaze jerked from his face to the can she still clutched in a death grip. Blush deepening, she hastily thrust it beneath the counter. Her gaze fell to his hands. One set of knuckles was scraped and had bled slightly.

"Your hand." She faltered, and he glanced at it.

"I'm sure his jaw feels worse." He paused. "Your face is pretty bruised. Does it hurt yet?"

Rae lifted her fingers to explore cheek and jaw, wincing in pained surprise. "Yes." She wriggled her shoulders, took a deep breath. "Tea. I need a cup of tea. I'll call the police, then put on a kettle. Would you like some tea while you explain what you're doing spying on me, Mr. Myers?"

"Call me Caleb," he replied cheerfully. "If you'll show me your kitchen, I'll heat the water so you can look around your store after you call. Don't touch anything, okay? They'll want to dust for fingerprints."

Chapter Five

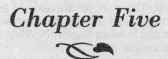

Caleb filled a tarnished brass kettle with water and put it on an old gas stove top to boil. Then he prowled around Rae Prescott's living quarters while she checked out the store. The FBI guys had already confirmed she had lived alone for the past three years, since her paternal uncle, Floyd Prescott, died. There was an older brother, but no address was available yet.

In a room that looked like a cozy Victorian parlor he found the only photographs in sight. One was of an elderly man with a magnificent snow-white mustache, cane in one hand, the other arm wrapped around a younger Rae's shoulders.

Next to that photograph was a framed snapshot of a lanky man with gangly arms and legs. He was standing by a flashy red sports car, an expression of smug pride on his face. The same brown hair, long narrow nose and stubborn chin as Rae identified him as the brother. Caleb looked on the back, but there was nothing written to corroborate his conclusion. He put it down, smiling. Rae's arms and legs looked just about as long, slender and unwieldy as her brother's. They had probably been teased unmercifully. Rae still moved with a sort of awkward grace, as though she had never quite learned what to do with all her limbs.

On the other hand, the lady had fought off her attacker with a gutsy determination, but the memory still congealed Caleb's blood to ice. He picked up the photo of Rae with her uncle and studied it. Long limbs, long hair, long narrow nose—actually, she reminded him of a long-haired Siamese cat, with gray eyes instead of blue. Her expression was filled with the same combination of intelligence and wariness. Caleb grinned. Of course, *cats* were inherently graceful.

He continued his prowling, tucking away nuggets of information. No pets. Lots of plants. A mixture of antique and modern furniture, most of which needed dusting. Several framed scripture verses like the one over the fireplace in the store. Most of these were from Psalms. The quiet proclamation of her faith in the privacy of her home reassured Caleb. Her faith was more than a carefully orchestrated outward display. Nodding, he moved out of the parlor into another room.

It was her bedroom. A cursory search assured him that it was empty of intruders, though he did lift a brow at her crammed, overflowing closet. The quality of the clothes was top-notch, the majority of the labels those of world famous designers, including a couple that made both Caleb's eyebrows shoot up. All the styles, however, were several years old, some more outdated. Not a single article was new. Caleb grinned at what his three sisters would have said about *that* sorry state of affairs.

So. At some point in the past, Rae Prescott had enjoyed significant material wealth, but apparently those days were long gone. While that could be construed in a suspicious light, Caleb found himself liking her even more because she seemed to have accepted her present circumstances with the same pluckiness she had summoned to fend off her assailant.

Before he left the bedroom, Caleb picked up the phone on her bedside table, verified the line was free and the phone clean of bugs, then made a quick call.

The last room had no furniture except for the biggest grand piano he'd ever seen. It sat in dusty splendor in the middle of the room. Music was piled everywhere. On the floor, in boxes, on the piano, on the bench by the piano...

Caleb smiled with self-directed irony, shaking his head as he quietly made his way to the kitchen. He had conducted hundreds of investigations over the years, and most of them involved women at some point. Many of those women had been attractive, even beautiful, but none of them had ever meant anything to Caleb beyond a professional level. He could instantly call up a detailed physical description of any of the women he'd dated casually—and not so casually. Not a single one had ever made his pulse race. Until now.

Rae Prescott was not beautiful, and made no pretensions otherwise, yet for some reason she made his blood pressure shoot skyward every time he looked at her. It was disconcerting and puzzling—and impossible to ignore, because there was a slim possibility that the intriguing Ms. Prescott was not precisely who she appeared to be. *You better watch your step with this one real close, pal.*

When he walked into the galley kitchen, Rae was opening a tin and taking out two tea bags. Her face was pale, hostile, the huge gray eyes smudged with suspicion.

"Did you enjoy your...tour?" she asked, dumping the tea bags into a couple of mugs.

"I'm sorry." Caleb took the kettle and poured. "I needed to make sure you didn't have anybody hiding behind a door or in a closet. Did you think I was casing the joint?"

"Yes, I did. Are you going to try to convince me otherwise?"

He put the kettle on the stove and they sat at an attractive maple trestle table. "I think I told you that your home is an impressive place the first time I was here, didn't I? I really like the way you've kept the integrity of the rooms in spite of having to turn half of them into a store."

"Thank you."

She sat there, glaring at him with wavering eyes as if she couldn't decide whether to smile graciously—or fetch that can of Mace.

Caleb sighed. Rae Prescott might be a gutsy lady, but unless he missed his guess, the lady hovered right on the edge of hysteria...or volcanic rage. Maybe both. He stared at the distasteful brew while he considered what approach to take to preserve her dignity—and his cover. "I saw your Bible verses, in your bedroom. They're some of my favorites, as well. David was quite a songwriter, wasn't he? Every emotion known to mankind...from reverence to rage and everything in between. Somehow he'd figured out that God didn't mind, and would remain faithful regardless of David's mood at the time."

He waited while she slowly registered the implication. "You know, we originally planned to discontinue the surveillance last night. But I had this feeling—now I figure it was God's way of getting my attention—because I told the team I'd watch one more night. Amazing, isn't it?''

She stared at him. ''Are you saying...that you're a Christian, too?'' She searched his face as though trying to crawl inside his brain. ''I mean...you're not just trying to feed me a line or worm your way into my confidence for your own purposes?''

''Yes, I'm a Christian.'' He winked at her. ''And even if I *had* planned to worm my way into your confidence, I'd think twice about it after seeing you in action against that prowler.''

A tentative smile slowly lit the bruised and swollen face.

Caleb fought down the first stirrings of deep uneasiness. Those prowlers might very well be nothing more than a couple of thugs out to rob a vulnerable woman. But he didn't think so. Instinct warned him that they had finally stumbled over the first real lead in the Starseeker case...which landed Rae Prescott right in the middle of it all. He forced himself to take a swallow of tea, then smiled across the table. ''Will you try to trust me a little now, Rae? It will make the next weeks—and possibly months—a lot easier on both of us.''

The police were a lot more thorough than they had been the last two times. Bemused, Rae watched them spill out of the cars, and wondered aloud why they'd sent so many. It was a multiple response, Caleb Myers told her, in the hopes that the burglars could still be chased down and caught.

Some of the officers stayed outside to search the area, but it seemed as if her kitchen and store were suddenly overrun by a swarm of stone-faced, intent professionals. A couple of men in rumpled civilian suits slipped inside as Rae was giving her account of the assault to a police officer holding a clipboard stuffed with report forms.

After giving his statement and showing his ID, Caleb stayed out of the way. He and two plainclothesmen clustered in a corner of the store, talking quietly. Caleb looked relaxed, casual, as if he was discussing the latest Broncos game with a couple of friends. Every now and then he looked at Rae, but she averted her head each time, uncertain of her feelings toward her rescuer.

The policeman thanked her for her statement and moved off.

Rae sat tensely on the stairs leading to the second floor while she watched the activity going on around her. She felt detached, almost anesthetized. Like a fourth-grade boy observing an ant farm. The only time she spoke was to make a rather tart request that they please be careful not to disarrange the music.

After the swarm of police officers finished poking and prying around the store, the sandy-haired one who had written up Rae's account strolled over. He brought along a short, trim man with iron gray hair and shrewd blue eyes. The police officer introduced him as Detective Pete Grabowski. Slowly Rae stood, eyeing both men uncertainly, because Detective Grabowski was looking her over like a piece of fresh fruit at the farmer's market.

"Ms. Prescott," he said in a surprisingly deep tone, "I know you've given Officer Hanley your statement, but would you mind telling me what happened again? Try to remember every detail, regardless of how insignificant you think it may be."

Rae suppressed a long-suffering sigh. "I spent the evening with my friend Karen. She owns Gibson Girl." The detective nodded, so Rae continued without elaborating, though she shuddered at the prospect of Karen's response to the events of this night. "I was walking home a little after eleven—I waited till the rain quit. Just after I crossed the street, I saw someone inside my store."

"You've confirmed that to the best of your knowledge nothing has been stolen?"

She nodded, mouth quirking wryly. "It makes this whole mess more bewildering. What could they have wanted in a music store? I don't keep money in the cash register after I close...."

One of the plainclothesmen who had been conferring with Caleb Myers walked over. Detective Grabowski turned and they spoke in low syllables Rae could not hear. The lines furrowing the detective's head deepened. When he turned to Rae she sensed a coldness, almost hostility.

"Ms. Prescott." He spoke slowly, as if measuring each word. "You live here alone, and you have on display in your store objects worth thousands of dollars. Yet you have taken only the most rudimentary precautions to safeguard them. After the past few weeks I find that extremely foolish."

"I don't have the funds necessary to install the alarms and newer locks your associates recommended." Rae kept her tone civil with difficulty. Why on earth was *she* being made to feel as though she was the one on trial? A hot coal lodged in the pit of her stomach, and she had to clasp her hands tightly together to keep from playing Bach on the stair railing. "Besides, if someone wants to steal anything, they'll find a way regardless of elaborate and or costly protective measures."

"And you would realize a substantial insurance settlement?" Detective Grabowski suggested.

The live coal glowing in her stomach burst into flames. "Detective, I resent your implications—"

"When was the last time you saw your father, Ms. Prescott?"

Rae felt all the indignant color drain out of her face, felt as though she'd been catapulted backward in time to Carnegie Hall. She could almost hear the applause in the background as two hard-eyed men destroyed her world. It was also the same night Uncle Floyd suffered the first heart attack. "My father," she repeated in a dead voice, wrapping her fingers around the top of the griffin's head so tightly her knuckles gleamed bone white.

"I've just been informed that your father, Raymond M. Prescott, is wanted by the FBI for a number of crimes, including extortion and grand larceny," Grabowski said in that cold, level voice that raised welts on Rae's frost-bitten nerves. "Ms. Prescott—is it possible your lack of precaution is intended? That the open display of all these items is so your—"

"How are things going over here, Grabowski?" Caleb Myers was suddenly there, his eyes on Rae as he moved between her and the detective. Rae braced herself. Masculine warmth and power radiated from him with such force she felt suffocated— yet oddly shielded. "Ms. Prescott doesn't look like she's holding up too well," Caleb commented. "Maybe the rest of it could wait until morning?"

"I'm fine," Rae began, yet she did not pull away from the hand urging her to sit down on the stairs. It felt so warm, and she was so cold her teeth were chattering. She was also angry, on a deep, primitive level, and the emotional contradictions left her faintly nauseated. Clamping her lips together, she slid a single swift glance at Caleb Myers.

"She's had a rough time of it," he continued mildly. "Besides, that would also give your people time to gather some mug shots for a photo lineup."

Detective Grabowski suddenly looked a lot less intimidating. "Ms. Prescott claims she wouldn't be able to recognize her attacker. There won't be a lineup unless it's for you, Myers." He paused, then added with the same deliberate lack of inflection, "Ramirez was just telling me about the background check on the Prescott family."

Caleb suddenly dropped down in front of Rae, balancing gracefully on the balls of his feet, his expression intent, probing. "Rae, will you tell me about your father?" he asked, but his voice compelled rather than demanded.

I don't want to talk about my father, she wanted to yell. But fatigue and bewilderment were overpowering the anger, and she felt all her defenses collapsing. She didn't understand this golden-eyed guardian angel who had swooped into her life, turning it completely upside down. She could have fought hostility and suspicion—by the time she entered fourth grade she was a veteran at facing down the slurs and taunts of others. But kindness...in the face of kindness she was helpless. "I don't know anything about my father," she admitted stiffly. "He deserted us when I was four."

"You haven't seen or heard from him since?"

"No. The FBI questioned us the last time he surfaced. We couldn't help then, either. My father—" she lifted her chin "—as far as I'm concerned, my father is as dead to me as his family is to him. He's made absolutely no contact that I'm aware of." She turned her head away, furious all of a sudden because the compassion in Caleb's eyes smacked more of pity.

Her gaze fell on a delicate antique hat-pin holder full of assorted pins, perched on top of Uncle Floyd's ancient Victrola. She'd rather have those pins digging into her scalp than be the object of Mr. Magnanimous Myers's *pity*. The sudden uprush of heady temper brought her to her feet to confront Detective Grabowski. "Detective, my lack of security is *not* intended as a flashing neon sign for thieves. In point of fact, I wouldn't realize a penny if anything were stolen. The only insurance I carry is for the house itself. At the time I took out the policy, carrying a personal articles floater was not an option."

A ferocious scowl furrowed the detective's forehead. Looking thoroughly impatient, he opened his mouth as though preparing to verbally skewer Rae. Then he caught Caleb's eye and swallowed the words in an indecipherable grumble. Still glaring at the detective, Rae started when Caleb's hand dropped onto her shoulder.

"Rae," he informed her quietly, "the reason you feel like you're on the wrong end of an interrogation is because you might be involved—unknowingly, of course—in a case I'm working on with the FBI, the OSI and now the Colorado Springs Police Department."

"You're divulging information that might be inappropriate at this time, under the circumstances," Grabowski warned.

Caleb didn't budge. "Your original purpose here, remember, is to investigate a crime committed *against* Ms. Prescott, not *by* her. The fact that her father—a man she claims not to have seen since she was four—is wanted by the FBI may or may not be germane. She deserves more than your suspicions, Grabowski."

"I also deserve an explanation as to why you've had my house under surveillance. Not to mention why you think my father has something to do with the break-in tonight." Rae's lips were stiff, while her knees possessed an unnerving resemblance to water.

She watched Grabowski and Caleb Myers exchange glances and wondered all of a sudden how she must appear to this gathering of stone-faced, cynical men. Hardened professionals who were more accustomed to liars and thieves and muggers than an innocent woman whose behavior vacillated between short-tempered grizzly and trembling mouse. She had taken the time to twist her hair into a chignon before the police arrived, but she knew after a horrified glimpse in the mirror earlier that the only color left in her face was from the swelling bruise. There were dark smudges on her throat, as well.

After an electric moment of silence, Grabowski wordlessly yielded the floor with an irritated swipe of his hand. Did Caleb get his way in everything? Rae wondered.

Just then one of Grabowski's men approached. "We're all through here, sir." The young man had been dusting for prints. He glanced sympathetically at Rae. Grabowski barked out orders and instructions, and the young cop left.

The detective turned to her. His face was not sympathetic. "Mr. Myers obviously feels the need to enlighten you, Ms. Prescott, so I will leave him to it." He paused, then added levelly,

"You aren't planning to go anywhere in the next few weeks, are you?"

"Hardly." Rae smiled sweetly. "I don't have enough money for a vacation, either. Perhaps I could burn down the store? I *do* carry fire insurance."

Chapter Six

After the police finally trooped out several moments later, Caleb folded his arms over his chest and settled his shoulders against the wall. Rae turned from shutting the door and almost ran into him. "What happened to the practice of turning the other cheek, Ms. Prescott?" he teased her, nodding at the closed door. "The detective does have a job to do, and in his defense, he doesn't know you any better than you know him."

"My cheeks have suffered enough for one night," Rae retorted, then she sighed, waving a hand. "Sorry. I know you all have a job to do. Normally I control my temper better, but I guess everything sort of overwhelmed me." She glanced at Caleb. "You may have noticed, I have lapses of what my brother irreverently refers to as a prima donna temperament."

"I noticed." He noticed a lot more than he wanted to concerning this young woman. Including the fact that she was trying very hard to maintain a semblance of control when she still bordered on an eruption of Mount Saint Helens proportions.

"Mr. Myers—"

"Caleb." He shouldered away from the wall and stood there studying her in the dim light of the hall sconces. "Call me Caleb, all right?"

Rae inclined her head. "Caleb...I apologize for the sarcastic crack I made to Detective Gar—Graw...whatever. But—"

"Grabowski. His name's Grabowski, and you don't have to apologize to me, but if you'll take a bit of advice—always co-operate with the police, as much as lies within you." The corner of his mouth lifted. "Even more so, since these guys are all that stand between you and that dirtbag who tried to steamroll you into the ground."

Way to go, Myers. The last thing she needed was a lecture, no matter how deserved. Talk about foot-in-mouth disease... If he could have, he would have delivered a swift kick to himself.

"I'll remember." He saw her swallow hard a time or two and inwardly winced at the purpling smudges marring the fine skin. "Caleb, I'd really appreciate it if you could tell me what's going on. I feel like I fell off the tour bus in the middle of the set of one of those prime-time detective shows." Her voice cracked on the last word.

"Why don't we go in the kitchen," Caleb suggested. "It's a lot warmer. I'll heat the water and we can have another cup of tea." His voice deepened with amusement. "I saw all your canisters and cartons. You must stock every kind of tea on the market."

"Tea is a very versatile drink."

He watched her move with wraithlike efficiency around the kitchen, though her movements were stiff and fumbling. Caleb sprawled along the trestle bench, obliging her by staying out of the way, eyes hooded while she struggled to reestablish control of her domain. He wondered how much to tell her, and if what he did tell her would finally shatter that fragile control. When Rae finally set down his mug of tea, then slid into the seat across from him, Caleb offered up a swift prayer for wisdom—and discretion.

"I believed I mentioned working with the FBI at the moment," he began immediately, so Rae wouldn't feel like she had to pry information with a pickax. "Technically speaking I'm still a computer security consultant in the private sector, though I've done a lot of work for most of the government agencies. So when a friend of mine who owns a corporation specializing in the development of state-of-the-art space-tracking technologies called, asking for my help, the FBI agreed to bring me in as a consultant." He grinned sheepishly. "Seems I've acquired something of a reputation in the field of computer fraud and sabotage.''

''Ah. Your friend thinks someone is sabotaging the computers in his company?''

''Not exactly.'' Caleb began fiddling with his watchband. If he was wrong about Rae Prescott, his name would be mud, and his career would take a potentially permanent nosedive. But there was something about those wide unblinking eyes, the nimbleness of her brain. She had followed where his words were going with surprising quickness. ''Someone is sabotaging the contract that Polaris—my friend's company—has with the Air Force, and that's where the problem has surfaced. We have reason to believe the individual or individuals are longtime employees of Polaris. That's where I come in—trying to find out who it is.''

''So it's just one person?'' Rae stared at him. ''Is my father—''

''Whoa.'' He reached across to brush her knuckles with his fingers. ''You're getting a little ahead of me here. Right now, let's table the matter of your father, because I don't know any more about him than you.'' He waited until she nodded. ''Okay, then. We don't know how many people are involved yet in the Polaris case. Could be one, could be an entire ring. We have suspects and we're following leads. The OSI—that's the Air Force equivalent of the FBI—is handling the active duty guys, but the FBI gets the rest. Everyone's getting a little shirty, because every official from the defense department down, both military and civilian, is screaming for results.'' He ran a hand through his hair. ''Which is why I'm trying to be...ah...nice to them all, tiptoeing through the tangles doing my *own* investigating.''

Rae sipped her tea. She wouldn't look at him. ''I still don't understand why you've had my house under surveillance, unless it's because you think my father is involved.''

She couldn't let it go, Caleb realized. Of course, if *his* father was on the FBI's most-wanted list, he supposed he wouldn't be able to let it go, either. He remembered the pain and humiliation in Rae's face when she tried to disavow all ties to the man responsible for giving her life. What, he wondered suddenly, had happened to Rae's mother? Her brother?

''I don't know about your father's involvement,'' he repeated gently. "The background check's still in the preliminary stages, which is a little unusual and possibly the reason for Grabowski's irritability."

"Background check?" Rae echoed. "The FBI has been checking up on me—on my family?" The ugly bruises stood out like smears of charcoal on a white sheet as she stared across the table.

Stalling, Caleb took a sip of his drink, struggling to keep a straight face. She had given him some aromatic herb tea that tasted like crushed dandelions. Swallowing an intense desire for a plain old-fashioned mug of hot chocolate, he manfully took another sip of tea, then faced Rae. In for a penny, in for a pound. "It's all part of the reason we've had your place under surveillance," he explained. "One of the suspects has come to your store several times in the last few weeks. Then, on a routine check with the police, we found out about the footprints in the snow. I guess Tray ordered the check after that. He's the FBI agent who's been assigned to head up the case locally— What are you doing with your hands?"

The restless movements of her fingers stopped abruptly, and she wrapped her hands around the mug. "Nothing," she muttered in a stifled voice. Caleb suppressed the urge to cover the nervous fingers with his. "So because one of the suspects in your sabotage case has stopped by Joyful Noise, that justifies a background investigation on my family?"

Caleb winced. "Sounds pretty intrusive, I know—but that's because I can only fill you in on part of the picture." He tilted his head. "I could tell you everything, but then I'd have to shoot you," he quipped, hoping to coax at least a small smile, relax her....

"You're all paranoid!" Rae snapped. She shoved away from the table and stood. "I don't believe this!"

"We have to follow up on any lead, no matter how slim or ludicrous." He sat back, relaxed and peaceable. Nonaggressive. "So far, you represent the best contact yet. The suspect could be coming here just out of a love for music, but it could also be something else—especially after hearing about your prowlers."

"I suppose they're planting top secret information in my music," Rae snapped. "Microchips in the bass and treble clef notes. And don't forget—I'm leaving all my most cherished possessions scattered about so they can help themselves after they plant their information.''

''Possibly.''

Rae threw up her hands. ''That's absurd! I was joking.'' She hesitated, adding slowly, ''You—you're not joking....''

''About the microchips, perhaps,'' Caleb conceded. ''But when you've been in the business as long as I have, you learn just how creative and twisted the human mind can be. Anything's possible for God's noblest creation.'' *Careful, Myers. Your cynicism's showing.*

He looked at Rae, whose indignation had disappeared, leaving behind a battered woman who, he observed dispassionately, had had just about all she could take. ''I think a good night's sleep will add a little sanity and perspective back in your life.''

''If you think I'll sleep a wink after this—''

''Would you like me to arrange for a patrolman to come out for the rest of the night? Under the circumstances, I think I can arrange it without too much official squawkings.''

''No. Thank you. I'll just—'' She stopped, took a deep breath, her fingers pleating the fabric of her slacks in a restless movement. ''I'll be fine.''

He stood watching with a frown between his eyes while Rae tried to shore up her defenses. For the first time in years, he didn't know what to do. All his life, he had had to console three younger sisters in all sorts of circumstances, ranging from skinned knees to heartbreak. Nurturing females was as natural to Caleb as breathing, by inclination as well as upbringing. He had a protective instinct as massive and ingrained as the Rockies, which infuriated the women in his life even though he was always the first person they ran to for help.

But he had a feeling if he offered Rae Prescott a shoulder, he'd be lucky to leave with his head still fastened. The lady had been sorely used by the male of the species, and the man who gained her trust would face an uphill battle.

Of course, he'd never been able to resist a challenge—or a puzzle. And Rae Prescott promised both. He stuffed his hands in his hip pockets. ''I'm something of a night owl myself,'' he mused to the ceiling. Then he dropped his gaze to her face. ''That's why I told Tray I'd cover the night shifts. Stakeouts are the worst duty to draw. Guys go to any lengths to avoid them, because they're boring, tedious, and it's impossible to maintain a constant vigilance and keep your sanity.''

"So why did you volunteer?'' Rae asked. She still looked as prickly as a hedgehog, so Caleb merely shrugged.

"My mind is too active to get bored very often. And when I get sleepy, I...well, actually I pray out loud.'' He gave her a sheepish grin. "It helps, and we both know the Lord's always awake. At any rate, I'm there until morning. The FBI takes over during the day. I sleep four or five hours, then follow my own leads.''

"Why are you telling me all this?''

"Testing the waters,'' he confessed candidly. "I was working my way around to seeing if you'd like *me* to stick around the rest of the night, since you're uncomfortable bothering the police again.'' He hesitated, "Rae...I'd like to help, if you'll let me.''

"Why?''

"Because I owe you one. I blew it earlier tonight—had no idea there was anyone over here until I saw you fighting for your life.'' Quick thinking, Myers. Plausible, but nonthreatening.

"According to the police, they came in a window on the side. You wouldn't have been able to see even if it wasn't dark.'' Suddenly she turned, grabbed the mugs and carried them to the sink. "Thank you, but I'll be fine.'' Her voice was brisk. "Don't worry about me, Caleb. I'm used to being alone.'' She turned, produced a tight smile. "I've been alone most of my life. You go ahead—play whatever games you have to play. Dig up whatever dirt you can find on the infamous Prescott family. The door's through there. Good night.''

So much for plausible explanations. Ah, well—he'd asked for it, but even so, her rejection still stung. "A cold compress might help the worst of the bruises.'' He walked to where she stood by the sink, ramrod straight "Take care, Rae Prescott.'' His gaze touched on her swollen cheek, the purpling bruises at her throat, and his hand lifted as though with a will of its own, his fingers brushing the soft skin just beneath her jaw. "I'll be in touch.''

Thirty minutes later, he settled in the nest he'd made on the upper story across the street. He doubted the vigilance was necessary, but he knew it was useless to return to his motel when his mind was spinning like an out-of-control CD.

Mom had prayed for years that God would drop a woman in his life who could shake him out of his comfortably nomadic life-style. Well, had that day arrived? Settling in an old automobile seat he'd dragged upstairs, Caleb mentally added up everything he had learned about Rae Prescott since their first inauspicious meeting almost two weeks ago. He was not encouraged. Lord, what could he do to help this very independent, very vulnerable woman who had just been tossed in the middle of a hornet's nest? *And as You already know—I'm going to have to do something...so any and all help will be appreciated.*

Matters would become even more dicey if Raymond Meikleham Prescott had decided to return to his daughter's life—especially if that return was evinced in a highly unpleasant, highly illegal manner. Caleb mulled over everything Tray Ramirez had told him and decided that, regardless of the thorns, he had no choice but to try his best to protect the prickly Rae Prescott. Ray—and Rae. Why, Caleb wondered idly, hadn't the man named his *son* after him instead of his daughter?

He checked his watch, then dug in the backpack stashed at his side for a candy bar. While he contentedly munched, he thought about the woman across the street. Right now Rae definitely could not be compared to a sleek Siamese cat. She was more like...like the delicate, spindly cat's claw, a wildflower that grew in abundance over the meadows behind his grandparents' Florida panhandle home. Dainty and flimsy to look at, the stems were covered with minute hooked thorns that could lacerate anyone unwary enough to try to pick them. A grin kicked up the corner of his mouth. Next he'd be spouting poetry and sending her flowers and candy.

Rae Prescott. And Ray Meikleham Prescott, her father. The grin faded as Caleb channeled his thinking into official lines. The Starseeker case had just corkscrewed again, and Caleb set his formidable memory to work recalling everything he had read about individuals involved with IOS. If Rae's father was involved, Caleb planned to find out how, and why.

* * *

She couldn't sleep. After tossing and turning and watching the clock until the illuminated hands passed the hour of two, Rae threw back the covers. Her fingers fumbled on the floor until they closed around the poker she had placed by the bed. Only then did she turn on the light. For several moments she sat, fighting the fear, the shame...the anger. She felt as though she had been emotionally violated, and she didn't know what to do. Finally she jerkily pulled on her robe and made her way to her piano.

For a while she played old gospel songs, hymn arrangements, even the music from the Easter musical. Eyes closed, her fingers flowed over the keyboard, and the music filling the lonely night might have made the angels weep, but it didn't help Rae. After thirty minutes she sighed and rose. It would have to be classical. Nothing else was complicated enough, challenging enough to keep her mind from churning over the events of the evening.

She never knew what prompted the impulse, but for some reason Rae decided to play the choral song from Beethoven's Ninth Symphony—the one that woman had wrongly placed in Beethoven's Fifth. Yeah...that would lift her mood. The soaring "Ode to Joy" could also help remind her of God's eternal care, even when His presence seemed—on the surface, anyway—to be as far off as a distant star.

While she was at it, she just might play the Fifth, as well. She could release a lot of pent-up emotion with *that* one.

A brief search through the cluttered piles of music did not yield a copy of either symphony, and Rae ground her teeth in exasperation. She didn't feel like pawing through piles the rest of the night, so she padded down the hall and let herself into the store, defying the ripple of foreboding spiking her nerves. She was perfectly safe, of *course* she was safe.

She glided across the floor to the classical music section, poker at the ready, pausing only to flick on a squat *Gone With The Wind* lamp that had been converted to electricity. Everything looked normal and in order, in spite of the frenetic activity earlier. A smile hovered as Rae riffled through the *B*s in the classical music, remembering how she had followed one of the cops around like an overprotective mother, reminding him to be careful with her music—

The smile froze. Goose bumps roughed her skin in a waterfall of apprehension.

Everything looked normal, on the surface, but something was radically wrong. All her copies of Beethoven's Fifth and Ninth had vanished.

Chapter Seven

"Whaddaya think, Myers? Both father and daughter—it's too much to be coincidence." Tray Ramirez paced back and forth across a threadbare dirty gray carpet, his normally pleasant face creased in a scowl. Thick black hair and an olive skin tone attested to his Latin heritage. "Maybe she's innocent and really hasn't seen her old man in over twenty years. But you gotta admit Ms. Prescott is in this thing up to her dainty little ears."

"I'm convinced the involvement is planned—but without Rae's knowledge. She was blown away when Grabowski dropped the bomb about her father." Caleb's voice was deceptively lazy.

"She could be a good actress."

Caleb shook his head. He remembered with disturbing clarity a pair of gray eyes almost unfocused with pain and shock, a wide mouth that trembled in spite of concerted efforts to keep it still. "I don't think so. She was attacked, assaulted—on her way down when I rescued her." He grinned. He remembered a few other memorable details about Rae, as well. "She also ripped a strip off me for taking so long to get there. Then she grilled me like a veteran interrogator before she was convinced I was on the side of the angels. She was terrified when I made her wait outside while I made sure the premises were safe—but when I came back for her, she was *singing*." Albeit not very well...

Ramirez stopped at his desk, white teeth flashing in a reciprocal smile. "I admit she's a little unorthodox. Did you see her
stand over one of the police officers and lecture him for not being
careful with her music? But I fail to see what her personal idi-
osyncrasies have to do with—"

"When Grabowski told her about her father I thought she was
going to pass out. Not even the best actress in the world could
have faked that reaction." Caleb shoved the irritating hair off
his forehead, then leaned forward in the chair where he had been
sitting. "Tray, she's an innocent victim. We need to protect her,
not persecute her."

The FBI agent slammed his hand on the desk. "You tell me
how, man! We've had men watching the store—you've been
taking the nights for two weeks—and none of us spotted anything!" He paused, adding heavily, "You do realize your timely
rescue will raise more questions—with the wrong people. If the
Prescott woman is a dupe instead of the victim of assault, your
interference is going to make her situation even worse."

Caleb's fingers slid under his watchband and restlessly twisted.
"I know. IOS flunkies don't care who gets in the way."

"You're convinced they're behind this? According to my reports, they don't like going after the government." His mouth
twitched. "We still have more money and manpower than most
of the local cops."

"I know, but the m.o. of the situation out at Falcon is almost
identical to the sabotage of a program Polaris was perfecting for
the Navy a couple of years ago." Caleb laced his hands behind
his head. "The Navy contract was canceled due to supposedly
faulty software. Software that turned up later in a company with
definite IOS connections."

"I don't like it," Ramirez said reluctantly. "Until we get a
definite lead on one of the Starseeker personnel out at Falcon,
we're walking in traffic blindfolded and handcuffed."

"I'm going to talk to Rae Prescott again. She might have
remembered something now that she's had a night to sleep on
it."

"You're sure you didn't recognize the assailant, either?"

Caleb shook his head, and rose. "He wasn't one of the three
we've been keeping tabs on, no." He headed for the door, adding

very softly, "But you can be sure I'll recognize the gentleman the next time."

"What do you want?" Rae pulled the folding doors shut behind her, muffling the sound of nine-year-old Angela MacVeese playing a spirited boogie. Her first impulse had been to throw her arms around him and beg him to hold her, just for a moment. Her second, far safer impulse had been to shut the doors in Caleb Myers's face.

Unperturbed by her lack of welcome, he cocked his head toward the room behind her. "A student? You teach piano lessons as well as run Joyful Noise?" He looked relaxed and capable in a heather wool sweater and pleat-front cords—more like a winter tourist than an undercover agent for some federal organization Rae had never heard of. She knew he claimed to be a private computer security consultant, but she wasn't ready to believe him.

Instinctively she'd gone on the offense. "You mean you didn't already know? I'm also the primary accompanist for our church...and if you like I can show you my driver's license, although you probably know all that information, too."

He smiled, a dazzling smile warm enough to melt concrete. "Well, I must say I hadn't exactly hoped for the fatted calf, but I didn't expect a verbal assault the next time we saw each other, either." His eyes moved over her in frank masculine survey, then softened. "Not much sleep, huh?"

Rae had a feeling he was memorizing every bruise and every freckle, and blushed. "Not much," she admitted. "As you see, I'm also in the middle of a lesson." Trying to think about teaching, instead of the million or so unanswered questions.

Without warning his hand lifted, and his fingers skimmed with the lightness of gauze over her bruised face. "Hurt pretty bad still?"

The light touch punctured her pride in a single stroke. She had never known, until Caleb Myers burst into her life, how gentle a man's touch could be. "Only when I smile, which is another reason I'm being such a grouch." Caleb laughed, and Rae reluctantly smiled—though it *did* hurt. "Everyone thinks I'm extremely lucky."

"You were, even though I'd call it something besides luck."

She focused on the strong-looking tendons of his throat. "I know," she whispered. *God, why did You have to put a man like this in my path?* A committed Christian, radiating compassion and competence. Regardless of his profession, he was too good to be true, and Rae resolved to keep her distance in spite of her yearnings. Caleb Myers spelled trouble, any way you looked at it. Besides, she had learned by the time she was seventeen that nice men wouldn't risk any kind of commitment with a woman like her. After all, she *might* turn out to be like her mother, her father. Perhaps both.

With a brisk shake of her head, Rae turned around and slid the door open a crack. "Angela, remember to practice feeling the rhythm. Emphasize the left hand a little more. I'll be there in a minute." She turned to Caleb, in control once more. "I do have to go."

"I need to talk to you. Can I stop by when Joyful Noise closes and take you out to dinner?"

"I don't—"

"It concerns your father, Rae."

Though the words were gently spoken, she sensed a force of will behind them that more than matched her own. He was circling her patiently, but if she didn't fall in with his wishes Rae realized he was implacable enough to take her arm and usher her out the door—politely, of course. Oh, well. Why not get it over with? He wasn't asking for a date. He wanted information for his investigation. She had questions of her own. Maybe if she didn't make him beg for his answers, he'd afford the same courtesy to her. Of course, she'd have to dump her whole sordid background in his lap. He probably already knew most of it anyway. She sighed. "Six-thirty, then. And just for dinner."

"Such enthusiasm for my company."

"I'm as enthusiastic as you are."

"Ah." Dancing lights sparked through his eyes. "In that case, it should be a very...rewarding evening."

He swiveled on his heel and was out the door before Rae thought up an appropriate retort. The bell laughed merrily at her, and with an impatient head toss Rae went to compliment Angela on her playing.

* * *

Two hours later, she gratefully flipped the sign to Closed and was in the process of locking up when a man in a navy blue suit strode swiftly up the steps. Rae opened the door for him and he stepped inside the store. "Ms. Prescott?" He held up a badge. "Detective Jamison. Will you come with me to the station, please?"

Irritated both by his manner and the inconvenience, Rae moved to the revolving popular music display to give herself time to think. "Someone is meeting me at six-thirty," she said as her hands automatically straightened music. "Why do you need me at the station again? I was told this morning that I wouldn't need to come back."

"We brought in a suspect. We'd like to see if you recognize him."

Her hands stilled. "I told Detective Grabowski I didn't think I'd be able to recognize him—it was too dark and happened too fast."

Swift impatience crossed the detective's face. "Nonetheless, we need you to check out the lineup. If you'll come with me, you'll be back in plenty of time for your date." He held the door open.

Rae did not correct his assumption that she had a date. She could see an unmarked car parked at the curb, with a suit-clad driver waiting behind the wheel. "Let me get my coat and purse."

Alarm bells were clanging in her head, but she felt ridiculous voicing them to this aloof, cold-voiced detective. His brusqueness was even more daunting than the detective from last night. Shrugging, Rae gathered her possessions and locked the door. As she climbed into the back seat, she wondered why Detective Grabowski hadn't come himself. Didn't the police observe some kind of protocol concerning who was in charge of investigations? She started to ask, but with a guttural roar the car pulled away from the curb.

Detective Jamison turned to Rae. In his hand was a short, ugly-looking gun, and he was pointing it straight at her heart. The car careened around the corner and down the street. The driver twisted his head around very briefly, an evil smirk on his face and Rae's eyes widened. It was *him*. The man who attacked her!

"I don't think," the bogus detective Jamison stated softly,

"that we need to make that trip to the station, do we, Ms. Prescott?"

"What do you want?" Rae asked. Calm. She must remain calm. *This isn't real. It isn't really happening.* She kept her eyes fastened on Jamison.

Her captor relaxed in the seat, but the gun did not waver. "I'm a messenger, Ms. Prescott." Suddenly he leaned forward and the cold barrel of the gun slid lightly over Rae's bruised cheeks, her throat. "A goodwill messenger sent to keep you from acquiring any more of these."

Rae shrank back instinctively, but then the man laughed—and a burst of glorious anger surged through her. "You're making a mistake—"

"Shut up and listen," The man leaned forward, weasel eyes narrowing. "And don't give me any more lip."

Her heart was racing, and she had to twine icy hands in a death grip in her lap to keep them still, but Rae managed to stare coldly back after she gave a short nod. She didn't speak again.

Satisfied, the man settled back with a grunt. "If you want to stay healthy, Ms. Prescott, and you don't want to see that ugly palace of yours burned to the ground, you'll keep your mouth shut about anything you see or hear." He leaned forward again, crowding Rae against the door so that her spine pressed painfully into the handle. "Take my friend here. I know you *think* you recognized him. But I also know that you were mistaken." The cruel thin lips bared in a macabre smile. "You were mistaken, weren't you?"

Slowly, Rae nodded.

"I thought so. Just keep practicing that wide-eyed innocence...or next time he won't be as gentle with you."

Rae tried to lick her parched lips, but her mouth was too dry. "Who are you?" she demanded, then flinched when the gun waved a hairbreadth from her face.

"No questions." His head swiveled. "Slow down, you fool!" he snapped furiously. "Do you want every traffic cop in town on our tail?"

The respite from the opaque deadness of his eyes was such a relief Rae drew a shuddering breath. Without thought she lifted a hand to her hair, and the man's head whipped around. Quick as a striking rattlesnake his free hand shot out, the grip biting into her wrist. He twisted it hard, causing Rae to gasp in pain. "Unless you want to be dumped on your back doorstep in a trash bag, keep your hands in your lap and don't move again."

He released her, leaving white and red imprints on her throbbing wrist. Rae didn't move. She couldn't take a breath, couldn't do anything but pray a jumbled entreaty for her safety. The physical assault the previous night had not frightened her as badly as the threat emanating from this walking death machine sitting beside her.

Five minutes later the car pulled into a crowded mall parking lot and stopped in one of the lots with fewer people milling about. "Remember—" the word reached her roaring ears "—no police, no blabbing. Keep your nose where it belongs, and just maybe it will stay there—in one piece." He leaned across her, opened the door and shoved her out. "And just in case you're lying, we'll be watching you to make sure, Ms. Prescott." The dead eyes bored into her. "Watching you."

The door slammed in her face. The car left, weaving sedately out of the parking lot onto the main street.

Twenty minutes later Molly Ferguson, the music director's wife, dropped her off at home. She smilingly waved away Rae's stammered thanks, her plump face concerned but tactful. "If you change your mind and need to talk give us a call, okay?"

"Thanks, Molly." Rae forced her voice to calmness, but she avoided the older woman's eyes.

It was a little before seven o'clock. Caleb was waiting on the front porch, and so, Rae saw with a sinking heart, was Karen. She might have known her friend would use the opportunity to meet the man she insisted on calling Rae's date, especially when Rae hadn't been out with anyone but Barry Weathering in the past six months.

She clutched her purse and hurried up the brick walk. Caleb's expression, while not impatient, was nonetheless questioning. Karen waved, her fire-engine red poncho practically glowing in the gathering dusk.

"It's a good thing you called and asked me to explain to your date, honey. When I got here Caleb was ready to send for the cavalry or whatever 'cause you weren't here." She flashed Caleb a beguiling grin and poked him in the ribs with her elbow before turning to Rae. "Guess he forgot one of the primary rules—woman always keeps man waiting. Where did you say your car was?"

Rae forced a smile. "Thanks, Karen. You can go back to the restaurant now. I'll tell you all about it later."

Karen's brows lifted. "By all means, excuse me, honey. Three's a crowd and all that." She blew Caleb a kiss. "Nice chattin' with you—ya'll come on down if you want decent food instead of—"

"Karen!"

"I'm going, I'm going!"

After she trotted laughingly down the walk and crossed the street, Rae gathered her courage and looked at Caleb. "Sorry I'm late." She lifted her chin. "I had to run an errand, and had some car trouble." There. She'd managed, and her voice hadn't even wobbled.

It was difficult to read Caleb's expression in the diffuse yellow porch light she had mercifully turned on before her "trip." He wasn't angry, but something hovered behind the light smiling eyes, something watchful, waiting. He glanced around as if searching the shadows, then put a hand under her elbow.

"Do you need to freshen up before we go?"

Rae stared blankly at him a split second. "Ah, yes," she finally muttered. "I—I do need to freshen up." She gestured awkwardly to the three-year-old suit she'd been wearing when he stopped by earlier that afternoon. The cashmere sweater underneath itched with trickles of perspiration. "I, uh, I didn't take time to change, earlier."

There was a pause, then Caleb said easily, "All right, Rae. Take your time."

She barely suppressed a shudder of relief, though his placid acceptance was unnerving. She hurriedly unlocked the door and fled inside, her nerves twitching, as raw as a fresh-cut slab of meat. *They had said they'd be watching, all the time. Could they hear, as well?*

Ten minutes later, wearing the same suit but a fresh blouse, she was buckled snugly in the car beside Caleb. Her hands lay with deceptive calmness in her lap, but her stomach felt like it was doing cartwheels over her heart.

Over dinner Caleb kept up a light nonthreatening conversation that did not include any mention of her father, Rae's past, or the Starseeker case. Though baffled—since that was ostensibly the reason he'd asked her out in the first place—Rae was grateful for the opportunity to pull herself together. She was almost relaxed by the time they left the restaurant. Caleb Myers could charm the stripes off a tiger, when he chose. Soon, Rae knew, he'd turn on her and pounce, demanding answers, but for now—she needed the respite. Sitting back against the seat of the car, she gazed idly at the passing traffic and stores while Caleb related a funny story about his cat, Sheba.

Then the car pulled over onto a side street and stopped next to the curb. Caleb switched off the ignition and turned toward Rae, one hand dangling over the steering wheel, the other stretching across the back of the seat, only inches from her neck. "Tell me what happened this afternoon." Though spoken quietly, the words framed an order, not a request.

She had known this scene was inevitable, but he'd still caught her unprepared. "I don't want to talk about it." It was a childish response, one of which she was ashamed. Unfortunately, she'd always been a lousy liar.

Caleb heaved a sigh. "Rae, what's happened? Talk to me. Trust me." His hand dropped off the back of the seat and closed around her throbbing wrist. In spite of herself, a gasp of pain escaped. Caleb released her instantly. "What is it?"

"I—my wrist. I sprained it."

"How?"

Trapped, Rae stared at her lap, heart thudding heavily. She would have to lie—or tell the truth. If she lied he would know it, not only because she was lousy at it, but because Caleb Myers was not a stupid man. If she told the truth, *both* of them could end up dead. The fake Detective Jamison had not struck her as a man who issued idle threats.

Chapter Eight

Rae took a deep breath. "I really can't talk about it, Caleb." She looked him in the eye. "I'll tell you about my father, if you like. I know that's the only reason you asked me to dinner, even if you tactfully avoided bringing him up the whole meal."

"Are you in trouble?"

"No more so than I have been since I met you," she snapped pettishly. "Not to mention finding out just because my father is a crook, every law enforcement agency in the country assumes I'm in cahoots with him."

"Mmm." In the muted glow of the dash lights, she thought she saw him smile. "'In cahoots,' huh? That's I phrase I haven't heard in a while. I think I need to educate you in current cops-and-robbers argot."

Was he *laughing* at her? Control shedding, Rae clenched her hands, though her injured wrist twanged a protest. She wondered what it would feel like to plant a fist in Caleb Myers's handsome face.

"Not everyone assumes you've the same criminal tendencies as your father, Rae—least of all me. I didn't bring everything up at dinner because I hoped we could enjoy a nice quiet meal, relax, get to know each other better." He paused, then finished evenly, "I can see that didn't work. I can also see that you're hiding something from me." There was another, more uncomfortable pause. "If I felt the way you claim all those law enforcement guys feel about you, I'd be taking you down to the station about now for a bit of intensive interrogation—no, don't freeze up on me."

He ran a hand through his hair, and in the dim glow of a streetlight Rae glimpsed the leashed frustration hardening the angles and planes of his face. "Okay, we'll try it your way for the moment. I'll tell you everything I can about your father, and you tell me as much as you're comfortable with. Fair enough?"

Rae nodded once, unable to speak because her throat muscles felt as though they'd been bound up in piano wire.

After a long moment Caleb shrugged. "Your father was last arrested in San Francisco five years ago," he began, frustration still evident in his voice. "Charge was passing stolen goods. He jumped bond, hasn't been seen since."

"That seems to fit his usual pattern," Rae murmured.

"Do you remember him at all?"

God, You promised to help...I don't know if I can do this. It would have been easier to strip naked and walk through fire than sit here in the dark with a compelling, mysterious man who could reduce her to mush with a single look. At least for the moment, anyway, the kindness was noticeably absent. Somehow telling him was easier when he wasn't being kind. "I remember an impression of long hair and some kind of jacket with a fringe. The fringe tickled me and I giggled. That's all. My mother—" she hesitated, finished flatly "—my mother never gave up hoping he'd come back. For some reason, she loved him, even though he broke every promise he'd ever made to her, and finally abandoned her and both his children. I remember climbing up beside her on a window seat—I think we lived in an apartment somewhere in Oregon—and I'd sit there with her while she looked out the window. She was always crying." Her voice sounded harsh, strained. "She tried—I know she tried to take care of my brother and me, but she was..."

"It's all right, Rae."

She shook her head. It would never be all right. But she'd resolved to tell Caleb Myers every sordid detail so there would be no misunderstandings. She also needed to deflect his attention from the reason she'd been late for their dinner engagement. "My mother was...weak. Uncle Floyd told me once that she was one of the sweetest girls he'd ever met—he'd hoped she would tame my father. But it didn't work that way. I don't think she had the...the inner moral strength, is the only way I can phrase it. She'd believe anything, if it *sounded* plausible. It was the late sixties. I found her high school annual once, when I was playing in the attic. It was before she dropped out, as they used to say. I hardly recognized her. She looked so innocent in that picture, with her perfect pageboy...her Peter Pan collar white blouse with the gold initial pin. Just like all the other girls.'' She stopped, hearing the bitterness rising like bubbles in a soda bottle.

Two blocks away a police siren split the night. Suddenly lights flashed behind them, and seconds later a speeding car roared past, followed by the pursuing cops.

Rae didn't have time to take a breath. Even before the fleeing car squealed around the corner at the end of the block Caleb had grabbed her shoulders and hauled her forward, pressing her onto the seat as he covered her with his body. Then, just as suddenly, the heavy pressure of his weight lifted, and he was pulling her upright again.

The receding siren had almost faded into the distance when he finally spoke. ''Sorry about that. When I'm on an undercover job, instinct kicks in, I guess.''

Rae felt as though he'd slammed his fist into her stomach instead of smashing her nose against the seat. Somehow in the past few moments she'd forgotten who and what Caleb Myers was, and what he wasn't. *She was as gullible, as naïve as her mother.* ''Were you trying to protect me, or prevent me from escaping?'' she snapped. ''That was the getaway car, of course—only now I'll have to make other arrangements, won't I?'' Her voice heated, the anger licking through the words. ''I'll have to commend you for your professional instincts. One of them is lying well about your real profession. Computer security consultant? I don't think so. You don't miss a trick, do you?''

''Actually, I seem to have more of a talent for stuffing my foot in my mouth.'' His hand dropped over her tightly clenched fist. ''I didn't mean that like it sounded, Rae. I haven't lied to you about my job. If you'll—''

She yanked her hand free and turned to stare fixedly out the window.. ''Save it for some other gullible woman. Take me home, please, Mr. Myers,'' she added, wanting to wound.

He leaned back and folded his arms. "Not until you allow me to explain—and apologize."

"Don't bother with explanations. Apologize, and we can go. I'm sure you've wasted enough time for one evening."

"I'll apologize when you turn around, and I'll take you home when I'm good and ready." Tungsten steel underlay his words, though the quiet voice didn't convey even a hint of anger.

She jerked around, grateful for the darkness so she wouldn't have to see him while he lied to her. Or worse, pitied her.

"Rae, I am *not*—nor have I ever been—an agent of any kind. I've always been as fascinated by computers as I have by people. I want to understand how they work, why they quit working—I can't resist finding solutions, solving puzzles. But my folks wanted me to go to seminary. They thought I'd make a good preacher."

Rae opened her mouth, clamped it shut.

"I agree," Caleb said as though she'd spoken the derisive comment aloud. "I'd have made a terrible servant of the Lord as a preacher. At any rate, eventually I ended up with a consulting firm that did a lot of work for the government. A lot of the jobs dealt with top-secret information. There was risk involved—I had to learn, I suppose, how to think and react more like an undercover agent. I left that company, went into business on my own."

"Why?" Rae ventured after a moment. She was intrigued in spite of herself. He sounded so sincere. *A preacher?*

He stirred. "I...like my freedom. I like to decide which jobs to take, which ones I wouldn't touch regardless of the money." He hesitated, sounding almost sheepish. "I don't like to feel...chained. By people. By my job."

So. He was one of those. "Less responsibility that way," Rae observed.

"Probably." He didn't sound at all defensive. "Be patient. God isn't finished with me yet," he quipped.

For some reason, his serene acceptance of his flaws made her feel better. Lighter, somehow. Rae studied his face. She wanted to believe him, trust him. Oh, why not admit it? She *did* believe him. "Okay, so you're a hotshot independent. That still doesn't explain your reaction when that police car flew by."

"I wasn't trying to prevent your escape—I was trying to protect you. Instinct again. I have three younger sisters who razz me constantly about my protective instincts." She saw his shoulders lift in a shrug. "You'll just have to deal with it, Ms. Prescott. Besides, I *am* on a job. And after last night, I think you'd be the first to agree there's some physical danger involved. So...I apologize if I scared you, but I won't apologize for wanting to protect you."

"Just all part of the job, huh?"

She'd tossed the remark out lightly, but for some reason Caleb went completely still. So still Rae's skin tightened in primitive response. "I won't deny that part of the reason I took you out to dinner was official."

"I never looked at it any other way."

"But that wasn't the only reason I took you out."

"Yeah, right."

Abruptly he leaned forward, so close their noses almost touched and she could feel his warm breath against her cheek. "You have an impressive temper, little cat, but I'm not in the mood to be clawed right now, even though you think I deserve it." His finger stroked her hot cheek once, then he moved behind the wheel. "Let me know when you've got it together again, and we'll...talk."

The night closed around them in a dark cocoon. The muffled sound of traffic, the drone of a plane overhead, the nervous rustle of the wind all receded, leaving Rae alone in an increasingly uncomfortable silence. She was trapped. She wasn't immature enough to jump out of the car, much less engage in a losing battle with him by refusing to speak. And she couldn't even yell at him, because she refused to act like her mother.

Humiliation jabbed her, a hot poker to her stomach. She barely knew Caleb, yet she cared about his opinion of her. She didn't want him to think she was as weak as her mother. Another realization slammed into her. Caleb had known about her father. With all his connections, no doubt he already knew all about Daffodil Prescott, as well. Knew about the mood swings, her unrestrained displays of temper. That was why he'd warned Rae to control her simmering emotion. *Lord? Why are You doing this to me?* Right now, she almost would have preferred facing Dead Eyes and his loaded gun.

"I'm willing to stay here all night if you are."

She flinched. "I'm not going to lose my temper," she mumbled.

"I admit to relief." He smiled, a brief flash of white teeth. "Now...I know you didn't look on this evening as a date. To be honest, I didn't either, at first. But something happened during dinner, somewhere between you knocking over your water glass, and spilling pie in your lap." A low chuckle burned Rae's ears. "It's totally unprofessional, not to mention risky. But I've given up denying it. You're not just part of the Starseeker case, Rae Prescott. You're an intriguing, beguiling woman, and...I'd like to know you better."

"Why? My father's a criminal. My mother—I never finished telling you about my mother, although you probably already know all about her, too."

"No, I don't, other than what you shared earlier."

The gentleness was back, and Rae swallowed hard, steeling herself against responding. She wasn't weak, wasn't gullible. "Then I'll fill in the rest. After I do, you won't be able to take me home fast enough." She took a deep breath. "My mother was a drug addict." There, why bother to whitewash it? "She never meant to be, of course—she just couldn't help it. After my father left, the last time, she turned to drugs for consolation, instead of the time-honored denials found in alcohol, or even other men. She had just enough sense to bring us here. Uncle Floyd tried to help, but he'd just lost his wife to cancer a year or so earlier, and..." Rae shook her head, hating to even speak of the first nightmare years here in Colorado. "My mother died a year after we came here." She stared at Caleb, praying he would revert to the inflexible professional and take her home— yet terrified of that very response.

"I'm sorry. That's a rotten background to overcome. But, Rae—your parents' life-styles don't affect the person *you* are. Nor was their character a reflection of yours, especially now. You're a Christian—surely you know this."

"I know it—sometimes I have trouble...accepting it." His calm perception healed, sustained, and Rae relaxed a little. She had forgotten, for a while, the truly miraculous nature of God's love, enacted through the behavior of a fellow believer. So many people called themselves Christians—yet they seldom if ever allowed Christlike compassion to spill from their lives to others.

The last of her temper sputtered and died, carrying with it much of the shame of her revelation. Regardless of Caleb's primary agenda, Rae would always be grateful for the gift of his Christian understanding. She managed the first real smile of the evening. "I've mostly accepted my parents, my past. But—"

"But now it's rearing up like a fire-breathing dragon and trying to take a big bite out of you, huh?'

"Well...at least breathe its fiery bad breath on me."

They smiled at each other, and Caleb's hand lifted as if he was about to touch her face. Rae was sure she hadn't moved, but his hand stopped and dropped on the seat. "Do you remember the police coming to talk to your uncle once? You would have been about ten. I've read the report from Carnegie Hall, which incidentally was lousy timing."

"It was my father's fault, more than those agents. They were trying to catch him, and the longer they waited the worse their chances. Frankly, I appreciated their tact in waiting until after I performed." Uncle Floyd hadn't, though. Rae had never seen him so angry. "As for that other time, when I was ten—I don't remember. I'm sorry. I know someone came, because I asked this morning, at the station. But I don't remember." She bit her lip. "Caleb? Do you believe me?"

"About that, of course." He sighed. "Did they give you a hard time down at the station?"

"Everyone was very civil, but I don't think they believed that I've had no contact with my father."

"I know." The warmth in the simple phrase stroked her as palpably as a touch. "Rae, I can't tell you too much about the case. But I promise you when I find more definite information about your father, I'll let you know."

"Can you tell me *anything* about what's going on?"

There was a longer pause, and he bowed his head as if in prayer. Then he turned to Rae, and his eyes were very clear, almost glowing in the night. "I can tell you only that it could be even more dangerous than you've already experienced," he said slowly. "I think an organization known as IOS is involved. It's not organized crime, but they're equally deadly."

"IOS?"

His voice grim, Caleb explained. "It started as a bunch of renegade businessmen—powerful, executive-level men who had been fired or laid off. For revenge, a group of them banded together and started sabotaging the companies in a variety of ways—stealing information or technology and selling to rival corporations, manipulating stock. At first it was mostly white-collar crime. This is the third time in three years I've been on a case involving them. It's making some waves at the federal level now. They used to steer clear of anything involving the military. Security is so tight it's not worth the effort. But things have changed.''

''What happened?'' Rae asked, relieved at the subject change, but increasingly chilled by the implications.

''We're not quite sure, but about four years ago we think there was a major change in policy. Things started getting nasty—a couple of deaths by mysterious causes. Some arson, a case or two of blackmail. The members apparently got carried away by their power.''

''Is there one particular man in charge?''

His fingers drummed restlessly on the steering wheel. ''Again, we're not sure. By design the whole organization is loosely structured, the secrecy so well-maintained we have little to go on, even after several years. A name dropped here, a letter there—every now and then some sketchy tidbit from a snitch.''

I bet I could provide a clue or two. ''IOS is a strange name—what is it? Greek? Latin? Or just an acronym?''

He gave her an approving look that was mixed with gravity. ''I knew you were a smart lady the first time I met you. You're right on—it's a Greek word, and the simplest translation is *poison*. A corrosive, destructive kind of poison. Whoever came up with it as the organization's name has a brilliant mind, but a twisted sense of humor.''

Rae shuddered. ''You're right. That's sick.'' She shifted in the seat. ''You're telling me this because of what's happened at Joyful Noise. But my father—'' the realization was a knife thrust ''—you think it's possible that my father—*no*. He might not care about me, but my father wouldn't hurt me. He couldn't—''

Suddenly Caleb slid over, and his hand came down on her shoulder. ''Easy, Rae. Don't borrow trouble, all right? We don't know whether your father's involved, or how, so until we figure that out, the best thing you can do is—'' his hand squeezed briefly ''—not worry. And trust me.'' The warm teasing note disappeared. "I won't lie to you. I think you need to be extra careful, even if this turns out to not be IOS. But if they *are* behind it...well, they're dangerous. They've had a taste of power, as well as revenge. It's addictive." He shifted, turning so he could see Rae's face in the light of the street lamp. "Power, money, revenge...some of Satan's favorite tools."

Rae shivered again, and Caleb's hand slid behind her neck. He massaged the rigid tendons, his touch warm, firm, and Rae almost gasped at the sensations. She had never felt like this before, all jumpy and sizzling on the outside and melting like hot caramel inside. *This is bad, Rae. You're making a bad mistake—possibly the worst of your life. Of his.* "I need to go home."

"In a minute." The hand slid to her chin and gently turned it toward him. "Rae, I know you're hiding something from me. Are you sure you won't tell me what it is?"

Mutely, she shook her head. There was no way Caleb Myers could protect her twenty-four hours a day. And the only way she could protect *him* was with silence. "I'm fine."

"I don't believe you. You've been nervous, even frightened all evening. Knocking over your water glass and spilling pie in your lap might indicate a charming clumsiness on your part— but I think it goes way beyond that." He muttered something indecipherable beneath his breath. "Every time you look at me I want to take you in my arms, shield you from whatever it is that's frightening you—promise you that everything will be all right." He ignored her startled jump. "Believe me, it's not a feeling I'm comfortable with, either. You're blowing my concentration, little cat."

"Thanks. You're not doing much for me, either."

With a chuckle he moved to his side of the car, leaving Rae a tangled mass of regret and relief. Neither of them spoke on the drive home. But as he pulled into the driveway Caleb reached across a restraining hand. "I'll check out your house," he said. "Stay behind me."

Rae didn't protest. In the cold, early spring night the mansion—her home—filled the sky, looking dark, almost malevolent, hiding evil in every corner. She wanted to weep for her loss of innocence, but tears were a sign of weakness, not to mention a waste of time.

Caleb led her up the back stairs and took her key. She could practically feel his body humming with alertness and tension. In a barely audible voice he instructed Rae to stand just inside the door, and she waited—can of Mace at the ready—while he searched the rooms.

He returned moments later, glanced at the Mace, and a grin kicked up one corner of his mouth. "I'm going to check the store," he told her, gesturing for her to follow him down the hall. "Stay behind me, and wait here, at this door, out of sight."

Heart pounding, hands slippery on the can, Rae somehow managed a composed nod. This was the Caleb Myers who had appeared out of nowhere to rescue her, the frowning, deadly professional who looked as capable of protecting her as a sword-wielding Archangel Michael. While it was reassuring to have that protection, it wasn't exactly *comfortable*.

Once again he returned in only a few moments. "You can check to see if anything is missing, but everything looks to be in order, and there's no signs of forced entry," he announced, looking more relaxed.

Rae opened her mouth to tell him about the missing pieces of sheet music, then closed it. She wandered obediently around the store, and the insidious feeling crept over her again. Everything looked normal, in its proper place. Except—

She couldn't prevent the dismayed, clumsy gesture of her arm. Caleb was beside her instantly. "The quarter note there—" she pointed to the shiny brass note mounted on a marble stand "—and that music box. They've been moved."

"How can you tell? The police could have—"

"No." Her voice was firm. "Everything is arranged in a very specific position—I moved them all back after the police left." She met his gaze with a blend of self-consciousness and stubborn certainty. "I'm like that with these. Until he died my uncle gave me a different one every birthday since I was eight years old. I can always tell when someone has picked them up, as you just saw."

"Hmm." Understanding and a disconcerting tenderness lurked behind the watchfulness. "I do see."

More flustered now than she was by the unknown entities who had disarranged her precious keepsakes, Rae turned away, pretending to examine a bin of sheet music. When she felt Caleb's silent approach, she stiffened, but he didn't touch her.

"I'm going to look around again," he murmured. "It'll take a little while. Why don't you make yourself a cup of tea?"

Rae shook her head. "I'll wait."

He spent almost half an hour checking the store for signs of forced entry, wiretaps on her phone and concealed listening devices. There were none. He called someone, his voice soft but persuasive, then told Rae that an extra team would be detailed to watch the Prescott mansion.

Before he left, he stood at the back door for a long, uncomfortable moment, studying Rae. She didn't speak, because a plea for him not to leave her alone was crowding her throat, and she was afraid to open her mouth. Finally Caleb shook his head. His gaze rested one last time on Rae's bruised cheek. "You'll be safe enough," he promised. "But be careful. Something's going on here. Until we know what it is—" he stuffed his hands casually in the waistband of his slacks "—and until you bring yourself to share what you know...be careful. Independence is a worthy attribute, but it can be taken to extremes."

Two blocks from the Prescott mansion, Caleb pulled to the curb. After locking the car, he loped down the street, keeping in the shadows and dodging street lamps. The two men in the second story of the abandoned hardware store told him everything was quiet. They had seen nothing, and no one had tried to enter the house. Radio contact with two other undercover men confirmed the report. Caleb sympathized with their frustration and boredom. He had a feeling, however, that it might not last much longer.

His noisy instinct was especially loud. Rae's living quarters were comfortably cluttered and dusty, but she was meticulous to a fault about every aspect of Joyful Noise. If she claimed those two objects had been moved, Caleb was inclined to believe her. But who had moved them, and how had the intruder slipped inside undetected?

The question that nagged him the most ferociously was the one Rae had refused to answer. What had happened to her before he arrived to take her out to dinner?

Chapter Nine

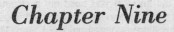

Another week passed. The Easter cantata was declared a success, but Rae shrugged aside the compliments she received for her accompaniment. God's grace alone had been responsible for the brilliance of her playing. Rae's mind—shamefully—had stayed elsewhere.

There had been no sign of the bogus detective or his henchman since the day they took her for a drive, but Rae felt their presence everywhere, even if she couldn't prove it. Her skin crawled from the sensation of being watched.

Caleb had stopped by twice. The last time, he told her he had to go out of town for a few days to check some leads. He didn't say what leads. He had promised to be back by the previous day. Since he hadn't called or come by, Rae had no way of knowing whether or not he really was back in town. She tried not to dwell on the implications of his conspicuous absence.

To pass the time she tried to catch up on bookkeeping and devoted more focused concentration to her students. There hadn't been a lot of customers that week. A lady who was teaching herself piano dropped by twice to purchase more music, and the balding man with thick-lensed glasses who collected old sheet music stopped by. This afternoon he lingered to converse, albeit diffidently.

"I wondered if you would mind if I just rummaged through

your music," he asked, mopping his balding head with a folded handkerchief.

Rae wondered why he was sweating. It was twenty-four degrees outside, and the radiators were unable to pull the indoor temperature much above sixty-eight. "Well..." She hesitated. In her experience customers who wanted to just look ended up creating after-hours work—and no revenues.

"I won't make a mess," he promised, voice anxious.

He made Rae feel small, so she smiled and told him to help himself. "Let me know if you need my assistance."

One of her favorite piano students arrived about then, and Rae forgot about the funny stoop-shouldered man. He was gone the next time she checked.

The following day proceeded much the same. Caleb still hadn't called or stopped by. Customers were still sparse, though one of them was the raspy-voiced woman who thought "Ode to Joy" was from Beethoven's Fifth. Today her request startled Rae, since she looked as impatient as she had her previous visit. "I'm looking for a piece of religious music," she said. "It's called 'The Lord Is My Light and My Salvation.' Do you have it?"

"Why, yes," Rae replied, wondering if the woman knew any more about this song than she did "Ode to Joy." "That's always been one of my favorites."

The woman did not look impressed. She coughed as she followed Rae, her eyes darting everywhere. She hadn't struck Rae as a particularly devout woman, but then, appearances really *could* be deceiving. After paying for the music, she hurried out of the store without so much as a thank-you, and Rae decided to drop the mix-up over Beethoven. Such a strange, almost ill-tempered woman would doubtless not take to correction kindly.

Rae was writing the entry in her log book when the bell jingled and a man wearing the uniform of the phone company sauntered in.

"Got a report that your phone's out of order," he announced.

Rae reached for the phone under the counter. She listened to the dial tone and looked at the man. "There's nothing wrong with my phone. You must have the wrong address."

The man scowled. "This place is Joyful Noise, ain't it? Well, I got orders to check your phones."

Rae stared. "Orders from who?"

"The President of the U.S.," he replied sardonically. "What kind of dumb question is that, lady? Orders from the phone company, okay?"

Rae studied the surly man, suddenly afraid without quite knowing why. He might be a rude serviceman. On the other hand... "Why don't you tell me the name of your supervisor and let me call and confirm the order?" She reached for the phone.

He gave her a thoroughly disgusted look. "You want to check my fingerprints, too? Forget it, lady. I got too many other calls to waste time waiting on you." He picked up the metal toolbox he had dumped on the floor. "Don't blame me when your phone won't work."

Well, Rae thought after he stomped out the door. So much for courteous, friendly service. She started to call the phone company anyway, but at that moment a customer entered the store, then the phone rang, and by the time she had another opportunity Rae had decided to shrug the matter aside.

That night she woke abruptly out of a sound sleep. For several moments she lay rigidly in bed, head pressed into the pillow, eyes wide open. There it was again—the creaking of a floorboard somewhere up front. The crawling sensation of danger suddenly jolted her spine like a thousand bolts of electricity, and for a moment Rae was afraid she was going to be ill. Then the anger arrived in a boiling flood.

She tossed back the covers and snatched on her robe, furiously tying it closed over her flimsy silk gown. After grabbing the poker, she tiptoed into the hall. *Not this time.* If they thought she'd tamely sit back while they wreaked havoc in her world, they were in for a rude shock, because regardless of their threats she was *not* going to cower in a corner.

The door to the store was still locked, but even through the thick oak panels Rae could hear the faint shuffling sound. Someone was in the store. Again.

The anger exploded. She lifted the poker over her head, heedless of consequences. "Get out of here!" she shouted. "I'm calling the po—" She stopped, breathing hard. She had been warned not to call the police. "I have a shotgun!" she yelled, resolving to purchase one immediately. "And I know how to use it." Well, surely all you had to do was pull the trigger.

From the other side of the door came the muffled sound of clanging tools and scrambling footsteps. They thudded across the floor away from Rae, and she heard the painful screech from one of the windows, unopened since summer.

Then there was silence.

Rae's arms flopped to her sides, the anger evaporated. Her fingers were so nerveless she almost dropped the poker. Moving on unsteady feet, she made her way into the kitchen and put on the kettle. Then she sat down, flipped her nighttime braid over her shoulder and tried to figure out what to do. She'd threatened to call the police, and she could only hope she'd swallowed that threat in time. Unfortunately, the one about the nonexistent shotgun had been screamed loudly enough for Karen to have heard all the way down the block.

She couldn't handle this alone, and it was the height of stupidity to pretend otherwise.

After a few minutes she went to the bedroom and looked in her purse. Caleb Myers had given her his card, writing down on the back the number of the motel where he was staying. It was two o'clock in the morning. Was he there, and if he was, how would he react to being awakened out of a sound sleep? She knew how she had reacted. *You have the survival instincts of a lemon rind, Prescott.*

The kettle was whistling, but its merry, homey sound dragged across her nerves. She turned off the gas and stood at the stove, holding her hands over the burner, vainly hoping the heat would warm her icy fingers. Her mouth twisted because she couldn't keep them still.

Caleb had more or less told her she was too independent. *All right, Mr. Private Consultant Secret Agent Wannabe Myers, let's see how you react when someone disturbs you unexpectedly.* She dialed the number and asked the sleepy clerk to connect her with his room.

He answered on the second ring. "Myers."

"Caleb?"

"Rae? Is that you?" The calm voice was alert instantly. "What's the matter—your voice is trembling."

"I hate to bother you, but—" she chewed on her lip, then

confessed in a tumbled rush of words ''—someone broke into the store again. I thought I could scare them off but I was prob-ably...I mean, I did a really dumb thing. Can you—''

''Where are you calling from?''

''The kitchen. He ran—''

''Stay there. Turn on all the lights. I'll be there in five minutes. Did you call the police?''

''No!'' Her voice was too sharp, and she tried to modify the panicked tone. ''I don't want to call the police. I can't. They said—'' She stopped, but it was too late.

''Who said?'' Caleb asked very quietly.

''N-nothing. I meant—I...''

''Don't move. I'll be there in five minutes.'' He paused, then added, ''If you have hot chocolate, I'd rather have that than tea.''

Four and a half minutes later she opened the door after his voice softly called out his name, and she recognized the calm, crisp tone. He looked so strong, so capable, that she fought the urge to throw herself into his arms.

Her face must have revealed the childish longing, for he smiled crookedly and held his arms wide. ''Come here,'' he prompted.

She took a step, then stopped, stiffening her shoulders. *If you give in now, it will be even harder after he's gone.* ''I'm fine.'' An even bigger lie than the one about the shotgun.

''Let's go to the kitchen,'' Caleb suggested, looking resigned.

Rae explained what happened with what she decided was com-mendable calm. On the other hand, she couldn't bear being left alone, and after a swift perusal of her face, Caleb allowed her to accompany him to the store. He poked around carefully, his ex-pression remote, focused. Then he turned to Rae and gestured for them to go to the kitchen.

''Your phone has been tapped,'' he said. ''Is the one here on the same line as the store?''

She nodded slowly. ''An extra line costs too much.'' Her smile wobbled. ''I sound like a broken record, don't I? Actually, the Lord has lived up to His promise about providing my needs, because I have a roof over my head, food to eat, and I can pay all my bills. I hope you—''

''Rae...it's going to be all right. I'm here.'' His hand moved to the pager at his side, then stopped. He cast another of those swift, measuring glances over Rae. "But I do have to leave you for a few minutes," he told her, his voice calm, matter-of-fact. "Three minutes, max. Stay here in the kitchen and drink your tea. Watch the clock—that's a nice one, isn't it? I've always loved the old pendulum wall clocks." He took her arm, led her to the trestle table and gently pressed her down. "Three minutes, and I'll be back. You just sit tight right here. Can you do that for me?"

"Where are you going?"

He didn't answer, just stood above her, the warm ginger-colored eyes shuttered. "I'll be back as soon as I can," he repeated.

Rae throttled the incipient panic. At least she hadn't taken up his earlier offer for comfort. "I'm perfectly all right," she promised. "You can go play all the spy games you want without fear that I'll dissolve into a gibbering idiot. If I can handle being—" She stopped, bitterly aware that she was perilously close to the gibbering idiot label.

Caleb dropped onto the bench opposite. "All right, Rae." He was calm, but firm. "Tell me what's happened. And don't try to fob me off with evasions or a plausible lie." He looked at her. "You're lousy at lying, as I expect you know."

"I wouldn't be much of a Christian if I was good at it, would I?" Rae startled herself by smiling ruefully. Ah, well. Why not admit it? Caleb's presence made her feel incredibly brave. She was a fool on any number of levels, but there was nothing to do now but tough it out. "I've probably behaved stupidly, but then I'm not used to being held at gunpoint."

"What?" All the color left his face. For once the imperturbable Caleb Myers looked completely knocked off balance, and Rae felt a brief sting of satisfaction. It was nice, not being the only one off balance.

"Last week—the night you took me out to dinner." She told the whole story calmly. "At the time I was too frightened to think properly, which of course is what they counted on. I'd do just about anything to keep someone from burning or trashing my home. It's been a week since it happened, and until a few minutes ago I was hoping everything was back to normal." Her hands lifted in a futile gesture. "Which makes me naïve, along with dumb, I know. A cop's worst nightmare.'' She looked away, swallowing hard. ''Have you or the others had any leads?''

''Not until now.'' His voice was grim. ''I trust this time you have a fair idea of what they look like. Grabowski will want to set up another photo lineup at their detective bureau. Can you describe the car?''

Sheepishly Rae shook her head. ''It was a—a car.'' She blushed when Caleb groaned. ''I'm sorry. I just never notice things like that much. About all I can tell you is that it reminded me of the kind of car all you undercover types seem to prefer.''

''Will you stop saying things like that? I'm a *consultant*.'' Caleb brushed aside the errant lock of hair dangling over his forehead. ''Rae, why didn't you tell me when this happened? I know you were afraid, but—'' Mercifully he bit back further words of censure.

She didn't want to look at him. ''I couldn't. I should have, but at the time I just couldn't.''

After a moment his face softened. ''All right. I do understand—but we're calling the police in now.'' He tilted his head, studied her somberly. ''What would you have done if I hadn't been in the motel when you called?''

She shivered. ''I don't know.'' Her chin lifted. ''But I would have managed. I yelled through the door that I had a shotgun, and I aim to purchase one first thing in the morning.''

The tender look returned, glimmering in his golden eyes and turning her poker of a spine to flimsy straw. ''I imagine you would,'' he murmured. His finger touched the end of her nose. ''Don't move. I'll be back as soon as I can.''

Chapter Ten

Caleb ran lightly across the street, making no sound as he slipped in and out of the shadows. The two FBI men on duty were as steamed—and perturbed—as Caleb. They notified Grabowski, and everyone converged minutes later at Rae's back porch.

Caleb watched her greet everyone with resigned aplomb. She had combed her hair and twisted it up, and was now dressed in a soft pink warm-up suit instead of her robe and nightgown, for which Caleb was privately relieved. He was still uncomfortable with his feelings toward her, but he had admitted to himself days ago that there was no sense fighting a losing battle. He faced enough of a battle with Rae's insecurities and inconsistencies.

Take right now, for instance—the pale blank face of a DaVinci madonna, with the marks of old bruises faded now to an unbecoming green and yellow. Proud, capable businesswoman and accomplished musician. Vulnerable, terrified young girl, trying to survive her free-fall into a reality no decent human being should have to face. She watched, gray eyes still and dark, while Caleb pointed out the nasty, unobtrusive induction coil planted under the counter. When he described her brief abduction by car the previous week she didn't stir, though Caleb knew she was fighting both fear and humility.

Grabowski looked as if he had been sleeping in his clothes.

He was scowling, irritable and short-tempered, though to give him credit, he moderated his response to Rae's lack of wisdom in not calling the police immediately after her abduction. Caleb kept his voice smooth, quietly matter-of-fact as he explained what he knew. All of them held a low-voiced discussion on the difficulty of maintaining a surveillance over a structure with as many angles and sides as the Prescott mansion. Grabowski's surliness flattened out a little, and he questioned Rae with surprising patience.

They fought a brief but furious battle over whether or not to leave the bug in place. Thanks to Rae, the police and the FBI won.

Elbows akimbo with her fists bunched on either side of her waist, Rae stubbornly refused to listen to Caleb at all. "I'm already in danger—and I don't see how I could possibly be more terrified than I was that afternoon last week," she pointed out with what Caleb decided was mule-headed naïveté. "If they find out that—that eavesdropping device is gone, they'll know for sure I called the police."

"What about the phone call you made to me?" Caleb asked, pinning her in an intractable stare. "If anyone was listening, are they going to assume you felt like calling a male friend at two o'clock in the morning for no reason other than to have a chat?" So much for his famous detachment. Right now he was finding it almost impossible to keep from tossing Ms. Prescott over his shoulder and spiriting her away like a Scottish Highlander on a raid.

Rae held his gaze only briefly before hers slid away. He watched her hands move in restless patterns up and down the counter. "I don't know," she admitted finally. "But if you take it away, they'll know for sure I called the authorities. Being threatened was bad enough, but I couldn't stand it if they drove by one night and chucked a firebomb through the window."

"It wouldn't only be the Prescott mansion that suffered," Caleb growled. Little idiot! She might be innocent to the slime buckets and sharks of the world, but she could out-stubborn a fence post. Even though the trait made her difficult to protect, Caleb reluctantly admired her backbone. She definitely wasn't the kind of woman who buckled beneath adversity.

"Ms. Prescott's point is valid," Grabowski interjected, looking as frustrated about the situation as Caleb.

Rae tossed her head. "Well, I'll just make sure I don't conduct any incriminating conversations over the phone." She smiled grimly. "Maybe those guys will even learn something about music."

She stood by the cash register, cornered but game, fighting fear with humor. Caleb felt his insides twist. He wanted to haul her in his arms and kiss those ugly bruises, then her eyes, her mouth. The strength of his emotions amazed and appalled him.

A fresh-faced man with a shock of carrot red hair approached Grabowski. "Rest of the place is clean, sir. But it looks like Ms. Prescott probably interrupted a second placement." He glanced at Rae. "They were going to put it inside one of the music boxes."

Rae's whole body jerked. "Another one?" Her voice rose, and Caleb moved to her side. She turned to Grabowski. "Why are they doing this? Why?"

Her hands flew out, fluttering awkwardly like wounded birds. The long slender fingers, Caleb noted with a pang, ended in short, practically nonexistent nails. *God, please—help me to protect this woman.* Unfortunately, the world seemed determined to rattle her cage, and it was only a matter of time— He stopped the thought.

"Do you still think my father's involved?" she was asking. "Am I still under suspicion?"

"Ms. Prescott," Grabowski began awkwardly, looking uncomfortable.

"I've told her about her father—and I've also told her about IOS." Caleb put his hand on Rae's shoulder. This time she didn't object, and he wondered if she even felt his touch. Her eyes were staring into some private hell, a brilliant, glassy look turning them to black obsidian.

He waited, ignoring Grabowski's impatience, until he felt her relax a little. "Rae, let's look at this from another angle. Think about your customers over the past couple of weeks. Have any of them acted strangely, made unusual requests, looked suspicious? Anything? Think about it as long as you need to before you answer, and don't leave something out because you think it's silly or irrelevant."

While they waited he and Grabowski exchanged looks. Both

men were aware that, while wiretapping was a federal offense, the investigation for this incident still belonged to the local police. By rights the detective deserved to be conducting the interrogation, and Caleb appreciated Grabowski's restraint. Over the past weeks they had met together several times, and Grabowski had agreed to let Caleb handle Rae...for the moment. Tonight, the detective's restraint had been pushed to the limit, and Caleb knew it.

Rae finally spoke, though her expression was dubious and she was shaking her head. "Business has been slow," she said. Her hair, hastily pinned, was starting to slip. Caleb couldn't help it. His fingers moved up to her head, pushing the pins in place. Thick and soft, the shining strands smelled like lavender potpourri and fresh linens. So much for detachment.

Rae took a step away, and he dropped his hands. "About the only thing I remember," she mused, faint color washing across the bridge of her nose, "is this woman who wanted Beethoven's 'Ode to Joy,' but she got the right symphony mixed up with—wait."

She hesitated. Grabowski shifted impatiently. Joe, one of the FBI men from across the street, started to say something. Caleb lifted an eyebrow, and Joe shut his mouth.

"What, Rae?" he asked after a minute when he realized she was having difficulty deciding whether or not to speak her mind.

"There is something," she admitted slowly. "But it's silly." A startled look crossed her face, and she smiled at Caleb sheepishly. "But like you said... All right." She inhaled, as though steeling herself. "After the first break-in I did discover that all my copies of Beethoven's fifth and ninth symphonies were missing."

Unimpressed, Grabowski snorted. "With all this music, how on earth would you know?"

Rae bristled, and Caleb fought to suppress a grin. "Detective, music is my business. I *know*—you'll just have to take my word for it."

"You probably misfiled them after all the excitement. You were pretty rattled that day."

A faint band of red deepened until two red coins dotted her cheeks. "Detective Grabowski, I may be a little rattled, but *nothing* interferes with running my store. Not thieves or muggers or the entire police department. That music is not misplaced. It's missing.''

Caleb dropped his hand over hers, which was moving furiously up and down the counter. The claws were out again, however unwisely. He glanced at Grabowski's face, which was turning just about as red as Rae's. The man was a crackerjack detective, Caleb had determined, albeit a bit gruff. From what the other cops had told him, Grabowski kept himself under iron control and expected the same from others. He would have little patience for Rae's flash-fire temper.

''Grabowski.'' Caleb fixed a serene but commanding gaze upon him. Without altering his gaze he pressed Rae's fingers one last time, then removed his hand. ''Like we discussed earlier, we've determined that they must be using the store as a drop. It's the only explanation that makes sense.'' He propped his hip on the edge of the counter, adopting a relaxed, nonthreatening pose. ''I think Fisher's our man. Joe and Charlie told me he came to the store again this past week. He left empty-handed, unless he slipped something in his pocket.'' He twisted his head to glance at Rae. ''Do you remember selling anything to a man that was small enough to tuck inside a jacket or pants pocket?''

''Not that I recall. I stock stuff with a musical motif like pencils and erasers, key chains, magnets—mostly for little kids. Unless he shoplifted, the man you're talking about isn't anyone I remember selling those items to.''

Caleb turned to Grabowski, who like Rae had cooled down considerably. Caleb thought, then mused aloud, ''He could have been leaving something behind.''

''There's something else.'' One of the Bureau guys spoke up. Charlie was a good-looking guy in his late twenties, a young Turk who liked to strut but who knew his job. He was staring at Rae with a brooding, calculating look that unaccountably irritated Caleb. ''Ms. Prescott is being tailed,'' he announced, glancing at Grabowski. ''And not by us. Are they some of yours?''

Grabowski's eyes narrowed. ''Describe the tail.''

''Male, average height, slightly overweight. Dark hair, wears a blue and yellow ski jacket or a red plaid lumber jacket. Joe got a picture of him the other day. So far no ID.''

Grabowski cursed under his breath. He whipped out his radio and spoke rapidly.

"I haven't noticed anybody like that," Rae said, faltering.

"Why should you?" Hiding his concern, Caleb straightened, jerked his chin slightly and eyed the stairs. The two FBI men started toward them.

"Where are they going? There's nothing up there." Rae darted from behind the counter as they reached the landing. "Just boxes and some old furniture. I keep it closed."

"Relax, Rae," Caleb said, snagging her elbow as she sailed by. She turned to gaze at him with a heartbreaking blend of fear, puzzlement—and wariness. *Don't look at me like that, sweetheart,* Caleb wanted to tell her. *It makes me want all sorts of things I can't afford to ask of you—or do to you—right now.* He contented himself with stroking his thumb over the inside of her elbow, carefully positioning his body so that the gentling caress wasn't witnessed. "It would be a good place to stash a few things, wouldn't it? When's the last time you went up there?"

"We checked it after the first break-in," Grabowski snapped. "It's clean."

Rae's mouth quirked. She stepped away from Caleb, her rejection graceful but final. "It's hardly that. I bet there's three years' worth of dirt and dust all over everything. I keep meaning to go over everything at least once a year, but time sort of gets away from me."

Joe and Charlie returned a few minutes later, dusting their hands on their slacks and sneezing. Caleb and Grabowski met them at the bottom of the stairs for a brief consultation. In a few minutes Caleb returned to Rae, who was studying her dainty ballerina shoes as though they held the secret of the Sphinx in their toes. Caleb waited until she lifted her head.

"It's still—clean." His eyes twinkled briefly. "In one capacity, anyway." He gestured to the watching men. "Rae, the FBI guys are going to give you a number to call in an emergency. It reaches the agents across the street. They have a modular phone set up. We hope you'll feel a little safer." He tried a small smile. "I know *I'll* feel a lot better."

Rae swallowed. "All right. I—thank you."

"Just remember it's for emergencies only. If you can get to

another phone to call, do so, since we're leaving the tap on your phone.''

"That does make sense," she said slowly, after a minute. "What can I do to help?"

Go on an extended vacation, Caleb wanted to say, but didn't. As it stood, Rae's guardian angels would have to work double time to keep her from dashing her foot against a whole truckload of stones, because even though he would have liked to become her shadow...watchdog...bodyguard, *anything* to keep her safe—he couldn't. Sometimes acting on faith was blasted difficult. "Just try to act normally. That means," he elaborated sternly, "that you continue to play the part of a musician, and leave the detective work to those who have trained for it."

Grabowski had other ideas. "It might help if you start keeping a written description of every customer, especially if they act peculiar in any way." He glanced at Caleb. "And keep the information hidden. Don't leave it lying around for anyone to find. And whatever you do, don't forget to take it out of the store at night."

The phone rang. Rae jumped violently, and without thought Caleb wrapped a protective arm around her shoulders. "Go ahead and answer it," he told her, giving her an encouraging smile, amazed when she didn't immediately pull free.

He felt her back straighten, saw her chin rise. The hand that reached out was calm as a peaceful Sunday morning. On the other hand, Caleb thought wryly, *his* feelings resembled a Saturday night play-off game.

"Hello?" Anxiety colored the syllables. After a second her eyes flew to Grabowski. "No—no, it's all right. I'm fine, Nancy," she responded with cheerful confidence as her fingers drummed up and down the counter. "I just thought I heard that prowler again, and they came to investigate. I'm sorry to cause such drama, but I promise everything's under control. Yes, it has been something of a shock...I will. Thanks for calling."

She hung up, staring at the phone as if it was a snake before her gaze moved slowly around the room, stopping on Grabowski. Incredibly, Caleb felt her lean into his chest as though seeking support.

He wrapped his arm around her shoulders and held her as though her action was the most natural thing in the world. "You did pretty well for an unworldly musician, Ms. Prescott. And without telling a lie, too.''

She seemed to realize all at once where she was, and stiffened. Caleb dropped his arm but could not resist winking at her. Rae blushed, swatting him, and everyone in the room relaxed. Then Grabowski's pager squawked. ''I'll be back,'' he said tersely, and left to call in by radio.

When he returned a few minutes later, he stood in the doorway for a moment, his grim face looking gray with fatigue. ''An unmarked car was stolen from our inventory nine days ago. We just found it. It's probably the one in which Ms. Prescott was abducted. No clues. No prints. It's been wiped clean as a car on the showroom floor.''

Chapter Eleven

"It won't look right. Everyone will think you and I—that you're—" Rae threw up her hands in exasperation. "Stop grinning at me like that! You know good and well what they'll think when you show up at choir with me and just sit there."

Caleb shrugged. "I don't care if everyone does think that. In fact, I think it's an idea with a lot of merit."

Rae sighed, too weary to debate the issue. She began the tedious process of closing Joyful Noise for the day, locking the doors, turning the sign, switching off lights. "It's a ridiculous idea founded on a premise too flimsy to be plausible. We both know you're not interested in any kind of dating relationship. Besides which, the whole church is resigned to me being a politically correct, independent, single career woman of the nineties."

"Hogwash. You're an independent, single career woman due to necessity and circumstances, not ideological bent. What puzzles me is why the men in your life are so blind. According to Karen, you've only casually dated the past couple of years, and so infrequently that it barely passes for dating."

Rae began straightening music, not looking at him. "I haven't had time—and it's not exactly as though I'm Delilah enticing Samson. There's also the monumental hurdle of my family ties."

"Few men want a Delilah. Look what happened to Samson.

As for your family, I thought we'd settled that already. Frankly, I'm beginning to think you throw your parents up as a convenient barrier."

Rae quit straightening music and produced what she hoped was a sophisticated smile. "Caleb, it's all right. You're not going to hurt my vanity by keeping our relationship strictly professional. I know you and Detective Grabowski and Agent Ram—Rom...whatever his name is—"

"Ramirez. Tray Ramirez," Caleb provided patiently.

Rae waved an indifferent hand. "Ramirez. I know you all think I need a bodyguard."

"My interest is not," Caleb replied just as patiently, "merely professional." He subjected her to a lazy, masculine appraisal that flustered Rae completely.

"Caleb, you're embarrassing me," she blurted. She lifted her hands in a sweeping gesture. "Look at me—my hair's a mess because I never take time to have it cut and styled. My nose is too long, my face is too pale...and even after all the ballet lessons Uncle Floyd insisted I take I'm about as graceful as a goose. Tyler—that's my brother—he used to call me Spiderlegs."

"I imagine a stockbroker wouldn't have much of an imagination," Caleb murmured, moving to stand in front of her.

Rae froze. "How did you know my brother was a stockbroker?"

He hesitated, then leaned against the music bin, crossing his legs. "Part of the background check. It's been ongoing—I thought you realized."

"Why should I?" she flared. "Of all the sneaky—you could have at least warned me!" Outraged, hurt, she pushed by him. "I'm still a suspect, right? Because of my father! All along, you've been lying about believing me. You don't want to protect me at all—you just want to *spy* on me! See if I have a contact at—at *church*."

It was always the same. Always. She should have known better, should have listened to her instincts. But Caleb was a far better actor than she'd realized, and stupidly she had trusted him. "It might even be the minister—or Jerry, the music director. I see him all the time, you know—don't *touch* me!" She darted around the bin when he reached for her. "If you think you can trot tamely off to church with me now—"

Caleb followed after her, the golden eyes intent, determined, and Rae realized with a pang that in cat-and-mouse dodging, she didn't stand a chance. Pride and temper gave her the impetus to stand her ground. "Just because I turn into a marshmallow with a touch doesn't mean you can bully me into—mmf—"

With dizzying swiftness his hands tugged her into his embrace, and his mouth came down on hers. As a first kiss, it was extremely thorough, and when Caleb lifted his mouth at last, all she could do was stare into the incandescent brightness of his eyes. Her brain had floated off somewhere in a soggy sea of sensation.

"I've been wanting to do that since the night I rescued you and you chastized me for not getting there sooner." His hands, those warm, clever-fingered hands, lifted and held her face in a tender cage. "You're beautiful where it counts, Rae—inside *and* out. I want you to start believing it. I also want you to believe that I'm not going to let anything or anyone defile what you are."

"You don't know me as well as you think," she whispered miserably. Her hands clung to his shoulders. He felt good—a strong, decent man—and the temptation to accept that strength was powerful because she was weak. Gullible and spineless—trapped in an endless circle. The sins of the fathers—and mothers, it seemed—were unavoidable. God's grace would have to wait for three more generations.

"Hmm...well I think I know you more than you think I know," Caleb teased her, nuzzling her nose. "Now pay attention." Her nose received a swift kiss. "I'm your bodyguard because I want to be. It would doubtless surprise you, but half a dozen cops and agents were all vying for the honor." He smiled into her eyes, finishing in quiet satisfaction, "I won."

Rae dropped her gaze to the top button of his chamois shirt. "You won," she echoed. "What you've won, I'm afraid, is a bucketload of trouble."

"Maybe so. But there's a few compensations." His head lowered again. "For instance...I need to practice being your significant other a little more in depth." He brushed his lips across hers, then took her mouth in a burning kiss.

If he practiced any better, Rae thought muzzily, she would melt into a puddle on the floor. He ended the kiss, but then his lips traveled all over her face with the softness of a snowflake. Rae wanted to cry from the sweetness of it. She was soaring, caught up in a kind of music she had only been able to create at the keyboard.

After a while, in a warm gust of laughter, Caleb murmured against her mouth, "Don't you think you better finish closing the store? We don't want to be late for choir practice."

Over the ensuing weeks, Caleb became her constant shadow. Rae eventually became accustomed not only to his presence, but the inevitable teasing and bantering they both endured at church. She tried to take each day as it came, tried to let go and let God control her destiny, tried to be a good Christian in the lion-strewn arena of life. Unfortunately, Caleb's attitude only exacerbated her situation. He played the part of attentive boyfriend with convincing realism, to the point that even Karen was won over. He treated Rae like a cherished possession, like a rare, original edition of music, but he was careful not to take advantage of her vulnerability. His kisses were the soul of discretion and respectability. He touched Rae frequently, but seldom with passion.

He was so careful with her that he was almost detached—an actor playing his part. In fact, sometimes he reminded Rae of a chameleon. With her, he was devoted, gently bullying and tactfully unobtrusive. When he talked with the FBI or the police, he slipped into the role of professional agent like feet into a pair of old slippers. Rae was constantly amazed at the level of deference accorded him, since he was assigned to the Starseeker case as a consultant. Probably it was because he seemed to know everything and everybody, from clerks to colonels. His contacts, Tray Ramirez told her once, were the envy of every consulting firm in the country.

In fact, Caleb Myers was...perfect. *Too* perfect, and Rae woke every morning wondering if this would be the day both shoes would fall, and his clay feet would be revealed. Just once, she found herself thinking as the days passed, just once she wished he'd lose that infernal self-confidence. That—that annoying *de-*

tachment. Sometimes she wondered if anything every really touched him.

Was that an offshoot of his bone-deep faith—or did he really just not care about anything that deeply?

Rae struggled to emulate his unruffled demeanor. She was convinced that his behavior that day in the store—when he had held her and kissed her and promised her that he really *felt* something for her—had all been an act. So she acted to the hilt as well. Right now she needed someone like Caleb Myers to keep her body healthy, safe from harm. But her heart was her responsibility, and to that end she could remain as *detached* from her feelings as Mr. Myers.

Two weeks passed without incident, and the situation assumed the overtones of a game. Rae pretended she was an ignorant bystander who had never heard of IOS, whose only connection to the FBI was through television shows. The police were distant players, driving their blue and white units around the city streets, nabbing speeders and keeping innocent individuals like herself safe.

On her walks to and from Gibson Girl with Caleb she fell into the habit of surreptitiously trying to pick out which strolling individual had been assigned to tail her. Which car held Agent Ramirez's men. And, of course, who in the never-ending crowd that strolled Old Colorado City were the bad guys.

That was impossible. The gaping tourist with his camera could be an IOS thug. The thick, middle-aged man strolling with apparent enjoyment down the street could have placed an illegal wiretap on her phone. It could even be a woman. After two weeks, Rae was heartily sick of the whole game, and quit pretending that she enjoyed playing cops and robbers. Instead she channeled her energy and focused on her store, her students and her music. When she thought about it, occasionally she prayed for peace of mind.

Toward the end of April, Caleb had to fly to Chicago, then to D.C. He didn't explain why, and Rae didn't ask. While he was gone, on a bright springlike morning with the forsythias bursting in butter yellow blossoms, Agent Ramirez and an FBI agent she had never met came to the store.

"Rob." She put an apologetic hand on the shoulder of her favorite piano student. "I need to talk to these two gentlemen in private." She hesitated. Rob was a gifted, intelligent high school senior who had arranged his schedule to have morning lessons so he could work after school. He was more than capable of watching over Joyful Noise for a few minutes. "Would you mind staying in the store and taking care of any customers? I can't afford to leave it unguarded."

"No worries, Rae." Rob was determined to go to Australia one day. "Take your time." He glanced into the other room. "You're not in any trouble, are you? Those two dudes don't look exactly like they're dying to hear Beethoven or Bach."

"Everything's just ducky, mate," Rae responded, and Rob grinned at her, oblivious to her quaking knees and the icy knot building in the pit of her stomach.

She led the two men wearing their revolvers beneath their suit jackets to her parlor, and wanted to giggle at the incongruity of such alien creatures in the comfortable, cluttered, Victorian-looking room. "Would you like some iced tea, a soda?"

"No, thanks." Agent Ramirez did not smile at her like he usually did. The cola-brown eyes were somber, watchful.

Rae glanced at the other man. He was taller, lanky, with a hard face and lighter brown eyes flicking around the room. "Is something wrong?" she asked into the growing silence.

"Ms. Prescott," Agent Ramirez began without warning, "can you explain who is responsible for the monthly payments you've received in a Denver bank over the last three years?"

He might as well have accused her of *robbing* a Denver bank. "I'm sorry, but I don't have any idea what you're talking about. I don't have an account in a Denver bank. Monthly payments are being made, you say?" She surreptitiously wiped her damp palms on her slacks.

"That's right," the other man confirmed in a gravelly bass voice. "Fifteen hundred dollars a month, to be exact. Deposited in a checking account for Rae Meikleham Prescott."

"You have a nice little pile accumulated," Ramirez observed. "More than enough to negate all the claims you've made about lack of accessible cash."

Rae sank into the old overstuffed easy chair that had been Uncle Floyd's favorite. "I don't know about any money." She looked at her knees. The five-year-old nubby silk designer slacks had a snag. Her whole life had hit a snag. "I have no idea what account you're talking about," she repeated, and pressed her lips tightly together. For once, caution and shock kept her temper under control.

"Ms. Prescott, I know Caleb has warned you that IOS is a ruthless, amoral organization. If they've managed to trap you some way—blackmail, threats of physical violence—you're not going to be safe by keeping your mouth shut."

The tall man stepped to the chair, looming over her. "Are you aware of the possible penalties for committing crimes against the United States government?" he asked, each word setting off tiny explosions of panic deep inside Rae. "The Starseeker program out at Falcon is considered a prototype. The sabotage of it has made a lot of people very angry." He folded his arms across his chest. "How would you like to spend the rest of your life in a federal prison, Ms. Prescott?"

Jackson Overstreet sat back in his chair and crossed his legs. His heavy jowls and broad forehead gave him the look of an aging bulldog. Right now the lines creasing his face were deeper than normal. "You can't be sure you didn't blow your cover a month ago—and that's why the whole thing has bogged down, Cal." He paused, then added, "In all the years I've known you, you've never allowed emotions to get in the way of your investigations before. I appreciate the FBI calling you in, but I'm not too happy right now. Polaris stands to lose more than just money."

Caleb stood in front of Jackson's huge plate glass window, his gaze on the Chicago skyline, hands clasped behind his back. He turned to face Jack. "My emotions aren't getting in the way," he promised. "But I'm not going to apologize for my actions toward Rae Prescott. Top-secret investigation or not, I was not about to be a pharisaical witness to the assault and possible death of an innocent young woman." He watched a commercial jetliner climb until it disappeared in a cloud, then explained with careful neutrality, "And she is innocent, Jack. Tray and I discussed it from every angle. We both agreed that playing the part of boyfriend is a lot easier cover than having a plainclothesman tagging along after her—especially when she spends the bulk of her time in her store or in church, where high visibility is unavoidable. Unfortunately, that's the procedure when I'm not available, regardless of the risk. But on the whole, becoming Ms. Prescott's attentive escort seems to be working pretty well."

Jack's hands slammed on the desk. "Well, now isn't that convenient—that really makes me happy! What are you going to do when your pretended relationship ends up blinding you to the facts? In spite of your assertion, there's still a strong possibility that Ms. Prescott's as dirty as her old man."

Caleb eyed his friend calmly. "I'll continue to do the best job I can—regardless of the facts." He steepled his fingers, deliberately prolonging the pause. "I still don't think Rae's involved criminally, but trust me—even if she were, I can handle it. I want the truth as much as you do, Jack." A fleeting image of Rae crossed his mind, but he suppressed it. He had a job to do, a puzzle to solve, and he refused to cloud his thinking over a woman. Even Rae Prescott. Their separation this past week had been good for him, he decided, because it had given him a needed opportunity to retreat from the dangerous ground upon which he'd found himself.

Overstreet slumped, expelling his breath in a noisy gust. "All right, I was out of line," he admitted. "I know you only want to uncover the truth—it's as much a gospel with you as your religion."

"Faith in Christ isn't a religion, Jack," Caleb informed him with a smile. "And you're not going to get a rise out of me on that tired old chestnut, either."

Overstreet's mouth flickered in response. "I don't know why I keep trying. I guess this whole mess is getting to me more than I realized. But Cal, regardless of your feelings or lack of them for Ms. Prescott, her father's been on the FBI's wanted list for fifteen years. Now you tell me she's been having monthly deposits made in a Denver bank for the past three years, yet you *still* claim she's innocent. Sounds like emotions to me, pal—but then, I could be wrong."

Caleb idly toyed with his watchband. "Rae hasn't heard from her father since she was four. He deserted the wife, Rae and Rae's older brother, as well. I haven't learned all the details yet, but apparently Prescott and his wife were sixties hippies. That whole scene might be looked upon with indulgence nowadays, but I can understand Rae's reluctance to discuss her background." Wounded, wary gray eyes filled his mental vision, and he shook his head to banish the image. "I haven't confronted her about the money yet—Tray just called me this morning."

"It's a little too much to be circumstantial, Cal." Overstreet hesitated, then asked bluntly, "You say you can keep personal feelings out of it, and I believe you, since I've known you over fifteen years. But is there a chance you might have to take yourself off the case anyway? Every time you insist on her innocence in the face of the evidence, it weakens your—and consequently Polaris's—position."

"No." Caleb strolled over and dropped down in one of the leather chairs across from his friend. "I'm convinced the evidence is circumstantial. Rae Prescott is innocent, Jack, but my conviction is based on training and instinct, not emotion." Right then, he still believed it.

Jack wouldn't let it go. "I don't see how you—"

"Okay, let's try it from this angle. Over the past weeks I've gotten to know her, watch her on a daily basis. You've accepted that my Christian faith is real, so you'll have to take my word for this, as well. Rae's that kind of Christian, too, even if she's struggling with it a little right now. She's not one of the Sunday morning bench-warmer crowd—she lives her faith as best she can, which means there is no way she'd *intentionally* involve herself in something illegal."

Jack emitted a rude noise.

Caleb leaned to stare directly into the other man's skeptical eyes. "Jack, do you think *I* could be involved in illegal behavior of any kind?"

He waited, and after an uncomfortable pause Jack reluctantly conceded, "You're the most honest, ethical man I know, and I know you claim the quality of your life-style is because you're a Christian. That's why I backed down earlier. But—''

''Forget the buts. Rae is innocent, a pawn. I'm pretty sure her father is behind it, but his daughter needs our help—not harassment. Give me a little more time, okay? This case has more sides than a prism. I'm hoping to find out about Rae's father when I fly to Washington.''

Overstreet picked up a gold pen and twirled it irritably. ''All right, Cal. I won't beat the horse to death. Go on—get out of here. Keep me posted on what you find out in D.C.'' He shook his head. ''And good luck in the Springs.''

Chapter Twelve

Caleb stopped by his apartment long enough to check the mail and Sheba, who as usual was entrenched in the manager's apartment. Then he packed more clothes, flew to Washington and spent two days with a liaison agent poring over mountainous files at the FBI. He then flew to Colorado Springs, catching the first flight out to make a meeting with Tray, Admiral Vale and Archie Cohen, the civilian contractor from Polaris in charge at Falcon Air Force Station.

After checking into a new motel, he tossed on cords and a lightweight pullover, then drove to Joyful Noise. It was a little before five on a cool, windy Friday afternoon, and in spite of his resolve he realized he was eager to watch Rae's response to his return. Would she maintain the indulgent, distant pose she had adopted these past weeks? He had tolerated the pose mainly because he hadn't wanted her to feel any more trapped than she already did, though several times he'd been tempted to smash the barriers with another mind-blowing kiss.

On one hand, the depth of his feelings made him uncomfortable enough to realize he wasn't ready for what those physical demonstrations indicated. He liked his freedom, liked the lack of responsibility for another person. If he was honest with himself, he'd have to admit that his past unwillingness to invest emotional energy into any serious relationship with a woman was incredibly selfish. On the other hand, what woman wanted to share his nomadic life-style, never knowing where he might be working on any given day? For that matter, what woman would tolerate being totally ignored when he was deep into an interesting puzzle, which—according to his family—was one of Caleb's worst character flaws?

Whoa, there, Myers. Back up, fella. Just because she stuck in his mind like cat hairs stuck to navy slacks didn't mean he was ready for a long-term relationship. Besides, any man willing to take on Rae had to take on the burden of her guilt over her family, as well. The thought of Raymond Prescott was an unwelcome reminder, even though it allowed Caleb to direct his thoughts to more comfortable matters—his job. As he maneuvered through the heavy afternoon traffic, he replayed the conversation in the hall with Tray Ramirez after they'd left the admiral's office. It had not been pleasant, and Caleb was debating what to do when he pulled up in front of Rae's store.

Joyful Noise was closed, though it was twenty minutes before the scheduled closing time. Rae did not respond to his knocks, either on the store door or the back door.

As a child, Caleb had sometimes considered his photographic memory more curse than blessing. Now, sprinting down the street to a public phone in front of a convenience store, he fervently thanked God for the gift. Rapidly he fed in a quarter and punched out the number for the agents stationed across the street from Rae's house.

"This is Myers. What's up? The store is closed." Thankfully Rae had given permission for the FBI to put their own tap on her phone.

"She got a call about some old sheet music—Broadway show tunes, I think. The old lady was leaving town in the morning, so Ms. Prescott closed up early to pick up the stuff."

"Who went with her?"

"Two guys from the Springs intelligence unit are tailing her—she refused to wait for Chuck to go with her in her car. Said it would look too suspicious." Joe's voice plainly revealed what he thought about such gross stubbornness.

Caleb was not used to feeling fear for another person. "What was the address?" A metallic taste trickled down his throat, soured his clenched stomach. "When did she leave?"

The agent played the tape. A scratchy, quavering voice directed Rae to a house in southwest Colorado Springs. Caleb told Joe he'd be in touch and to check with Grabowski. He borrowed a city map from the convenience store clerk, pinpointed the address and the route Rae would doubtless take.

"You need to buy it?" the clerk asked.

"No." He almost grinned. "I won't be needing it now."

Traffic was appalling—slow, irritating, noisy. Caleb forced himself to remain calm. Grabowski's men were tailing her, it was definitely an old lady's voice—*it wasn't a trap.*

Twenty minutes later he turned off a major thoroughfare onto a narrow two-lane street, his muscles relaxing a little when the traffic finally thinned. A few minutes later he turned onto the street where the elderly woman lived. Eighty-year-old trees lined cracked sidewalks and shaded the small but stately-looking older homes. Several cars were parked on either side, all of them older but well-kept mid-size sedans—except for Rae's mud-splattered hatchback parked halfway down the block. Caleb drove past, mouth softening briefly as his eye caught on the shiny black quarter note painted on the door.

He pulled into a driveway four houses down, then casually reversed into the street. Grabowski's men waited in a medium gray sedan, parked inconspicuously next to the drive where Caleb had turned around. They exchanged brief glances, then Caleb pulled to the curb and parked across the street from Rae's car. After turning off the engine he slouched in the seat, looking as if he might be settling for a catnap. His eyes, however, though almost closed, ceaselessly roamed the surroundings. Adrenaline had kicked his pulse rate into high alert.

Several minutes crawled by, and only two cars passed. Caleb noted the models and colors, then returned his gaze for another sweep of the house where Rae purportedly was visiting. Another car went by. Suddenly, Caleb twisted and glanced out the back window. Not two minutes earlier, that chocolate brown sedan had passed him traveling the other way.

Movement across the street jerked his head around. It was Rae, coming out of the house, her hands clutching a large manila envelope. She smiled at a short, tottering old lady, waved goodbye, then followed the slate path toward her car.

Down the street an engine revved.

Caleb shot out of his car and sprinted across the street even as the sedan hurtled toward Rae like a deadly avalanche. Rae fumbled obliviously with the envelope while she unlocked her door.

Tires squealed, and a hot wind buffeted his back as Caleb grabbed Rae around her waist and hurled both of them over the hood of her car. They knocked against the metal and tumbled in a tangle of limbs into the gutter. Tires squealed again as the car disappeared around the corner.

In the sudden silence, Caleb's ear caught the sound of running footsteps, and he rolled swiftly, shielding Rae with his body. The two plainclothesmen skidded to a halt, faces pale.

"Are you all right?" J.W. asked while MacArthur talked urgently into his radio.

Caleb nodded shortly and turned to Rae, who still clutched the manila envelope to her chest. The backs of her hands were scraped raw, oozing. Her pupils were dilated, her face blank with shock. Caleb swiftly checked for broken bones or a head injury, then lifted her in his arms. "It's all right, Rae," he murmured, carrying her to his car. J.W. opened the back door, and Caleb gently set her on the seat. He searched her face. "Can you tell me if you hurt anywhere? You've got some nasty scrapes on your hands."

She responded automatically, like a wind-up toy. "My knees and my right elbow sting. Probably just scraped, like my hands, and my hip aches." Her mouth curved in a pathetic imitation of a smile. "It wasn't an accident, was it? Guess I'm a popular punching bag for those guys." She stared from Caleb to J.W., back to Caleb. "It *was* IOS, wasn't it?" A shudder rippled over her body.

J.W. glanced at Caleb, cleared his throat. "Ms. Prescott, do you need medical treatment?"

"No. I'm okay. You're not going to tell me, right? Fine." She shoved Caleb, who was crouched at her feet in the open car door. "How nice to see you. Now go away. Thanks for another splendid rescue, Superman. Send me a bill."

Caleb studied her, trying to determine if her fractious temper was shock induced. "Rae, sit here a minute until you've recovered."

"I'm not hurt. I want to go home. I've got some music to

catalog.'' She thrust the manila envelope in front of Caleb's nose. ''Broadway show tunes—classics. *South Pacific, Oklahoma.* They're all in the original covers. I hope they're okay.''

She started to open the envelope, and Caleb covered her injured hands with one of his. ''Rae—honey. Relax. You're safe now.''

''You sure she didn't hit her head?''

Caleb tightened his hold on her hands, keeping her still. Her eyes were wide and strained, still staring blankly, but at least the pupils were evenly dilated. A smudge of dirt smeared one cheek, and some of the pins holding her braids on top of her head had fallen, allowing one of the braids to slip over her ear. ''Hold still,'' he ordered. He released her hands, lifted his to her head. With careful fingers he probed beneath the heavy mass of hair, freeing more pins until the whole mass unraveled across his forearms.

''Now look what you've done,'' Rae snapped. ''It takes *hours* to fix it right.'' She drew a shallow, quivering breath. Then, ''Sorry. I'm all right, Caleb. Really. Just—give me a moment alone. Please.''

Caleb stood and backed away. ''Sure.'' He motioned to the detective and they walked to the front of the car. ''I don't think she wants us to see her break down,'' he informed the puzzled man wryly. ''In spite of her temper—or maybe *because* of it— she's got this obsession about staying in control, or at least appearing to the world as though she's always in control.'' He waited until Evan McArthur approached, his normally pleasant black face wearing an intimidating scowl. ''Did you get the license number radioed in?''

''I could only make out the first three numbers,'' MacArthur grumbled in disgust.

''That's okay—I got it.'' Caleb ignored Evan's astonishment and reeled off the number. *So I memorized the number instantly. Big fat hairy deal.* There wasn't anything they could do about it right now.

Frustrated, still shaken from the encounter, he turned abruptly and slammed his palms against the hood of the car to vent some of his pent-up emotion. It was too much of a risk to pursue the car because neither the police nor the FBI could afford to blow their cover—especially when there was a good chance the incident had been designed to frighten, not kill, Rae. But how many times would the intent be to just frighten, if he kept charging to her rescue? The thought was not a pleasant one. Smoldering, he fought the urge to kick the tires, jamming his fists inside his pockets instead.

"I know how you feel, Myers," J.W. offered sympathetically. "This case is one big headache. We tail her for protection—but we can't follow up on a lead because we can't afford to let IOS know we're tailing her."

He clapped Caleb's back, glanced at his partner. "We better get back—don't need to risk being seen. You sure you can handle Ms. Prescott? She doesn't look so hot." He half-grinned. "Feisty when she's caught off guard, isn't she? I don't envy you the next couple of hours, when the shock wears off."

Caleb shoved his hands deeper in his pants pockets. "I can take care of Ms. Prescott."

The two agents loped down the street, and Caleb shook his head at his confidence. Probably more like arrogance...or perhaps pride? Slowly he returned to the other side of the car, wondering if he was about to learn one of the more humbling lessons of his life. Though her hands noticeably trembled, Rae was struggling to braid her hair. Her eyes had focused somewhere in the middle distance, while her lips moved in what Caleb realized was a desperate prayer.

"I need You to help me," he heard her whisper, and he stopped, not wanting to intrude. "Help me remember You've promised to stay with me...even when I don't feel You, and everyone else has walked away—*God!* I'm so alone. So...scared."

Before he could help himself, Caleb lifted her to her feet and gathered her in his arms, hugging her close. "How ya doing?" he inquired, as though he'd just arrived.

She stiffened. "I'm...okay. I think. At any rate, I'm not a child. I haven't asked, and I don't want your—your pity."

"Glad you haven't asked for pity, because I'm not offering any. As for this—" He cupped her shoulders and gave her a gentle shake. "I'm trying to comfort and reassure you, as any, ah, proper guardian angel would under similar circumstances." He dropped a light kiss on her brow. "Doesn't matter whether you're eight or twenty-eight or eighty. You had a rude shock—

you need comfort, and so do I, for that matter. You know, if this keeps up, I'm going to have to petition the Lord for a *real* guardian angel to take up the slack.'' Good, Caleb thought. The light touch was working. He could feel the brittle tension easing, and she was relaxing in his undemanding embrace.

''I suppose rescuing me all the time would get pretty wearing.'' Suddenly, with an inarticulate little exclamation, she buried her head against his chest, and her hands lifted to clutch fistfuls of his shirt. ''I'm sorry, Caleb. I—I'll be all right in a minute, but if you don't mind, hold me. Just...hold me, for a few moments.''

He gathered her close, bending over her, rocking her while he murmured reassurances in her ear. His hands stroked her hair, her back. A wave of protective compassion so strong it almost knocked the wind out of him washed over him. It was not an entirely comfortable emotion, because though he had felt compassion for hurting souls any number of times in the course of his life, the feeling had never been coupled with physical desire. A desire that multiplied every time he was near her, and even when he was separated by a couple of thousand miles.

Face it, Myers. You're in big trouble. The lady didn't need that complication right now, and neither did he. What she *did* need was understanding and protection. But while he might be able to suppress the desire enough to provide the big-brother understanding she craved, it was humanly impossible for him to protect Rae twenty-four hours a day, regardless of all his skill and professional training.

Chapter Thirteen

"**Y**ou're a right proper mess." Karen plonked a mug of chamomile tea in front of Rae. "But you say he only kissed your *palms* before he left?"

Rae wrapped her sore hands around the mug and carefully crossed her skinned knee over the unskinned one. Scabs were already forming on all the scraped areas, but between redness and the Merthiolate Caleb so liberally applied, she looked like a refugee from a Red Cross demonstration. There was a new bruise the size of Delaware on her hip.

It was a sunny morning, with balmy April breezes and a predicted high in the sixties. But the hot mug of tea was exactly what Rae needed, and Karen knew it. What she didn't need was Karen's irritating one-track mind. "Karen, do you ever think of anything else? Caleb has a job to do, and just because..."

"Yes?" Karen drawled, one eyebrow raised and her hand resting knowingly on her hip. "Just because the last six weeks or so he's stuck closer to you than eggs on a hot sidewalk, and just because he can't keep from touching you as though you're one of your precious pieces of antique china—even if last night all he did was kiss your hands...you're going to tell me his behavior is all in the line of duty?"

She dropped down across from Rae, propping her chin in her hands. "Honey, take it from an old pro. The pair of ya'll have it bad, even if neither one of you wants to admit it. And while Caleb Myers might not be the first guy you'd pick out of a crowd of available men, he's got—'' she frowned, then shrugged ''—presence is the word that comes to mind. Sort of a quiet power, like a sleeping lion.''

Rae sipped her tea and avoided meeting Karen's eloquent gaze. ''I'd hate to be around when he got awakened,'' she muttered, thinking of the expression on Caleb's face when he'd left her the previous night. She sighed, pushed the mug aside and rose. ''I better get to the store. It's almost nine.''

''How long are you going to ignore what you feel, Rae?''

''Karen, I accepted years ago not to trust my feelings when it comes to men. Yes, I know my rationale is wrong, but this isn't the time—or the man—to try and change for. Eventually, please God, this—this nightmare will be over, but do you honestly think Caleb will stick around? No—don't give me that look. You know I'm right, so be my friend? Let it go. Right now it's the only way I can keep my sanity. I've been mugged, threatened, almost run down—and the authorities suspect me of everything from conspiracy to fraud to sabotage. If I start brooding over Caleb's personal feelings for me and mine for him, I don't think I'd be able to stay in control.''

''Great. Lose control. It'd be good for you. You're not your mother, Rae. Even if you threw a teapot across the room, you wouldn't be your mother.''

''See you later, Karen. Thanks for the tea.''

''I thought you were supposed to let *God* be in control,'' Karen yelled after her as she started down the steps.

Rae stiffened, hesitated, then kept walking. ''He takes care of the big things,'' she called over her shoulder. ''I take care of my life.''

She opened the store, her mood subdued, pensive. Karen's words bothered her, even rankled a little. Ever since she was a child, she had determined the course of her life. Never again did she plan to feel the yawning helplessness, the frightening uncertainty that had scarred her early years. A quiet joy and a measure of peace had gradually healed her soul after she accepted Christ as her Savior and adopted His life for the role model she'd never known.

But then Caleb Myers, IOS and the Starseeker case erupted in her life.

Quit brooding, and apply your energy to work. Some things she could change—some she couldn't. One of these years perhaps she'd attain the wisdom to know the difference between them. Until then...she checked all the music, dusted the shelves and her treasures and tried to pretend everything was normal. When the bell tinkled thirty minutes later, she looked up from the counter in relief at the young woman with a mop of short blond curls capping her head. "Good morning. How can I help you?"

The young woman smiled brightly, practically bouncing over to the counter. Though at least in her mid-twenties, her manner more resembled an effervescent teenager's. "This is the most awesome store! I heard about it from a friend." She propped her elbows on the countertop, confiding with engaging candor, "Everyone at my church keeps begging me to do a miniconcert, and my friend Elaine promised me you have the best selection of contemporary Christian music in the Springs. So—" she waved her arm "—I need at least half a dozen songs—I've got some, but I'd like to try some new stuff. I'll need the soundtracks, too. You do carry those, don't you? Say, what happened to your hands?"

"I scraped them." Rae came around the counter and headed for the appropriate room. "All the music you'll need will be in here. Why don't you tell me some of the songs you've done, and we'll take it from there?"

A pleasant half hour went by, with a satisfactory pile of sheet music accumulating. Occasionally the customer's attention strayed, her eyes darting around the store as she asked friendly questions. How long had Rae lived there? What was her training? Why didn't she want to move?

Eventually the inquisitive, talkative young woman decided she had enough music. Rae gathered everything up, then tallied the total and waited while the girl rummaged in her purse for the money. "That's a lovely necklace you're wearing," Rae commented. "Very unusual." A fleeting memory surfaced, and she frowned, struggling to capture it. "Are you sure you've never been in here before? For some reason, your necklace looks familiar."

The young woman's hand flew to the necklace, then dropped. "No," she answered, laughing what sounded to Rae a bright, false laugh. "But I'm sure you'll remember me after today, won't you? How many customers buy as much music as I have?" She laughed again, but the eyes watching Rae were narrow, almost calculating, at odds with the throwaway comment.

Rae took the proffered bills and busied herself at the cash register. "Actually, I'm not too good with faces," she confessed, handing back some change. "But your necklace *is* unusual—I haven't seen one like that. Or at least—"

"I have to be going. Thanks for your help." The young woman scooped up the music and walked swiftly out.

Rae shook her head, furious with the serious character flaw she couldn't seem to help, especially now when she needed to be remembering every little detail about people. Detective Grabowski had not been able to hide his frustration and impatience with her lack of observation skills, and even Caleb teased her. Grumbling to herself, she walked to the religious section to straighten the music. Maybe she should enroll in detective school or something. Not only could she better help with the Starseeker case—she could *definitely* improve her customer relations.

She paused, examining her scraped hands. On the other hand, maybe her lack of awareness was the only reason she was nursing a few scrapes instead of lying in the morgue. Sighing, Rae went back to the counter and picked up the phone to call Karen and share the wonderful news of her eighty-seven-dollar sale. She'd also call Jerry at church and chat with him awhile. If nothing else, she could bore IOS to death forcing them to listen to her decidedly nonintriguing conversations.

What she would *not* do was think about her relationship with Caleb.

Caleb pulled up in front of the FBI field office in the Springs, where he had arranged to have a meeting with Tray. He was restless today, his internal radar sending out disquieting signals, and a few minutes later he found out why.

"It's not looking so hot for Ms. Prescott," Tray greeted him bluntly. He indicated a report on his desk, and Caleb picked it up, memorizing the contents while Tray talked. "As you see,

Fisher's had two deposits of twenty-five thousand dollars in the past two months—and the same amount has been withdrawn from the checking account in Denver Ms. Prescott claims she knows nothing about.''

''I'll ask her about it when I see her later, but I'm not going to push.'' Caleb stared at the other man. ''Cut her some slack, Tray. You and your people have been riding her pretty hard lately.''

''I understand how you feel, Myers, but the account *is* in her name.'' The phone buzzed, and the FBI agent snatched it up, spoke briefly, then hung up. He studied Caleb thoughtfully. ''Let's discuss Fisher a few minutes, since Rae Prescott is such a touchy issue.''

Caleb dropped into a chair. He'd just as soon not discuss Rae out loud, either, but if Tray thought the issue of her innocence had been settled, the man was in for a rude awakening. ''Suits me. What in particular?'' He tugged on the lock of hair falling over his forehead while he listened to Tray.

''You're more familiar with computers and computer personality types. Why would Fisher jeopardize his career, get involved with IOS? His record's clean, and his personal life sounds positively dull. Married out of college, divorced three years later. No discernible relationships since. Friends and colleagues think he's your average quiet, retiring-type guy. Nobody's ever labeled him a troublemaker. So why get involved with a vicious gang of traitors?''

Caleb relaxed in the chair, stretching out his legs. ''Any number of reasons,'' he mused, eyeing the ceiling while Fisher's nondescript features floated across his mind's eye. ''In Fisher's case, my guess is that it goes beyond money, although that probably figures in it, as well.''

''Doesn't it always?''

''It's almost a cliché, isn't it?'' Caleb agreed. ''Even Aldrich Ames sold his country and countless lives down the river, for love of money.'' He exchanged world-weary looks with the FBI agent. ''Anyway—you've seen Fisher. Unassuming, balding, slight. The antithesis of the Hollywood hunk. I read an article on computer viruses and their perpetrators years ago when viruses first started appearing. At the time, the author theorized about a pattern of personalities he dubbed the 'nerd syndrome.'

Granted, the entire industrial world has gone so computer-obsessed that article's probably not viable for the most part. On the other hand, Fisher's history fits the pattern, particularly concerning the poor social integration skills—he had few friends all through school, spent all his spare time with computers."

Tray leaned back, hands over his head. "I got labeled as a Latino troublemaker when I was in high school." He looked at Caleb. "But I didn't turn into a statistic. Maybe Fisher had a lousy childhood—and I'm sorry. But even a self-styled geek can overcome the label."

"People have different breaking points," Caleb murmured. "Cruel name-calling may not break bones, but it has been known to break spirits." He shrugged. "I'm not condoning him, Tray—just trying to walk a mile in his moccasins, so to speak, to better find a way to run him down. Strikes me that he could have devised a virus program as a simple prank that deteriorated to the sabotage. I've cross-checked all Fisher's records, though. Like you say, there's no history of aberrant or malicious behavior." He paused, finishing quietly, "We'll just have to keep digging. I'm as convinced Fisher is involved as I'm convinced Rae Prescott is not. I don't think, however, that Fisher has the personality or profile to mark him as the man in charge."

"What about Ray Prescott, Rae's father?" Tray queried, riffling through some files. He tugged one out and scanned it briefly. "He's definitely got the criminal mind, though his profile doesn't fit an IOS exec. And this name business. Why didn't he name the *son* Ray, Junior?"

"I've had the same question myself," Caleb admitted. "When I put it to Rae, she told me she thought it had to do with the parents' general rebellion against all tradition. Instead of the oldest son, they named the youngest daughter after the father." The two men exchanged looks.

"Makes sense, in a crazy kind of way," Tray said. His fingers fiddled with a paper clip. "There's still something we're missing here, Myers—and a lot of us are convinced it's Ms. Prescott."

"Then a lot of you are wrong."

There was a short, crackling silence, then Ramirez threw up his hands. "I *know* she's the stereotypical picture of innocence. I *know* she's gone out of her way to cooperate." He leveled a piercing look at Caleb. "And I know your emotions have gotten involved. The only reason I haven't demanded that you be thrown off the case is the strength of your reputation. Your objectivity in a case is a byword from here to D.C."

"Thanks. Then perhaps you'll bear that in mind when I continue to reject her willing involvement with IOS? How long since the Denver guys checked on the signature or signatures that can authorize the withdrawal of deposits from Rae's account?"

"They should get back to me by this afternoon. Dennis Hoffman's our liaison. He's supposed to contact me."

"I'd appreciate the update. I'm heading out to Falcon now to talk with Archie Cohen again. They're still trying to track the virus and how it made it to the mainframe, and I promised to see what I could do. It'll probably take several hours. If I'm not at Joyful Noise or my motel room later, just leave a message with the agents staking out the store."

"It would help if you wore a beeper all the time."

"I'm not a trained pug waiting quietly for the summons of my electronic leash, pal." He rose and headed for the door. "That's one of the reasons I'm content being an independent consultant."

Behind him, Ramirez laughed and called him a rude name. Caleb was almost in the hall when the other man called him back. Caleb suppressed a sigh and retraced his steps.

"What makes you so sure the Prescott woman is innocent?" Tray asked. "I need to write something in my report, and I'd like it to make more sense than Myers's gut instincts." His voice was conciliatory, genuinely curious.

Caleb's hand went to the lock of hair while he tried to decide whether or not to give Tray a pat answer—or the unvarnished truth. He settled on the latter. "Because I can see all the way into her soul when I look in her eyes. She doesn't have the right kind of defenses for a criminal, Tray. She hasn't needed to cultivate any, considering the kind of life she leads."

"Just because she's religious and runs a music store doesn't make her incapable of treachery."

"I'd agree with you if Rae was merely religious," Caleb retorted very softly. "But she's not. She's a Christian." His gaze bore into the confused eyes of the agent. "Think about it, Tray.

And while you're at it, think about this, If any of your guys relax their guard, and Rae suffers because of it—I'll be on your back faster than a bolt of chain lightning.''

He closed the door with ominous gentleness.

Chapter Fourteen

Rae was sipping tea and reading a how-to book on basic self-defense when Caleb arrived. She waited until he rang the bell and knocked in the distinctive pattern they had devised, then scurried down the short hall to let him in.

"A month ago I would have felt silly taking these elaborate precautions," she confessed as they walked to the kitchen. *Did he know about the bank account?* Caleb gave her one of his looks—the one where his smile lurked somewhere in the backs of those amber eyes, his mouth would soften and one corner tilt. The look that turned her knees and her brain to mush. Rae busied herself by fixing him a glass of lemonade.

"Precautions are never silly, especially in today's world. Sometimes survival—especially for a woman—can depend on a little bit of street smarts." He came up behind her, and his hand brushed lightly over her cheek. "How are you doing? Did all your students and customers make a fuss over your latest battle wounds?"

Rae rolled her eyes, her smile barely forced. "Two students insisted I should be in bed, probably because neither one of them had practiced. Most of the customers were either too polite to say anything, or they didn't care. Karen, on the other hand..."

"I don't think I want to hear what Karen had to say," Caleb

answered. "She probably thinks we ought to call out the National Guard and have them trail you in perfect formation."

"That about sums it up." Except for her pointed remarks about the nonstatus of hers and Caleb's relationship, Rae added to herself. No way she would bring that up, however. She led the way to the parlor.

"What have you been reading?" He wandered over to Uncle Floyd's chair and picked up the book she had been reading. "Sweetheart, it's impossible to learn adequate self-defense from a book."

"I'm quite aware of that," Rae retorted, her face heating. He knew every trick. Toss out a patronizing comment, but soften it with a glib endearment. Softhead that she was, she knew—and responded anyway. *When was he going to mention that account?* "I'm trying to cultivate my—what was it you said? My street smarts. Beside, it's better than feeling like a sitting duck all the time." She took a sip of lukewarm tea, grimacing, trying to figure out his strange mood. He was, if possible, more enigmatic than usual, and with inward trepidation Rae decided to probe. "Have you found out anything new, Caleb? That you can share with me?"

He sat on the couch and patted the cushion beside him, but Rae sank in the chair, her hands tense on the mug. All the indulgent warmth had fled from his face. "You do know something, don't you? Is it about my father? Or—or something else?"

Caleb took his time responding, propping his elbows on his knees and resting his chin on the palm of his hand. "Rae, will you tell me more about your childhood? There has to be more than you've shared with me, especially concerning your parents, but every time the subject comes up, you shut down like a computer given the control-alt-delete command." The intelligence and gentleness in the amber eyes all but destroyed her crumbling defenses. "Actually...I like that analogy of you better than an earlier one I entertained." A corner of his mouth curled up. "You're so determined to stay in control by deleting your past and altering your present circumstances—yet what you've ended up with is a blank screen."

Rae focused on Caleb's fingers. "I don't discuss my past because it *is* irrelevant to the person I am now. It's also very painful, as I've told you before."

"The last thing I want to do," Caleb said, "is to cause you more pain. But, Rae...your father *is* involved with IOS. Regardless of whether or not your own involvement in the Starseeker case is incidental or planned, you're still pivotal to the investigation. It would help us both if you'd be more honest and open with me about your memories of him."

She should have known. "I am not a criminal!" Rae sputtered, the sting of betrayal burning deep. "I thought, until now, that you believed me. Believed that my father's illegal activities don't make me a criminal, too. All these weeks—" She surged to her feet. "It's that stupid account, isn't it? Agent Ramirez told you about that account, and now you think—you're trying to maneuver me into admitting—"

She had to stop before her voice broke and betrayed the depth of her hurt. She had learned by the time she was four years old that men were an undependable lot of self-serving egotists, but Caleb had started to change her way of thinking. Until this moment. She couldn't believe she'd been so blind.

You can't depend on anyone, even someone who calls himself a Christian. This must be what Jesus meant when he said that everyone who followed Him would be betrayed, by family and friends...by the world. Sometimes she wondered why she continued to put her faith in a God who always seemed to demand more of her than she was capable of giving.

Caleb had risen, as well, coming across to put his hands on her shoulders. "You misunderstood me," he started to say, but Rae pulled free.

"All these weeks, leading me on, treating me like—like I was someone special. Or at least as though I were a decent citizen trapped by circumstances beyond my control." She raked him head to foot in a blistering glare. "But I'm not decent, am I? Why haven't you told the police to go ahead and put me behind bars already, seeing what a dangerous felon you've uncovered with your brilliant mind?"

Caleb stuffed his hands in the back pockets of his wheat-colored jeans and pretended an absorption in the photographs on the table. "Actually, I think your temper is far more dangerous than your nefarious tendencies," he mused. "Especially when you jump to conclusions." His eyes focused on Rae, and their intensity burned a molten gold path into her soul. "I believe you when you say you don't know anything about that bank account, Rae.''

Without warning his arms hauled her into a close embrace with such lazy but bewildering speed Rae didn't have time to struggle. One of his hands wrapped around the braid spilling down her back, and he tugged her head until her face was lifted to his. What she saw, flickering deep in the burning brightness of his eyes, flummoxed her completely. Too late, she realized that her wayward tongue had finally stung the sleeping lion one too many times.

''I believe in your innocence totally, little termagant,'' he breathed, his mouth hovering just above hers. ''And I'm spending every hour I'm not with you trying to establish it beyond doubt with everyone else.''

''Caleb—''

''But you're going to have to trust me, both as a man—and as a Christian.'' His grip tightened, and he held her a little way away. ''If I can see Christ's love shining out of your eyes, won't you try to see the same thing in mine?'' His thumbs began rotating around her shoulders, a caressing motion that threatened to make her knees buckle.

Rae swallowed, dizzy with the sensations bombarding her senses. ''I...I can't see anything when you hold me like this,'' she muttered, dazed. Then, with a helpless laugh over her absurd confession, she surrendered, relaxing to rest quietly against his chest. ''You don't play fair, Mr. Myers.''

A reciprocal chuckle floated past her ear. ''How so, Ms. Prescott?'' His hand released her braid to cup her cheek, the fingers pressing with restrained tenderness.

Rae took a shallow breath. ''I've never known a man like you.'' Her fingers, graceful only at the piano, lifted to hesitantly touch his hard cheekbone. ''Do you really believe that I'm innocent, Caleb?''

She watched the tiny laugh lines at the corners of his eyes deepen. ''So much that I put my career on the line over it,'' he admitted cheerfully, balling his hand to chuck her gently under the chin before he dropped a swift kiss on the end of her nose. In spite of his casual playfulness, Rae felt prickles of heat blossom from her flushed cheeks all the way down to her toes.

"Why?" she asked, unable to hold back the raw vulnerability. "Why would you risk your career for someone like me?"

The teasing laughter faded as he continued to study her up-turned face with a solemn intensity. "I've asked myself that question a lot lately," he replied thoughtfully. With almost absentminded gentleness he began stroking fallen wisps of hair from her face. "There's something about you.... I feel you pushing me away with one hand—but reaching out with the other. I see the evidence of your faith in the way you've chosen to live, in your inner strength...yet I sense a fear, almost as if you're afraid to even trust God to take care of you."

Abruptly he dropped his hands, sat down and took a long swallow of lemonade, then stared into the glass as if memorizing the position of the ice cubes. "To be honest—and I think I've confessed this before—what I feel for you is pretty uncomfortable. But every time I decide to ignore it or push it aside, the feelings just comes back stronger. It's almost as though God keeps using the circumstances to throw us together."

He took a hefty slug of lemonade, then lifted his gaze to capture hers in a look as potent as a touch. "Too much honesty, Rae? We've been playing a game, you and I, these past weeks—me as bodyguard pretending to be boyfriend, you as independent woman indulging the paranoid authorities. Don't you think it's time we faced a few home truths?"

Rae flopped down on the couch next to him. "I suppose," she agreed, though her pulse was racing and every instinct screamed that she was walking into a trap with no escape. "It's silly for me to deny that, physically, I'm pretty much helpless against you, on all levels. All you have to do is touch me." *Rae Prescott, how could you be so stupid, arming him with that kind of ammunition? God? Can You ever forgive me for being so weak? I'm not my mother...*

"It's nothing to be ashamed of," Caleb said, his voice gentle. "Physical attraction isn't the sin, Rae. Giving in to it without God's blessing is where most of us run amok. You and I haven't done anything that the Lord would find offensive."

"Caleb, I—" she gestured awkwardly with her hand and knocked the glass of lemonade off the end table where Caleb had put it. For a suspended moment she stared at the spreading puddle. "I don't believe I just did that—yes, I do. I'm certifiable. Absolutely, unequivocally certifiable."

The muttered self-abasement continued while she scuttled to the kitchen and cleaned up the mess. Caleb wisely stayed out of the way, keeping his mouth shut. But at least the mishap accomplished what, in a moment of brutal self-analysis, could only be termed a Freudian slip. By the time she returned to the parlor, Rae was in control, having successfully throttled the compulsion to confess any further secrets of her soul.

"Yes, I'm feeling pretty mixed up myself," she agreed. "The way I respond to you is doubtless no more than propinquity—or a variation of the white-knight syndrome. Doubtless I'd react that way to *any* man who repeatedly rescued me."

"Doubtless," Caleb intoned, steepling his fingers.

He looked unruffled, relaxed, practically asleep...except Rae made the mistake of looking directly into his eyes. Hastily she dropped her gaze. "Never mind. Let's go back to your belief in my innocence. Since you claim to be the only one who thinks I'm *not* part of the whole conspiracy, is the reason for the elaborate setup across the street merely for my protection? Or are your FBI cronies—not to mention the local police—hoping to catch me passing government secrets?" It was a colossal mistake to bait Caleb in this mood, but she had already lost any leverage she might have retained by keeping her mouth shut. "I'll be passing them along to my father, of course, who plans to sell them to the highest enemy foreign government willing to pay for the technology."

"I think we're back to square one," Caleb growled, leaning forward. "Listen to me, and try to take this at face value. Half the reason everyone is so suspicious of you is because of your adamant refusal to talk about your past."

"That's a lot of hogwash," Rae snapped. "Why don't *you* level with *me* for a change? My guilty fate is sealed because of a bank account of which I knew nothing."

Caleb groaned. "All right. All right! I'll level with you. The bank account is a major hurdle, and it's higher than ever, because we just discovered that over the past two months our chief suspect has had two large deposits into one of *his* accounts—with corresponding withdrawals from the checking account opened in your name."

''What?'' Rae gasped. A slap in the face would have been less of a blow. ''Caleb...'' Her voice hoarsened. ''I have no idea how that account came to be established. Please—you have to believe me....'' *It wasn't fair... Lord? This isn't fair.*

''I know.'' The words might have been reassuring, but as always Caleb's focus was unalterable. ''And I'm sorry I had to tell you. Can you see how I'm scrabbling for leads? *Any* details you could remember about your father could help, no matter how insignificant they may seem on the surface—no matter how painful an exercise the process may be. A name, a place...anything.'' He waited until she met his gaze. ''Rae, help me. Together we can prove your innocence.''

''I thought I was innocent until proven guilty.'' Her fingers played jerkily over the tabletop she'd just cleaned. ''I wonder if this is how Jesus used to feel. Everyone kept trying to frame Him, too.''

''He also promised the truth would set you free. Yes, it's my opinion that IOS is framing you, but unfortunately that's all I have at the moment—an opinion. And in spite of appearances nowadays, our country's legal system occasionally still tries to operate through the venue of substantiated facts instead of the court of public opinion that crucified Jesus. On the other hand, human nature hasn't changed much in the last two thousand years. So...I need your help. Before something worse happens to you than being framed.''

Beneath his quiet voice the discordant note of cynicism jarred her ears even as she felt an answering chord resound in her heart. Rae searched his grim face, feeling the bitterness, the despair well up and spill between them in a dark, ugly tide. ''I know all about human nature,'' she finally responded. ''Which means that, when IOS succeeds, all your cronies will finally agree that I really was an innocent pawn. They might even be sorry that I had to die to prove it. Maybe I should start planning my funeral now—draw up a list of the songs I'd like played.''

Caleb's face lightened, and he slouched in the seat, a slow smile gradually replacing the grimness. ''Don't be so melodramatic. Granted, you and your store are being watched for both reasons. We're pretty certain Joyful Noise is being used as a drop. When we figure out how, we ought to be able to pin some concrete evidence on the parties involved.'' The slow grin turned sheepish. "Should I have said 'substantiated facts,' for consistency?" He shook his head. "Everyone involved really is out to ensure your safety, Rae. But right now, the only avenue open is the one that seems to point to your guilt."

"That's very comforting. In the meantime I just sit around waiting for the next abduction, or a firebomb to be tossed through the window." His quiet confidence irrationally irritated her. Rae stood, her temper flaring because Caleb could sit there looking as laid-back as a cat in sunshine. "I don't like this, Caleb. I need to *do* something, not just sit around feeling helpless, exposed. Staked out like a tethered goat."

"I know. We're working around the clock on it."

"Work faster."

He snagged one of her arms and unhurriedly forced her to sit beside him. "We have a suspect, and it isn't you, so stuff a sock in it, Ms. Prescott." His finger pressed against her lips, then trailed up to tease a wayward strand of hair. "But the situation is actually similar to the one we face with you. We have a lot of hypotheses but still haven't established motive, method or the others involved. All that takes time. Months, but other suspects are also innocent until proven guilty, too, regardless of what our instincts—make that *my* instincts—are screaming."

His arm came around her shoulders. He hugged her to the warmth of his body, and Rae was unable to resist the craven need to sink into the calm and comfort he offered. It felt so good to be held. "I know," she admitted after a long moment of silence. "It's just that… I hate feeling like a coward, hate being afraid. And…well, I get angry with myself for not being able to claim all the promises God made to take care of us."

His embrace tightened. "I know."

She bit her lip. "I detest feeling so out of control, so unable to do anything concrete."

"I understand *exactly* how you feel."

Rae swiveled her head, puzzled by the nuance of fear she'd heard in that terse acknowledgment.

Caleb feathered a kiss across her forehead. "When I ran across the street yesterday and hurled us both in the gutter," he whispered against her temple, "I came as close to panic as I have in years." She felt his chest expand as he took a deep breath. "Maybe I *should* have trained as an agent instead of specializing in computer sabotage. I'd know more of the tricks of the trade of self-defense. Trouble is, I've also had to face the fact that I can't be here twenty-four hours a day to watch over you, keep you safe.''

A lump grew in Rae's throat, and her eyes began to burn. Nobody in her entire life had ever offered to protect her. Abandoned by her father, forsaken by her mother. Pampered by Uncle Floyd out of guilt and pity. Tolerated by her brother, Tyler. Even long and enduring friendships had not offered the promise implied in Caleb's low-voiced confession. Rae tried to speak but couldn't find the words, so she slid both arms around his waist and hugged him.

''I guess,'' Caleb concluded softly after a while, ''that we *both* better start leaning a little more on some of God's promises, hadn't we?''

Chapter Fifteen

Two days later a handwritten note from Caleb was in Rae's mail. *"No time to stop by, and you know I couldn't call. I have a lead on your father, and am flying to Calif. to follow up on it. Be careful, and keep your chin up. P.S. Read Psalm 32:7. Caleb."*

Rae's instinctive response was panic, followed in dizzying procession by resentment, humiliation, anger and—by the end of the day—resignation. For weeks she'd been fighting an internal battle between her heart and her head. For the second time in her life, her head lost. The first time, she had renounced a career as a concert pianist for the sake of the only salvageable part of her heritage. This time, she was falling in love, and she knew the consequences would prove to be far more cataclysmic.

Fortunately, the needs of her customers that day required little thought. Nobody seemed to notice or care about Rae's distracted air. A little before closing time, the bell jangled and the nervous little man who collected old sheet music scuttled crablike to the desk. For some reason—probably because she was already on edge—the man's diffidence rankled today. Rae dredged up a smile. "Hello."

His mouth twitched upward briefly. "I know it's late, but I was wondering if you'd let me rummage a few minutes." He glanced at his watch. "You close at five-thirty? That gives me about ten minutes."

Rae stifled the urge to tell him to try one of the chain stores at the mall if he wanted to poke about. "Were you looking for anything in particular?"

"Ah, not really—I mean, of course I'm always...Clementi," he stammered. "I'm looking for Clementi's...one of his piano sonatas." He avoided Rae's eye, and his wandering gaze fell across Caleb's note, lying beside the ledger.

Rae followed his glance. Before she could control it, her hand snatched it up, crumpling the stiff paper into a ball. To the casual observer, the note was perhaps intriguing. It certainly hadn't revealed Caleb's identity outside his oblique reference to a lead. All the same, she shouldn't have left it lying about. "Go ahead and look around," she muttered. "I'll finish some work here."

"Thanks." He looked from her clenched hand holding the wadded paper to her temper-heated face. "Problems?" he probed hesitantly.

"No, no. I'm just, uh, out of sorts today." She waved an irritable hand toward the classical room. "You better rummage if you're going to." Mr. Fowler—no, Fisher, he'd told her some weeks back, Rae finally remembered—scuttled off. She remembered his name because of the crablike way he walked. Crab, ocean, fish, Fisher. *Snap out of it, Rae.*

She tried to concentrate on the ledger, but Mr. Fisher kept darting her concerned glances, and Rae made three mistakes in as many minutes before she threw the pencil down. Between Caleb's disturbing note, Mr. Fisher's uncharacteristic interest in it and her uncomfortable revelation earlier, she was about as efficient as a piano missing half its keys. She picked up the offending note, glaring at it. In a wild fit of frustration, she ripped it into tiny pieces.

"Why are you tearing it up? What on earth made you so upset?"

Rae's head snapped up with a jerk. Mr. Fisher had come to the desk and was staring at her with a peculiar expression.

"It was a note. A *personal* note. It made me a little, ah, upset." She swept the minuscule scraps into her palm and dropped them with a flourish in the wastebasket. "Did you find any music you wanted?"

His gaze whipped from the trash to her face. He turned toward the classical music room, then abruptly stopped and looked back at her. "Not today," he replied, his voice as sharp and wary as Rae's.

Mr. Fisher's curiosity might be intrusive, but her behavior toward a customer was inexcusable. Rae bit her lip hard, then mentally ran through a half-dozen key signatures on the piano. "I'm sorry, Mr. Fisher," she said, her voice contrite. "I shouldn't have snapped at you. I've had a difficult day. But I had no right to take it out on someone interested enough to inquire."

"That's okay." He backed away, his glance moving almost furtively around the store.

Rae frowned. "Mr. Fisher? I really am sorry. Listen, I'm expecting a shipment of music from a store in Aurora that went out of business..."

"Um, yes. Well...I'll be back." He wiped his forehead, then scuttled out the door.

Restless and keyed up after a lonely supper, Rae decided to run errands. She carefully bolted and locked the back door, resisting the urge to wave at whomever was on duty in the upper level of her detached garage. That novelty had worn thin long ago, but tonight for some reason a dart of fear tickled her back, like skeleton fingers tiptoeing down her spine. She was always watched, never truly alone, and the knowledge taxed already painfully stretched nerves. Her skin crawled every time she left the house. It wasn't just the good guys wearing white hats watching her. Lurking somewhere in the darkness, IOS eyes watched as well.

She turned the car radio to the Christian station she listened to, reminding herself that God always had His eye trained upon her, too. Just as unseen, more often than not even unfelt—but nonetheless there. With sudden resolution, Rae changed lanes, then turned and headed for church. What she needed right now was music, not mindless errand running.

For several hours she played, working on the synthesizer, trying different blends, layering and relayering until she found combinations she liked. Then she moved to the piano, where she practiced for the coming Sunday's music for an hour. By nine o'clock she was tired enough for the last dregs of guilt over her outburst with Mr. Fisher to have dwindled, along with the nagging sense of uneasiness about Caleb's note.

Refreshed, she closed everything up, turned off all the lights, then set the church's alarm system. After she pulled the outside door closed, she lifted the key to turn the lock, which would activate the alarm.

Two men stepped forward out of the shadows.

"Ms. Prescott?"

Rae gasped, choking back a half-scream before it occurred to her that they must be the men assigned to follow her when Caleb wasn't available. "You nearly scared me to death!" she began, and stopped. Both the local police and the FBI were under orders not to approach her in any manner outside of a lifesaving gesture. She clutched the key in her hand, calculating furiously. First she'd have to lock the door, then *unlock* it. The alarm would sound within fifteen seconds if she didn't enter the code.

"If you're planning to rob me, I may as well warn you that I have little cash and no credit cards. If you're going to assault me—I can scream a high C and pierce your eardrums." Her tongue felt thick, unwieldy, and her pulse was racing, but she kept her voice light, almost indifferent. "Well?"

There was a split-second pause before the taller of the two men answered. "Feeling feisty, are we, Ms. Prescott? What a surprise, considering the boyfriend's out of town." His hand moved suddenly, lifting a flashlight and shining it directly in Rae's face. "All the bruises are gone. Maybe it's time to acquire some new ones?"

The other man, short and wide as a bulldozer, crowded Rae away from the door toward a dark corner the outside lighting failed to reach. So much for her grand plan to set off the alarm. A nauseating odor of sweat, cigar smoke and peppermint swirled up Rae's nostrils.

"What do you want?" she demanded, trying to shield her eyes from the flashlight.

The tall man laughed softly, and the sound raised the hairs on the back of Rae's neck. He turned off the flashlight, then casually reached out and enclosed her throat with large, smooth fingers that pressed against her windpipe with increasing weight. "You've made some people very nervous, Ms. Prescott. Just as nervous as me and my associate here are making you." The fingers pressed a little harder, and Rae flinched. At her back, hard hands closed over her shoulders, digging into the tender skin.

"You are nervous, aren't you, Ms. Prescott?" he murmured in a sibilant, seductive whisper.

"Petrified!" Rae gasped out. "You know it. Let go!" Surely they didn't mean to kill her, did they? If so, she deserved it for suicidally determining not to blow the cover of the men who were tailing her. "What do you want?" she asked again, the words emerging as a thin croak.

Another eerie chuckle grated in her roaring ears. "This is a second—friendly—warning, Ms. Prescott. Regardless of what you notice over the next couple of weeks, you better remember to keep your mouth shut. If you happen onto any, shall we say, information, that you're tempted to keep to yourself, let this friendly warning change your mind." The hand squeezed again, and Rae's hands reached up to claw. She might as well have tried to claw an iron pipe. "And," the voice added, "you better not destroy that information."

She was freed and sucked gulps of fresh night air into her depleted lungs. The hands crushing her shoulders in a vise squeezed one last time, and a gust of peppermint-laden breath choked off the gulps of fresh air. "One other matter, *Rae*. You better think up a way to keep your boyfriend's nose out of your business." Peppermint Breath's voice was rough, less polished than the taller man's.

Rae stumbled until she bumped into the brick wall, feeling the cold roughness scrape her elbows and shoulder blades. "My boyfriend?" she repeated hoarsely.

"He might enjoy playing hero, but the next time he comes to the rescue might be his last. Understand?"

Rae managed a jerky nod, but there were no further taunts. The men's bulky silhouettes faded into the night with a noiselessness more terrifying than a thundering herd of wild elephants. Her fingers shook so badly she was barely able to fit the key in the lock to activate the alarm; Rae briefly debated the efficacy of deliberately setting it off, just to see the response of the agents assigned to watch her. Had they even witnessed her latest threat?

After she finally gathered the courage to walk to her car, she collapsed behind the steering wheel and spent several moments thinking. Ever since she had almost been sideswiped the day she bought all that Broadway music from Mrs. Hayfield, Rae had been closely monitored. If Caleb wasn't with her, she couldn't even dash to the 7-Eleven without a discreet escort.

Since no one had charged to the rescue tonight, it was probably because they were willing to take the risk that she wasn't in mortal danger. Obviously the Starseeker case took precedence over a mere individual whose innocence was still questionable. Muttering beneath her breath, Rae started the engine and headed for home. She had just turned off Academy Boulevard when a flashing red light illuminated her rearview mirror. She pulled into a parking lot and stopped.

"What's wrong, Officer?" Rae only rolled the window down several inches. "There isn't a sign preventing a right turn on red at this intersection, and I know I wasn't speeding."

The patrolman responded with a slight smile. "I'm just delivering a message, Ms. Prescott. If you'll wheel into that fast-food restaurant and order yourself a milk shake, someone will happen along who wants to talk to you."

"I'll just bet they do!" Rae snapped huffily. She thanked the police officer, promised to go straight to the fast-food place, and admitted to gratitude in the privacy of her car when the patrolman followed at a discreet distance until she turned into the parking lot.

The only customers in the restaurant left as Rae sat down in a booth at the back. She took a sip of an unwanted milk shake, and waited. A few minutes later a short, compactly built man in jeans and a CSU T-shirt carried his tray down the aisle. Rae recognized the man as one of the detectives who had run to their aid after Caleb rescued her from being sideswiped. Ayers. His name was Ayers. Ha! She'd actually remembered a name. An overdose of adrenaline was good for something.

"Well, hello, Rae! Long time, no see." He slid into the booth opposite her. Without seeming to, his eye roved the deserted restaurant, and he relaxed infinitesimally. After taking a huge bite of chicken sandwich, he turned a shrewd gaze on Rae, studying her while he chewed. "Are you okay?" he asked quietly.

"I'm grateful to still be in one piece. Why the interest now?" Rae asked, now that he had confirmed her suspicion that he and his partner had witnessed the frightening episode but chosen not to intervene. "Where were you hiding out while you enjoyed the show?"

"Close enough to help if you really needed it," the detective promised.

"Oh, really? If they had wanted to stick a knife in my ribs, you could have materialized instantly to prevent it?"

A faint wince crossed his features. He leaned forward. "Listen, Ms. Prescott...Rae. It's fairly obvious that right now they don't want to kill you, because they're still too uncertain of your part in all of it. Now, can you tell me what they said? Try to remember exactly, so Ramirez and Grabowski won't override Myers and have you wired every time you leave your house."

Caleb hadn't mentioned anything about that. But then, Caleb rivaled the Egyptian Sphinx for being closemouthed when he chose. Rae shuddered at the thought of having every sneeze or cough recorded and decided that—in this instance, at least—she appreciated his silence. "I'll tell you what I can," she promised Detective Ayer, and dutifully scoured her memory for every detail, faintly apologetic when it was obvious she could provide nothing tangible for the authorities to use.

"It seems," she finished with a twisted smile, "as though my only useful part in this whole mess is to provide local IOS heavies with a punching bag." She stirred the thick shake with short, almost vicious swirls. "I realize you guys are desperate to catch whoever sabotaged that tracking program out at Falcon. But I wish everyone—including those IOS creeps—would accept that I don't know anything! I just want to be left alone."

The detective leaned back, his light gray eyes dissecting her with cool detachment. In that respect he reminded her of Caleb, though the dispassionate gaze lacked the ever-present nuance of compassion Caleb's gaze reflected. And her heart didn't miss a single beat, even though the man sitting across from her was an equally attractive specimen of manhood.

"As long as IOS thinks you might constitute a threat or be hatching some sort of double cross," he told her, "we can't afford to treat you merely as a dupe. Nor can we leave you alone. Especially when there's that account in Denver. And your father."

"It always comes back to that, doesn't it? I don't know why I waste my breath protesting anymore—"

He lifted a placating hand. "I know. Myers insists you're pure as the first snowfall on Pikes Peak, and if it's any consolation, I'm sort of inclined to agree with him."

"Thanks a bunch." Rae glared across the table, wondering what he would do if she kicked his shin as hard as she could with her sturdy Timberlands.

Suddenly he smiled. "You've got guts, Rae Prescott. I'll have to give you credit. Most women would have thrown a screaming fit, back there at your church, and Evan and I halfway expected you to yell for us, since you knew we'd be somewhere close."

"I didn't want to blow your cover." Color crept into her cheeks at his tacit compliment. Okay, so she shouldn't have entertained the notion of kicking his shin....

"We do appreciate that. I know you were scared." He paused, added more gently, "You know, it might help if you gave us the benefit of the doubt, too. If all we were interested in was the case, I wouldn't have bothered to arrange this meeting. I thought it might reassure you."

Most of the adrenaline had dissolved, and all of a sudden Rae was so tired she could have laid her head on the table and fallen asleep. She was also depressed, and toyed with the straw of her milk shake while Detective Ayer finished his sandwich. "Can you tell me if you've found out anything about the man responsible for planting the virus program?" she asked after several moments of silence.

Ayer's head lifted sharply. "How do you know it's a man? And who told you about the virus? Myers?" He muttered something beneath his breath Rae pretended not to hear.

"I assumed it was a man, which was probably archaic of me." She shoved the milk shake aside. "I'm involved in this case whether I invited it or not, and regardless of your need-to-know attitude toward the public, the less I know, the more precarious my safety. Caleb agreed, and yes, he did tell me a little bit about the case." She folded her arms and lifted her chin. "Though not nearly enough, in my opinion. I've also spent some time reading up on virus programs. I'm cooperating as much as I can, and I'd appreciate it very much if, in return, you at least pretended to believe that I'm innocent when you're talking to me."

One light brown eyebrow lifted. "I'm beginning to think Myers has met his match in you, Ms. Prescott, ma'am."

"Keep it in mind, Detective."

"How 'bout if you call me J.W. and I call you Rae? If we try hard enough, we might even work our way to mutual respect."

Rae reluctantly smiled, and the atmosphere subtly relaxed.

"You play the piano like a dream," J.W. commented as he polished off his sandwich and balled the paper. "I understand you were planning to go professional until your uncle died."

Rae nodded. "The trouble was, there was no money left after the dust settled, but about the only way I could have established a reputation—and thereby earned a substantial income—would have been to go on the road. I couldn't afford to let the house sit empty." She shrugged. "It wasn't easy, but if I had to make a choice all over again, I'd still keep the place. It's...home."

"What about your brother?"

"He couldn't shake the dust from his heels fast enough. He left Colorado when he was seventeen, went back East. I can count on one hand the number of times I've seen him since. We maintain a relationship largely over the phone. He still lectures me over my decision. Calls the Prescott mansion a financial albatross, among other things."

The detective nodded. He studied the pattern on the table, then looked at Rae, a self-conscious smile on his face. "There's a piece you play a lot at night, when Evan and I pull the graveyard shift over your garage. We can hear over the bugs you let the FBI plant in your living quarters. That piece...do you remember what it's called?"

Disconcerted, she stared at him. "Um, I play a lot of pieces. Can you hum a little of the one you're talking about?"

Red stained the bridge of his nose and cheeks. "I've got a voice like a cement mixer," he confessed. "The music goes all over the keyboard—sounds like you have about six hands."

"Mmm...probably not the Mozart, then. He's complex, not flamboyant. Might be the contemporary Christian, one from a Dino collection, possibly. I do play his arrangements a lot when I'm needing excessive emotion as well as energy." J.W. looked blank. "Let's see, I've been playing 'God and God Alone' a lot." She shoved the empty containers aside and played the opening bars on the table, singing the melody in a soft, clear voice. "Like that?"

"That's it—it's a religious song, then?"

"I think of it as a Christian song, and it's one of my favorites, too." She watched her fingers playing the table a second longer, then quit. "There's also another one that's an older song—one I heard as a teenager, when I first started going to church." She hummed and played on the table again. "That one's called 'The Lord Is My Light.' I guess I've been playing both of those a lot more lately, because of the words—they really help me right now. They remind me that I don't need to be afraid of anything, because God *is* omniscient and omnipresent, able and willing to take care of me." She wrinkled her nose. "Even when the police and FBI aren't."

J.W. shifted. "I never put much stock in that religious stuff," he admitted gruffly. "But I suppose if it helps you cope, I'm all for it."

"'That stuff,' as you label it, was all that kept me from having the screaming fit you expected at church earlier." A conciliatory smile filled her face, and after a moment, J.W. chuckled in response. "It's odd, now that I mention it. That last song, 'The Lord Is My Light,' has been on my mind over a month now, ever since this woman wanted a copy. She's been in a couple of times, and I never seem to remember *her,* just this necklace she wears. Then I had another customer..." Rae shook her head. "I'm rambling—sorry."

"What kind of necklace?"

Rae began gathering the trash. "It was an unusual necklace. I'd never seen one like it—until another customer came in wearing what I'm sure was an exact replica. I probably put my foot in it, because I think I made a comment. I haven't seen either one in a while now."

J.W. leaned across the table. "Describe the necklaces." His voice was level, but an undercurrent of excitement, almost urgency, rippled beneath the quiet words.

A little thrill of warning set her pulse racing. Rae closed her eyes, struggling to remember accurately. "It was silver and turquoise," she replied slowly, "also some pearl-like stone. Old Colorado has similar jewelry on practically every corner. But I'd never seen this particular design. It was unusual enough that I remember it." She opened her eyes wide, excitement building. "There was a large thunderbird at the bottom, with two small ones interspersed with whatever that other stone is on either side." She spread her hands helplessly. "I'm sorry. That's sort of a garbled description. You know how Detective Grabowski grumbles about my lamentable observation skills. But I—"

"You've done great." He was beaming at her, looking so pleased—even smug—that Rae's jaw dropped. His hand reached across and patted hers. "This just might be the break we're looking for."

At Rae's utter look of mystification, he relented. "Occasionally IOS females use that method to identify themselves."

"A thunderbird necklace?"

"Not necessarily *that* necklace—I'm referring to the use of jewelry as the ID code. According to Tray Ramirez, there have been two other recorded cases dealing with IOS where jewelry was used." He closely watched Rae. "Think. Can you describe the women wearing the necklaces? Anything at all?"

Rae closed her eyes again and tried to conjure a picture of either woman, but it was hopeless. She opened her eyes, feeling incredibly stupid. "One was probably in her late thirties—and she didn't know much about music. The other one was young—she bought a whole pile of music, almost ninety dollars' worth. Christian, mostly solos she said she planned to sing."

"Hair, eye color? Weight? Distinguishing marks?"

Rae ducked her head. "I can tell you the music they bought," she offered. "Title, publisher, date of publication and how much it cost. But as far as anything else…"

J.W. grimaced. "You're supposed to keep a record of your customers, as well as anything out of the ordinary." He picked up the trash Rae had gathered and stood. "Why haven't you mentioned the necklaces before?" An undercurrent of suspicion had replaced the growing camaraderie.

Rae wearily rose. "It just didn't occur to me," she replied, the words dragging. "At the time, I was being polite, making idle conversation. Now I suppose you think I'm deliberately concealing information."

"One of the things you learn when you've been on the street as long as I have," the detective returned just as wearily, "is that the most angelic face can hide a devil's soul." He looked at Rae. "Myers is a solid guy, for a civilian consultant. I'd be glad to have him at my back any time, in a fight or on a case. So I hope he's right about those guileless eyes of yours. He talks a good story about his Christian faith, and yours. Be nice if it meant more than a bunch of meaningless words.''

He nodded once, then sauntered out the door with the wily grace of an alley cat.

Chapter Sixteen

The L.A. precinct office where Caleb sat offered a relatively calm oasis compared to the chaos and noise emanating outside the semiprivate glassed-in walls. Drunks, dope peddlers, prostitutes, criminals, victims—all milling around, waiting with apathy or defiance for the system to take its grinding course. No wonder law enforcement struggled against cynicism, Caleb mused—they seldom associate with decent people in their work.

He gloomily contemplated a stack of reports about to slide off Lieutenant Zeingold's desk. Nowadays, with rampant relativism to cloud the issue, he wouldn't be surprised if "decent" people ended up in jail because their so-called standards violated the constitutional rights of everyone who wanted to change the definition of the word.

You're losing it, Myers. How about if you concentrate on the present reality, and try to remember that God's agenda doesn't have to be cleared with you. Caleb shifted his gaze to the man he'd come to see.

Lieutenant Harold Zeingold sipped a lukewarm cup of coffee and ran gnarled, ink-stained fingers through the thinning wisps of his black hair. Deep lines scored his forehead, ran down his nose to his mouth. It was the stubborn, jaded face of a man who had seen and heard everything, and Caleb felt an uncomfortable premonition that he was going to end up like the older man if he wasn't more careful with his thoughts.

"Sorry I can't do more for you," Zeingold offered in a rumbly bass voice, more matter-of-fact than apologetic. "But if the statement we got before he was blown away helps, I'm glad. T-bone was one of our more reliable snitches." He shook his head, shoved the report across the desk and watched while Caleb read the single-page document.

"I'll need a copy of this."

Zeingold waved his hand. "No problem. Keep me posted. Prescott's a sneaky, two-bit hustler, but unfortunately he's gotten himself some good connections. Since they're IOS connections, you guys have your work cut out for you." He leaned back and folded his hands across an ample girth. "Better you and the Colorado police than us. We've had a plateful, these past few years."

"I know," Caleb assented. He twisted his watchband. "I'm pretty sure Prescott will surface in Denver within the next couple of weeks. This—" he held up the statement from the dead informant "—pretty much insures that. I'm concerned about his daughter, though. I'm convinced Prescott is using her. I just don't know how or why, yet."

Zeingold grunted. "Are you still convinced the source leads down here?"

"Fisher doesn't have the personality to spearhead an operation this size. He could be the brains behind formatting and planting the virus, but I think IOS is calling the shots from another city. They wouldn't place any of their top people that close to their victim, especially when it's the U.S. government—and a top-secret project. It's too risky." He smiled ruefully. "Southern California has size as well as anonymity and plenty of targets for milking big bucks, which rates the area pretty high on a list of likely headquarters. Obviously there's others. That's what makes the investigation so tedious and lengthy."

And exhausting. Thankless. Frustrating. "It could just as easily be D.C. or Denver, Chicago or Miami. They might not even *have* a so-called corporate headquarters." He shifted his gaze to the opposite wall. Above cluttered metal desks and rows of filing cabinets, the wall was peppered with maps.

"Neither," Zeingold reminded him dryly, "does organized crime. IOS might not have their power yet, but I don't envy you the task of trying to run them to earth, much less getting a prosecution not based on endangerment or entrapment."

"We'll get as many of them as we can," Caleb promised grimly, even though privately he entertained monumental doubt. "DOD gets pretty hostile when someone messes around with multimillion dollar leading-edge space technology."

Outside the glassed walls, a truculent, slump-shouldered teenager hurled himself into a wooden chair, the violent action catching Caleb's attention. The boy, wearing gang colors, glared with hate-filled eyes at an impassive police officer. Despair lodged in Caleb's chest like a massive boulder. Sometimes he wondered why he didn't just delete his whole career and turn into a beach bum.

Then a picture of Rae filled his head, and he knew why he couldn't give in or give up.

"We're pretty sure," he told Zeingold slowly, "that there's someone in the area instructing Fisher, keeping him in line. They've also sent strong-arm thugs to harass and intimidate Rae Prescott. Any results yet on the descriptions I faxed you?"

"Nope. From what you've been telling me, though, I doubt they'd import dirtbags from this far. Have you checked Denver and Kansas City?"

"I'm flying to Denver this evening."

The door opened and the booking officer poked his head in. "There's a guy out here screaming brutality against Loomis, Lieutenant."

"Who is it?"

"Vinnie. Loomis caught him dealing to a couple of kids."

"Umph." Lieutenant Zeingold grimaced and rose. "Knowing Loomis, he might have done more than read him his rights." He paused, added dryly, "Knowing Vinnie, he probably deserved it. Of course, you didn't hear me say that." He glanced at Caleb. "I'll be there in a minute, Harris."

Caleb stood, as well. "Will you let me know if you hear anything else on IOS? No matter how flimsy or unsubstantiated? The information T-bone provided has been invaluable. I just wish it hadn't been at the cost of his life."

Zeingold shrugged. To the hardened detective, T-bone might have been a useful source of information, but as a human being he'd been a washout, not worth crying over.

It was enough to make a statue weep. Mood glum, Caleb shook the detective's hand. "I better get moving so I don't miss my flight. The sooner I get to Denver, the sooner I can get back to the Springs and we can collate all this information."

Zeingold snorted. "You feeling the heat, Myers?"

"Yeah...and I'm starting to sweat. If we don't get some kind of break soon, I have a feeling Congress is going to be screaming for some heads on a platter." He stuffed his hands in the hip pockets of his jeans. "Mine will probably be the first."

Dennis Hoffman, one of the Denver FBI agents, met him at the airport. It was eleven at night, and pouring rain. Hoffman grumbled about the abysmal weather on the long drive to the local Bureau offices as he maneuvered through the surprisingly heavy traffic.

In a conference room littered with paper coffee cups and crumpled cellophane wrappers, they joined the Denver section chief, Bob Taylor. He gestured Caleb to a chair, then slid a file across the table. "Rae Prescott's *brother* is responsible for the checking account," he announced as Caleb sank into the chair. "We finally got hold of him this morning. He hadn't told her about the account because he wanted it to be a cushion if the store bombed." He looked disgusted. "Only Tyler Prescott said *when* the store bombed. Supportive brother, huh?"

"They aren't that close," Hoffman put in. "From what we've learned, Tyler Prescott thinks his sister is too sentimental and idealistic. Not a practical bone in her body. At least he's got enough family feeling to make sure she doesn't end up on the street, homeless and broke."

Caleb rubbed the back of his hand over his mouth and gritty eyes. He had been seventeen hours without sleep, the flight from L.A. had been bumpy and exhausting, and incoming bad weather kept the plane circling the airport for almost an hour. Taylor's revelation poured over his weary bones like the balm of Gilead.

"Thank God," he murmured beneath his breath with heartfelt sincerity. At this point he didn't care if Tyler Prescott had the family feeling of a shark—at least Rae's innocence had been established as far as the Denver account was concerned.

His mouth relaxed into a relieved smile as he rapidly scanned the file. "You're positive the signature on the checks withdrawing the fifty thousand is forged?"

"Yes." Taylor leaned back, absently cracking his knuckles. "It was a professional job—our document examiner's one of the best on the west coast, and she's willing to swear that the original sample was done by a man, which pretty much absolves Ms. Prescott."

"You can sleep tonight, Myers," Dennis Hoffman gibed good-naturedly. "Your girlfriend's off the hook. Or maybe the two of you would rather...celebrate."

He was *not* in the mood for this. Caleb shifted slightly, leveling a gelid stare at the agent. After a silent moment of increasing tension, Hoffman shrugged and cleared his throat.

"Sorry," he muttered. "I guess that was out of line."

"Way out," Caleb agreed in a deceptively pleasant voice, and Hoffman backed a couple more steps. "Don't let it happen again."

"The word's out that your interest in the Prescott woman is more than just professional," Taylor intervened. "That's not smart, and you know it, Myers. You're opening yourself up to a sexual harassment suit. And she might have been telling the truth about the checking account, but there's still a good possibility she could be conspiring with her father."

"She's not conspiring with her father." Caleb casually leaned forward and planted his elbows on the table. His voice was low-key, deceptively soft. "As for your concern over a lawsuit, don't be." He looked both men in the eye. "My primary job, like yours, is finding out who's behind the virus that aborted the Starseeker program. But it's also our collective responsibility to make sure that innocent bystanders—like Rae Prescott—are protected. If I can help in that capacity, I plan to do so."

"Take it easy," Taylor counseled. His weary, watery blue eyes analyzed and accepted the threatening aura emanating from Caleb. "No one's implying anything unethical about the Prescott woman or you." He paused, then added flatly, "But you know we're going to dig as deep as we can and follow up on every lead, regardless of the individuals involved. I want to agree with your assessment of her innocence, but until it's established beyond doubt, we can't afford to rule her out."

"I'm aware of that." Caleb raked a hand through his hair. "Whose signature was forged—the brother's?"

"Yeah. He was pretty torqued about it. Especially when we had to warn him it might be his father."

"What did you learn about Ray Prescott, senior?" Dennis asked, his voice and stance back to normal.

Caleb produced the folded sheet from the inside pocket of his jacket. He handed it to Taylor. "A snitch happened to overhear a conversation in a bar between Prescott and an ex-employee of Chem-Con."

"Chem-Con...the corporation that pirated, then produced the stolen Polaris technology in that case a couple of years back that you told us about, right?"

Caleb nodded. "It's my opinion that the same thing is happening with the Starseeker technology. I think IOS is after the money and power available upon the sale of the technology more than they're out to sabotage the country's security. T-bone—the snitch—overheard enough of Prescott's conversation for us to establish reasonable proof of the IOS association."

Taylor lifted the paper, read it aloud. "'I heard him tell the other dude that IOS better come through with the goods. The other dude told him to shut up and never mention the name. He looked around—I saw Prescott put something in his suit pocket. They left.'"

For a long, somber moment the three men pondered in silence before Hoffman spoke.

"Prescott was sighted leaving a restaurant on Colfax Avenue last Tuesday," he told Caleb. "We lost him at a traffic light. He hasn't surfaced since."

"Any more funds disappear from Rae's account?"

Taylor shook his head. "There's only about four thousand left, anyway. Prescott probably wouldn't risk an investigation by depleting the account totally, much less for that trivial amount."

Caleb stretched, then rose with lithe coordination that belied the stiffness of his tired body. "I want to get back to the Springs." For an hour, he'd been feeling uneasy mental twinges—and they all concerned Rae. If God was trying to alert him to something, Caleb planned to listen and take action. "I'm concerned about Ms. Prescott."

Taylor loosened his tie and unbuttoned the collar of his rumpled shirt, then sighed and scratched the back of his head. "You could be right," he reluctantly admitted. "I talked to Ramirez earlier. They should have already tightened security around her—there's no need for you to knock yourself out tonight."

"I'm going to anyway."

"Are you crazy, man?" Dennis sputtered. "It's raining like the Last Flood, and it's past midnight."

A corner of Caleb's mouth tilted. "Guess I'll just have to hunt up a southbound ark."

Twenty minutes later, he was headed south on I-25 in an unmarked government car. Soggy with fatigue, eyes rid-rimmed and grittier than ever, he nonetheless still heard the small voice deep inside warning him more urgently of pending danger. "Okay, Lord." He talked out loud to keep alert, squinting through the rain-lashed windshield at the stygian blackness. "I'm going to need some help here, or I'll probably end up at the morgue instead of my motel."

Less than ten miles out of Denver the rain quit, and a weak yellow moon hovered over the black masses of the mountains, lighting up the midnight sky.

The crescendoing wail of sirens jarred Rae from a deep but restless sleep. An ominous reddish cast tinted the window, and she stumbled out of bed, tripping over her slippers as she staggered to the window. Sleep-clumsy fingers plucked aside enough slats in the miniblinds so she could peek outside, and the sight brought her to heart-pounding wakefulness. Her garage was on fire.

The agents! The agents hidden in the loft.

She thrust her arms inside her robe and crammed her feet in slippers. Praying desperate prayers, she yanked open the back door. The fire engine whose siren had awakened her was rumbling to a halt. Men jumped off and ran toward the garage, hoses unwinding across the lawn behind them. Eyes transfixed on the billowing smoke, Rae hugged the porch railing and stayed out of the way.

Forty minutes later it was over. No injuries to the agents. Rae thanked the Lord for His mercies, in spite of the bitter revelation of the fire's cause. One of the agents who had been on duty—Charlie?—had slipped her a note so she wouldn't panic. The fire had been set deliberately—a pile of trash ignited with a kerosene-soaked rag. Damage was minimal, except for the soot, ashes and puddles of oily water. The agents were safe, and even if the location of this stakeout had leaked somehow, they planned to remain until Agent Ramirez informed them otherwise. She was not to worry. This was just another scare tactic.

Rae thanked the firemen, reassured a police officer that she was all right and woodenly offered a statement to the arson investigator who made out the report. Finally she was allowed to go inside, and out of habit padded into the kitchen to put on the kettle. It was while she was waiting for the water to boil that a disquieting thought drifted into her mind. The fire had been deliberately set—but why? Could there be a reason other than to harass, warn them all of IOS knowledge of the stakeout location?

The fire had provided a good diversion, if they planned— *No!*

Heedlessly Rae ran down the hall, fingers so clumsy in her haste she barely managed to unlock the door to Joyful Noise. *Please,* she prayed desperately. *Please don't let anything have happened.* Her hand went automatically to the light switch and shoved it upward. Then she stood, hand frozen on the switch, while her gaze absorbed the sickening sight.

All her priceless ornaments, the figurines, the china, even the music boxes had been hurled to the floor. Everything lay scattered in thousands of pieces, mutilated, totally destroyed. Only the brass quarter note remained unbroken, gleaming dully on top of the shattered onyx base.

Nausea gushed upward, and a gray veil dimmed her vision. Weakly Rae leaned against the wall, fighting to keep from throwing up or fainting. Possibly both. One fist lifted to her mouth, the other pressed against her chest as if she was trying to keep her heart from leaping out. Her heritage. The best part of her past. All destroyed. Gone forever. She shook her head slowly, hearing a strange keening noise in her ears that she eventually realized was coming from her own mouth. "God, Father God," she whispered over and over. "Help me. I need You to help me."

Chapter Seventeen

Rae called in the police. Regardless of the consequences—merciful God, what else could IOS do that they hadn't done?—she wasn't going to pretend that nothing had happened. Probably IOS was waiting to see if she would do just that. There was even a chance that if she didn't call, their suspicions would be even *more* aroused. The police would certainly question her silence, and if Detective Grabowski discovered she hadn't reported—

She couldn't stand it. The pain, the betrayal and confusion were simply more than she could bear. *God? Where are You?* And where were the men who were supposed to be guarding her and the Prescott mansion?

She dialed the police as if in a trance, having to clear her throat twice before she could speak. "This is Rae Prescott," she told a bored-sounding dispatcher. "My store, Joyful Noise, has been—" She stopped, waited until she had herself under control. "My store has been vandalized."

The voice on the other end transfered her to the complaint clerk, who told Rae a unit would be dispatched to her address. Rae hung up, then stood staring at the phone for a long time. Eventually she turned, looking vaguely around at the mess. Somewhere inside she was screaming, and a deep quivering was working its way out, threatening to explode into hysteria. Busy. She needed to stay busy, do something productive, or she would go mad. And without thought her feet moved across the floor to the bins of sheet music.

Several scores protruded untidily, as though someone had rifled through the music and started to pull individual pieces out, then changed his mind. Rae carefully straightened them, then pulled out a couple of misplaced selections to play while she waited for the police. Destroying evidence never registered in her short-circuited brain.

The piano she leased from the store wasn't *hers,* so Rae wandered trancelike down the hall to her Steinway. *What if they had trashed her piano?* Bile surged in her throat, and Rae gulped convulsively several times. She was afraid to look, but when she flicked on the switch and saw her most precious possession undamaged, waiting for her in dignified splendor, tears filled her eyes. *No. You will not cry.* Her hands scrubbed over her eyes, and she forced herself to take several deep breaths. Then she sank onto the bench, arranged the music she had brought with her and began to play. When she turned the page, a folded piece of paper slipped out and floated to the floor.

Rae stopped playing and picked it up, unfolding it mechanically. Nothing but meaningless notations. Gibberish. Some customer probably using a piece of scrap paper for a marker. With a shrug, her fingers opened and the paper drifted to the floor.

The police arrived just as she lifted her hands to the keyboard, and she met them at the back door. More red lights, only this time, instead of firefighters, the two cars spilled forth what looked like an army of uniforms and plainclothesmen. One of them was Detective Grabowski. So. Her faithful watchdogs must have notified him about the garage. Would have been nice, some detached voice in her brain observed, if they'd noticed the activity going on inside Joyful Noise. She hugged her waist, standing on the threshold, waiting for the onslaught as though she was waiting for the curtain to draw back so the play could begin.

Across the street, the DeVrieses' lights turned on. Nancy had offered to stay with her after the fire, but Rae had persuaded the oversolicitous mother to go home. The last thing she wanted was to be treated like a three-year-old.

"Ms. Prescott? Rae?" Detective Grabowski materialized at her side. He peered into her face, opened his mouth, then shut it. "Are you all right?" he asked after a minute, the normally hard, gritty voice surprisingly gentle. He placed his hand on her arm and ushered her up the porch steps. Inside, he repeated his question.

"Not at the moment," Rae replied with ethereal candor. "I sort of feel like...I'm not really here."

Grabowski jerked his head, then steered Rae out of the way. The lab technician and Evan McArthur, Detective Grabowski's second in command, filed past. Another patrol officer loped across the lawn toward the DeVrieses'. A female officer, her rather rawboned, plain face softened by compassionate brown eyes, laid a comforting hand on Rae's shoulder.

"I'm Officer Dix, Ms. Prescott. Why don't we go in the kitchen?" she suggested. "You can tell me what happened."

Grabowski and Officer Dix exchanged looks, and Rae wondered why they looked so worried. She was all right, under control. She wasn't going to go to pieces on them.

"What's the status on Myers? He was scheduled to fly into Denver this evening," Grabowski said abruptly.

"He hasn't checked in with us."

They both looked at Rae again. At the mention of Caleb's name, Rae's fragile poise wavered. Caleb. She mustn't think of Caleb right now. If she did, she'd lose what little control she had left. The ice-coated fog returned, shrouding her in cold droplets of mist. She stared sightlessly down the hall, praying the mist would never lift. All the *good* memories she had so carefully preserved over the past twenty years were destroyed, lying scattered in millions of pieces all over the floor. She felt as though she had been erased, the essence of her personality crushed. She was nothing—a nobody. And she had nobody to turn to, to restore validity to her existence.

Uncle Floyd was dead. Tyler would say, "Good riddance. Now put the place up for sale and try to make a name for yourself as a concert pianist."

Karen would tell her that there were worse tragedies in life than the loss of material possessions. Divorce, for instance. Everyone at church would reinforce that sentiment. After all, they were just *things*. Rae was lucky to still be alive.

Dear God. *I know they were things, Lord.* But they had helped remind her that beauty could be created even from the ugliness of her past. The pain intensified, because it wasn't valid. She was a Christian. The power of Christ was supposed to have transformed her, maintained her. She shouldn't be hurting so over the loss of material possessions.

Her parents were failures. As a Christian, *she* was a failure.

Rae walked with the step of a somnambulist, into the kitchen with Officer Dix. Until a few months ago she would have proclaimed to the world her unshakable faith in a loving God and thanked Him for His blessings. What had she done wrong, for Him to allow these unspeakable circumstances?

"Ms. Prescott? Rae? Your kettle's boiling away here. Were you fixing yourself a drink before you called?"

The kind voice penetrated her icy reverie, and Rae finally focused on the concerned face across the table. Her silver nameplate glinted in the light. Rae took a shaky breath. "Tea. I want a cup of hot tea." Her lips felt strange, as though they'd been anesthetized

"I'll fix it," Officer Dix said. "Is this the mug you were going to use? It has a tea bag in it. How about if you sit down at your table, and I'll bring it to you. Then we'll talk."

Rae sat down. When the steaming mug appeared in front of her, she stared at it a moment, then looked vaguely at Officer Dix. "Thank you. What did you want to talk about?"

Step by step she was led through the night's events, including the note Charlie handed her during the fire in the garage. The words dribbled out in a slow but steady stream, shorn of emotion, until she tried to describe the state in which she found Joyful Noise. Officer Dix told her again to take her time and calmly waited until Rae could continue.

Detective Grabowski entered as she concluded. He walked wearily over to them. "They did a thorough job of trashing your trinkets, but they didn't touch anything else." He muttered a terse apology when Rae flinched. "I wonder why..."

"I'd have to concur with Rae's conclusion that they started a fire in the garage as a diversion," Officer Dix stated. "With all the activity and attention over that, the feds missed what was going on in the store."

"If the feds had been on the ball instead of joining in the three-ring circus, we might have learned some useful information." Grabowski scowled at the toe of his scuffed black shoes. "Nothing could have been done to keep them from destroying the valuables, but at least we might have picked up a lead on the perpetrators.''

Rae's chill intensified.

Officer Dix shrugged, rose to her feet. "Can't say I blame those guys too much. You know what a bummer pulling surveillance is. It's impossible to keep your eyes peeled every minute, even without a fire for a distraction."

Headlights flashed through the windows, then disappeared. Into the sudden silence came the faint sound of a car door slamming. Officer Dix slipped her revolver out of the belt rig and moved in front of Rae. Detective Grabowski glided out into the hall, a semiautomatic appearing as if by magic in his hand.

The back door burst open, and Caleb's voice echoed with sharp demand down the hall. "Rae! Where are you?"

Rae's heart had been lying at her feet, a shriveled, lifeless lump. Now it kicked all the way into her throat. Suddenly she lurched up, shoving Officer Dix aside as she hurled herself toward the sound of his voice. Later, she would have time to analyze, question—and regret the revealing response. But right now a force even more powerful than her pain propelled her toward the only man who offered her safety...and hope.

"Caleb!" Her voice was choked, the word emerging as a croak. Her eyes fastened on him and refused to turn away.

His hair was damp, shaggy, his clothes impossibly rumpled. His own eyes were bloodshot with exhaustion. But in spite of his obvious fatigue, danger emanated from him in a sizzling current. It electrified every person in the room. He spared Grabowski one swift, comprehensive glance, then turned to Rae. "Rae..." The greeting was hoarse, almost guttural.

She faltered to an uncertain halt, hovering in the doorway. Then Caleb lifted his arms, and she fled into them without hesitation. He enfolded her in a protective embrace, and she burrowed against his chest, hands clutching the soft cotton of his shirtfront. She couldn't speak for the tears clogging her throat, her nose, her eyes. The trembling she'd managed to conquer until now surged upward, causing her knees to buckle. Caleb's hold shifted until he was practically supporting her entire weight.

"What happened?" His voice, stripped for once of its low-key control, rumbled above her ear as his hands stroked her hair and back.

"Store got hit by vandals, doubtless courtesy of your IOS pals," Detective Grabowski answered. "They trashed all her knicknacks, yet left the music intact. We haven't determined if that was by accident or design. Offhand I'd say they were more out to teach some kind of lesson, bullies taunting, showing their power."

"Did the guys across the street get any pics? How about prints from your people?" Caleb's voice was equally terse, remote, even, but the hands holding her were imbued with warmth and strength. Rae absorbed it like a greedy sponge.

"They're just finishing up," the detective told him with heavily exaggerated courtesy. "But no pics. A trash fire was set in Ms. Prescott's garage to divert anyone who might have been interested in interrupting the party in her store. The feds on duty all felt obliged to join the general commotion at the garage, ostensibly to offer help if needed." Grabowski's opinion of their actions hovered unspoken in the air. "Of course, we wouldn't have interrupted even if the perpetrators *had* been seen. We can't afford to alert them that we've got the place—as well as Ms. Prescott—under surveillance in more than one location."

Then he added in the same dispassionate tone, "Strikes me that a possible motivation for tonight would be if IOS believes she's planning a double cross of some kind." The words hammered into Rae's body like blows.

Her head jerked up and she twisted around, though Caleb wouldn't let her go. "You know that's not true," she denied hoarsely. "Don't—I can't—"

"Shh...don't try to talk yet," Caleb ordered. He gently forced her head against his chest. "It's okay," he promised. "*You're* okay. That's more important than the case, or all your keepsakes. They didn't hurt *you* again."

Rae tore herself free, backing away. "You don't understand! Yes, they were things. I know they were just knickknacks and decorative items, inanimate objects. They didn't have a soul—I shouldn't place value in my possessions. My life is more important. But when they destroyed those *things*, they destroyed part of me!" She dragged air into her lungs, stared with burning eyes into Caleb's face. "All those objects were the only part of my past I could look at with pride."

"Rae, that's not—"

''No. Don't say anything else. I know I'm wrong—you don't have to lecture me on my sins. Oh, *God!* I'm sorry. Sorry!'' she burst out. ''I'm nothing now. He's punishing me because I coveted my possessions, but now I have nothing...nothing.'' She covered her face with her hands.

Then Caleb's hands covered hers and forced them to her sides. His gaze burned into her, the bloodshot amber eyes glittering, so commanding that she went utterly still. ''Those objects might have been a reflection of your life, but they were not worth your life. And God is *not* punishing you, Rae.'' He shook her wrists. ''Listen to me. Your grief is legitimate, and God understands. *I* understand. Now, I want you to go wash your face and wait for me in the parlor.'' The laser-beam gaze searched her face. ''I don't want to have to hunt you down, either,'' he warned, very softly.

He released her and turned to Detective Grabowski. ''I brought some info. I'll share it with you after I have a look at Rae's store, if you don't mind. Can you fill me in on everything else that's gone down?'' He sent Rae one last, unfathomable look before heading down the hall toward the store, Grabowski at his heels.

Rae stared after them, the icy mist disintegrating into a frostbite of hurt, confusion and despair. Eventually she trudged toward the bathroom. Her face probably did need washing.

Chapter Eighteen

She sat in Uncle Floyd's favorite chair, waiting. Officer Dix poked her head in briefly, and another policeman reminded her that they would need a list of all the destroyed valuables and that she should call her insurance agent first thing in the morning. Rae nodded. She had washed her face, wound her hair up on top of her head and dressed in a warm-up suit, but everyone still treated her as though she was in shock. Her fingers curled, the short nails biting into her palms.

Eventually Grabowski returned. He stood over her without speaking, the lines in his face deeper, his eyes speculative.

Rae straightened her back with a tired sigh. It was obvious the detective had been doing some thinking, as she had. "I suppose you're wondering if I did it myself." She spoke in a remote, indifferent voice.

"The thought occurred to me," he admitted. "Every time I turn around lately, you seem to be in trouble of some kind. I can't help but wonder if it's designed to keep the spotlight on you—instead of where it needs to be."

Even though Rae had anticipated the suspicion, hearing it verbalized exacerbated her already raw state. For the first time, anger stirred, and she lifted her wrists. "Well, why don't you go ahead and arrest me? I might do something really dangerous the next time. Who knows, maybe I'm building a bomb in the basement and I plan to hand it over to my father next week, so he could sell it on the international black market.''

"On the whole, I prefer dealing with your temper, but don't you think the bomb's a little extreme?" Caleb's voice, calm yet implacable, cut off Rae's sarcastic flow of words. He walked across the worn Oriental carpet, his gaze locked to Rae's. "What have you been saying to her, Grabowski?"

"Back off, Myers," the detective grumbled. "I'll run my investigations the way I see fit, and you run yours. If I have to question Ms. Prescott, I will."

"Agreed," Caleb assented, and Rae's temper fizzled at the latent threat icing his tone. "But while I'm protecting the lady—and since it involves the Starseeker case—I'd recommend you keep your questions...reasonable."

"You wouldn't be trying to threaten me, would you, Myers?"

Caleb smiled a shark's smile. "Not at all. That was by way of some well-intentioned advice."

Grabowski's brows lowered in a fierce scowl, then abruptly he gave a short laugh. "I'm getting too old for this," he muttered, shaking his head. "Have at her, son, but keep in mind what you've learned." He glanced at Rae. "You're right about one thing—I much prefer her in a temper myself, on the whole." Incredibly, he leaned to pat her hand. "Sorry about your things, Ms. Prescott."

After Grabowski left there was a moment of strained silence.

"What have you learned?" Rae finally asked, not looking at him.

"Nothing good," Caleb responded. He leaned over as though he was going to pull her to her feet, but froze when Rae flinched. "Rae, trust me, please. It's going to be all right. I know you're not a criminal."

"Well, you're probably the only one." She swallowed hard. Her fingernails were digging into her palms, but she forced herself to remain calm. "What's the nothing good you've learned? You may as well tell me. It can't possibly be any worse than what I've gone through tonight."

"That's why I'd rather not get into it now. You've had enough. I think it would be best if you went to bed, tried to sleep. Things won't look so black in the morning."

"Don't you *dare* patronize me!" she said angrily, calm for-

gotten. She stormed to her feet, planting her fists on her hips.
"If you don't want to talk, fine. Leave. I don't care. I don't need
you, and I'm sorry I threw myself at you earlier. Believe me, it
won't happen again." She stopped, breathing hard, reveling in
the turbulent feeling crashing through her. At least it reminded
her that she was still alive.

Flames licked through Caleb's amber eyes, turning them to
hot liquid gold. "Oh, I think it will happen again," he returned.
Then he reached out and pulled her close, wrapping his arms
around her waist and shoulders. Just as firmly, his head lowered
and his lips brushed her ear. "Don't scratch, little cat. I'm wiped
out. Seeing this place surrounded by squad cars aged me ten
years."

He began to press light, soothing kisses along her neck and
across her rigid jaw, and Rae's protest died in her throat, along
with the angry hurt. "It was pouring rain in Denver, but I wran-
gled a car and came anyway," he whispered. "I knew something
was wrong—I felt it. I knew you needed me. So even though I'd
been on my feet for eighteen hours, I came." A half-frustrated
chuckle escaped. "The FBI agents in Denver are convinced I'm
a lunatic. Maybe they're right. But over the years I've learned
not to ignore that little voice I sometimes hear, somewhere deep
inside. I prayed all the way down here." His arms tightened,
practically squeezing her in two. "I don't know what I would
have done if you'd been hurt...or worse."

Incredibly, he sounded almost...panicked? It was almost as
though he was clinging to Rae as much as...well, as much as
she wanted to cling to him. Panicked herself, Rae realized that
she wanted to sink into him, drown in the mesmerizing warmth
he offered. She wanted it with such frightening intensity her
knees threatened to give way like wet sand. But she couldn't risk
it. Every man in her entire life had always left her, and Caleb
was no different. Right now he was relieved that she was safe,
that was all. He was a good, decent man. But when the Starseeker
case was finally resolved, Caleb would be gone. It didn't matter
that she was falling in love with him. Somehow she had to find
the strength to stop that free-fall before she hit the bottom.

God was having to teach her many painful lessons. But as she
steeled herself against the warmth of Caleb's embrace, Rae realized that watching him walk away was going to be far more

devastating than the loss of all the treasures Uncle Floyd had given her. She turned her head aside from the persistent on-slaught of his gentle kisses. *Keep it casual, in control.*

Above all else, she needed to curb her temper.

She laughed, a light, woefully artificial sound, and tried to ignore the enticing pressure of his mouth. "I was just thinking that I'm really doing something wrong somewhere in my life, since God needs such extreme measures to teach me a lesson." For some reason the words were sticking in her throat. "Lately all my prayers seem to sink through the floorboards."

The caressing kisses stopped. Caleb held her away a little, tipping her chin up with his thumbs. "You know better than that."

"I used to think so." Her voice wavered, and the fierce intensity of his gaze softened. *Don't be kind,* Rae wanted to beg. She couldn't sustain the facade against the warmth of his compassion.

"Take it easy, sweetheart," he murmured, the thumbs continuing to stroke her chin. "You've had a rough time of it, haven't you? But it's going to be all right."

She closed her eyes in a vain attempt to keep from responding, but the need for comfort spilled up and out along with a flood of words. "It's gotten out of control, Caleb. My life, the store, this whole situation! Every time I turn around something else happens. I feel like my whole world is the house on shifting sand instead of the house built on rock." A sob caught her by surprise, erupting from her throat. "I had it all planned. Joyful Noise was finally making money. I'd done it, and Tyler would have to eat all his hateful words. I had everything under control. My past couldn't touch me anymore. I prayed so hard, thought God had answered all my prayers...."

"Rae." Caleb wrapped his arms around her and held her close, rocking her, calming her. "You're just not seeing clearly right now. You've forgotten the most fundamental truth of all. God's *unconditional* love. He offers love, sweetheart. It's life that deals out consequences. All these trials...well, I don't know why you're having to suffer them, but I do know God hasn't abandoned you." For a fraction of a beat he hesitated before adding gruffly, "I won't abandon you to IOS, either."

She shook her head against his chest, but couldn't bring herself to pull away. "If you do, I might as well make my funeral arrangements." Another watery sob escaped. "It's painfully clear that I'm no good at playing cops and robbers. I don't remember details, everyone but you suspects me of being in collusion with those despicable thugs, and I—I..." *Don't do this to yourself, Rae.* "I'm f-frightened all the time. I never thought I'd be a coward. But I am. I am." She closed her eyes in shame and despair.

"Ah, Rae, you're no coward." Gently, inexorably, he lifted her head, and his mouth covered hers, breath flowing across her tightly pressed lips. "You're one of the bravest women I know," he whispered between soft little kisses, and with a last despairing cry her heart gave up the battle.

She lifted her arms around his neck and kissed him. It was either kiss or weep. The deliberate yielding of herself into his care was terrifying, because she did it with the full awareness of inevitable loss. But that vulnerability was still preferable to the humiliation of cowardly tears. Besides, as long as he kept kissing her, she might be able to forget the shattering nightmare of the past hours and the nightmare that waited in the future.

Tomorrow would be soon enough to face the bitter consequences—she had fallen head over heels in love with a man who would disappear out of her life when the Starseeker case was eventually solved. And for the rest of her life, she would be alone.

She had become her mother.

Rae could only pray that God really hadn't abandoned her, because she needed all the divine help He chose to provide.

Karen was helping her clean the mess in her store the next day when the phone rang. Karen looked from a load of smashed glass she'd been emptying in the trash to Rae, who was sitting on the floor of the classical music room staring at the phone as if it was a rattlesnake. IOS, checking up? The police? A customer? Phone solicitation?

Caleb?

"You want me to answer it?" Karen asked after the fifth ring, her drawl more pronounced than usual.

Rae gave a short nod. Before he'd left the previous night,

Caleb had called Karen and asked if she could spend the rest of the night with Rae. Alarmed, Karen had flown up the street, bursting on the scene wearing a bright yellow caftan and looking like an enraged canary. Even Caleb had needed fifteen minutes to calm her down.

All in all, Rae reminded herself, her whirlwind of a friend had been a welcome lifeline. She called all Rae's piano students and canceled the lessons, then insisted that the store be closed for at least the day, regardless of Rae's protests. She even handled the reporter from the *Gazette* after Rae's tenuous composure fractured.

Rae nonetheless suffered a symphony of guilt over Karen's involvement in the deepening mess of her life. Now that she'd answered the phone, her friend's voice would be picked up by the IOS phone tap, and Karen would doubtless be investigated by IOS as thoroughly as the authorities were investigating Rae.

Unfortunately, it was too late now. "Hello, Joyful Noise," Karen chirped even as she rolled her eyes at Rae. She listened, a frown growing. "Just a minute. I'll see." She put her hand over the receiver. "Rae, this man claims he's your brother. You want me to ask a few pertinent questions to confirm that?"

Tyler! Rae gasped, her heart leaping in a gigantic thump of gratitude. Awkwardly scrambling up, she bumped her hip on the music bin in her haste. Just as she reached for the receiver, her brain belatedly clicked in. She motioned to Karen, thinking furiously. "Tell him I can't come to the phone right now. Tell him I'm—I'm going down to your place to help—to help plan for some background music for the restaurant. If it's important, he can call me there in a few minutes."

Karen looked baffled, but she relayed the message. "Okay, honey, give," she demanded after hanging up. "Ya got two minutes—then we have to boogie down to my place to supposedly plan some music." She gave Rae a quirky smile. "Y'know, that's not a half-bad idea, as I think about it."

Rae stashed the broom and dustpan in the closet beneath the stairs. "Let's go. I needed to get out of here, anyway." Her skin was crawling. Sometimes she wondered if she would ever feel clean again.

On the way down the street she told Karen about the bugged phone, aware that she was violating official instructions. Karen, with typical emotional fervor, shrieked in outrage, and Rae found herself arguing fast and furiously to convince Karen to keep her mouth shut. Rae shuddered to think of the implications, but she refused to drag her friend into danger wearing the blindfold of ignorance.

Tyler called five minutes after they climbed the stairs to Karen's apartment.

"What's going on?" he demanded irritably. "Why aren't you working in your store? It's ten o'clock out there, isn't it? If you want to run a successful business you can't afford to keep irregular hours, Rae."

Rae smiled, shaking her head. "Hi, Tyler. Thanks for the advice." Her fingers absently played on the countertop where Karen's phone sat. "Why are you calling? It's not Christmas or my birthday."

A long-suffering sigh blew over the phone. "I wanted to make sure you were okay," he said. "Have you, ah, have you talked to the FBI about our esteemed father?"

Rae groaned. "Oh, Tyler—you, too? I'm sorry. This is the biggest mess."

"Tell me about it. I'm sitting in my office, fat, dumb and happy, and some rock-faced fed in a three-piece suit lowers the boom. I'm still reeling from the blow." He covered the mouthpiece and Rae heard him speaking muffled words to someone. When he came on the line he irritably apologized. "Anyway, remember when we set up that Durable Financial Power of Attorney when you were eighteen?"

"The one that gave you legal power to take care of my finances?"

"Yeah. Anyway...I opened an account in your name a couple of years back, up in Denver. I didn't tell you cause I figured you'd sink it in that dumb house, and I meant for it to be used as a financial safety net for you."

"Tyler—" Flummoxed, Rae blinked rapidly. Never in her wildest dreams had she expected such a loving gesture from her older brother.

Tyler swept on, hiding his discomfort behind clipped impatience. "Then this guy, this fed, tells me that Dad stole checks from that account, forged the signature and depleted all but a crummy four thou."

''What?'' The rush of happiness shattered into shock. ''This account...it must be the one that the FBI—'' She closed her eyes, mentally grappling with the revelations being dropped into her lap like sticks of lighted dynamite. ''And it was our father. How...did he steal the checks and forge my signature, Tyler? Are you sure?''

''The feds are. I keep the checkbook here at work, locked in my desk. But it's crazy around here, and someone with dear old Dad's experience could pick the lock while I was at lunch. The stolen checks were near the back.''

''And my signature?''

''I don't know,'' he all but yelled. ''Quit grilling me, all right? Maybe the bank didn't bother to check. He was depositing the forged check into his own account, not taking cash. Talk to the feds. Let them explain.''

''It was our father,'' Rae repeated, struggling without success to quash the pain of betrayal.

''You bet your sweet little bearish market bottom,'' Tyler shot back before once again covering the phone to speak to someone else. ''Look—I gotta go in a few moments. Haven't you talked to that Myers guy? I spent half the day on the phone with the FBI guys out in Denver, and then Myers rings me up at home a little while ago and rakes me over the coals for not telling you about the account. He told me it's caused you a lot of trouble. If the tone of his voice was any indication, it's a good thing we weren't talking face to face. What's going on between the two of you, Sis?''

Rae laughed a hollow laugh. ''I have no idea, brother dear. But I do know that if it hadn't been for Caleb, I'd probably be in jail now.''

''Yeah, well, I guess maybe I should have told you about that account,'' he admitted awkwardly. His voice altered to the defensive whine that catapulted Rae fifteen years back. ''How was I supposed to know the old man would surface again after all these years, much less have the gall to pull some of his con tricks on his own family?''

''Don't start that old routine,'' Rae began, then stopped. ''Tyler? Has he ever gotten in touch with you?''

''Not even when he stole the checks right from under my nose. Some father, huh. After a stunt like that, I don't care if I ever talk to him, much less see him. Far as I'm concerned, the old goat's dead.'' After an uncomfortable pause, he added, ''I hate to admit it, but sometimes—especially after this stunt—I wish he was.''

''I understand,'' Rae nodded her thanks as Karen placed a mug of tea and two apple spice muffins on the table beside the phone. ''Tyler, did you know the FBI came to Uncle Floyd another time, when we were kids, to ask about Dad?''

''Yeah.'' He bit the word out. ''I knew. I was fourteen. The guys had been hassling me about our background pretty bad. When those two feds came, Uncle Floyd told me to ride my bike to the store for a candy bar, but I didn't go.''

Rae's heart went out to the sullen, rebellious teenager her brother had been. ''Where did you hide? In that hidden pantry under the stairs?''

''Uh-huh. I heard an earful, too. They wanted him for transfer of stolen goods across state lines, larceny, car theft.'' There was another long pause before he added roughly, ''I never told a soul, but I swore to myself that day I was going to leave and never look back. I was going to make a name for myself, and people would look at a Prescott with respect.''

''It was rough on me, too,'' Rae said gently. ''Even if I was too young to really understand. It's hard sometimes, even now. But it made such a difference when I—''

''Don't start all the Jesus stuff again. You know how I feel about that.''

''I know. And I don't mean to preach. It's just that lately I've begun to realize how much I *do* depend on my faith. God…God accepts me for what and who I am, even when I doubt, or mess things up—'' She stopped, impatient with herself. ''What I'm trying to say is that I'm learning that God doesn't keep score, and He doesn't hold the sins of our parents against us.''

''That's great. Look, I really have to go.''

''I know.'' She wound the phone cord around her little finger, wondering if she should have kept her mouth shut. And yet, even as the doubt surfaced, she felt an elusive sensation of renewed strength flowing softly into her soul. ''I don't have all the answers—and I've made a lot of mistakes—but in the past couple of months, I do know that if I hadn't had my faith in God, I wouldn't have made it at all.''

"Right. Whatever. Well...I just wanted to tell you about the account. Gotta go, Sis."

After he disconnected, Rae still sat, toying with the muffin. The gentle river of peace continued to flow, and after a while a smile spread across her face. Caleb had been right—she really hadn't been abandoned at all.

Chapter Nineteen

"Myers, we spend millions of the taxpayers' hard-earned dollars investigating people to avoid nonsense like the Starseeker sabotage. Now you sit there and tell me that this virus—this logic bomb or time bomb or whatever you called it—could have been planted in the software for over a year? It's unconscionable!"

Admiral Vale chomped on the end of a half-eaten cinnamon stick candy, narrow face mottled red, his eyes hard as stones. "And neither do I like your assertion about the difficulty of getting hard evidence on this Fisher character."

Caleb sat patiently, ignoring the smile Tray was trying to hide behind his hand. They had been called on the carpet over the debacle at Rae's store, the carpet being Admiral Vale's office at Peterson Air Force Base. "Sir," Caleb pointed out when the admiral finally ran down, "you've been aware for two months now of the difficulty in tracing the source of the virus. Thanks to the elaborate security measures the joint services utilize, we at least *have* been able to narrow it down to Fisher."

He offered the angry admiral a placating smile, fully understanding the man's frustration. "I can tell you that my experience with similar cases makes me pretty certain the virus had to be planted from the *inside*. Which means, Admiral, that there was little—if anything—your people could have done."

"The military is trained to defend against *outside* aggressors," Tray reminded him, "not insiders."

"I want Fisher picked up and dealt with now."

"You know we can't do that, sir. We haven't got enough concrete evidence to prove criminal intent, and without it there's no hope of conviction." Tray glanced at Caleb in an unspoken signal for help.

"Don't forget that Fisher is merely a tool—the inside access IOS needed to achieve the sabotage," Caleb continued with the blend of low-key authority and deference that in the past had kept the volatile admiral from erupting further. "We're after the principals, as well, or the whole effort will result in pretty much of a washout. IOS will just recruit someone else." He kept his gaze leveled directly on the scowling man. "Even more to the point, if we don't succeed in cutting off the head of this serpent, they won't think twice about hitting on the military again. The next time, the impact might be more devastating and far-reaching than the Starseeker sabotage."

"You don't need to remind me!" Admiral Vale growled. "These programs are closed systems, complex by nature as well as by design, complete with the latest in safeguards. That's why we could put the finger on the little creep—as you just reminded me, Myers! We'll learn from the incident and adjust security measures accordingly." With an abrupt, unconscious movement his fingers snagged another cinnamon stick out of the jar on his desk. "Unfortunately, criminals nowadays have gotten so sophisticated it's harder than ever to stay one jump ahead. They use the same technology we have to gain access, blast it!"

Caleb opened his mouth, and the admiral held up a hand.

"I've talked to the chief of computer security for the Department of Defense." He stuck the piece of candy between his teeth like a cigar. "He sent his regards, by the way, and promised me you're the best. But, young man, you're going to have to do better than you have been, to convince me."

"I'll do my best, Admiral," Caleb promised solemnly. He saw Tray cover a laugh behind a cough.

"He also assures me," Admiral Vale continued after slicing a censorious look toward Tray, "that any future attempts can nonetheless be detected and contained just as this one, because our technological control is still better than in the civilian sector.

We've also implemented a better password-checker program and will be making more frequent data backups."

"Yes, sir," Caleb agreed, though he wasn't assured. "Um, if I may return to the Starseeker case, I need to point out, sir, that if we don't persist in our efforts to uncover the kingpins, Polaris might be out a contract, with both the company *and* the Air Force suffering losses of considerable money and wasted time. IOS will be able to continue to do as they please with impunity."

Admiral Vale slammed his fist on the table. "It's so blasted frustrating! I feel like I'm on a destroyer trying to seek out and neutralize enemy subs—without sonar." His attention returned to Ramirez. "Since Fisher is a civilian, I suppose we won't be able to prosecute him under the Uniform Code of Military Justice. What are our options here, Tray?"

"The Attorney General will be trying for a conviction based on charges of harmful access to a computer." Ramirez leaned back in his chair and laced his fingers behind his head. "Lately we've had a lot more success in those cases." He glanced at Caleb, who nodded. "Also, if there's any way to utilize the Computer Fraud and Abuse Act Congress passed back in eighty-six, they'll go for it."

The admiral heaved a sigh and chomped on the candy. "I don't like all this clandestine maneuvering and namby-pamby political parleying." He quirked a thin gray eyebrow, his mouth curving in a wry half smile. "Guess I've been a military man too long. When the enemy is identified, I want to go after him."

"I tend to agree with you," Caleb murmured. Sometimes it was hard to remember God's admonition that vengeance belonged only to Him. He thought of his feelings after seeing Rae's store the previous night. After the fear, a cold, bloodthirsty rage had threatened to sweep away his civility, as well as his faith. The layers of aloofness that his personality had reinforced all his life had exploded, shocking him to the core. Because of Rae, he knew that his life had been somehow altered forever. It was an unnerving revelation.

"Tell me the latest info you've got," the admiral ordered abruptly, pulling Caleb from his uncomfortable thoughts. "I have a meeting in an hour over at NORAD."

"We think at least two women are involved. No description yet, but we're working on it," Tray supplied. "The Prescott woman happened onto what we think is an IOS identification code used on occasion by their female operatives."

"What about the Prescott woman?"

"We're still monitoring—"

"She's a pawn," Caleb answered, cutting across Tray's answer. "An innocent pawn drawn into this because her father's involved with IOS. So far we've been able to confirm that he's responsible for the funds used to pay off Fisher. He forged Rae's brother's signature to retrieve the funds out of the Denver checking account. The FBI have had a positive ID from the bank employee who gave him the money."

"He surfaced briefly in L.A. and Denver," Tray finished. "Dennis Hoffman told me this morning his car was spotted in San Francisco last night."

"At least, the car he was driving when he was spotted in Denver," Caleb added.

"Do you think he plans to approach his daughter?" Admiral Vale asked. "Is that why there's been no evidence that IOS has moved the drop site?"

Tray looked at Caleb, who contemplated his hands for a long moment. "I don't know," he finally admitted, the syllables dragging out. He lifted his head, met the gazes of both men. "I'm afraid there's a strong possibility they'll try and frame Ms. Prescott. They act like they're still not certain of exactly what she knows."

"And Fisher?"

Caleb stood, a disconcerting restlessness crawling over him. "Fisher doesn't have a criminal mind. He's highly intelligent, but he's not devious. He's been collecting old sheet music for some time, so he doubtless feels comfortable going to Joyful Noise. Possibly he's the reason the drop site hasn't been changed." He pondered the ceiling, thinking, assessing. "Maybe Fisher just dug his heels in and IOS right now is willing to comply. Only Fisher can supply the answer to that." The fear for Rae's safety filled him with ironclad resolution to protect her, regardless of personal consequences.

His gaze returned to the two men, and even the admiral shifted uneasily. "When we nail Fisher, I'll find out the details. If he chose Rae's store deliberately...if Rae's father is trying to set her up and IOS harms her person in *any* way—then God help them, and me.'' His voice dropped to a rustling whisper that seemed to bring down the room temperature by forty degrees. ''Because I'll track every last one of them down and nail their hides to the barn door. Permanently.''

With the store closed for the day and no piano students, time hung heavy on Rae's restless hands. After she and Karen parted, she indulged in a therapeutic bout of cleaning her living quarters for the first time in six months. When even that failed to help, she made herself some tea, then curled up in Uncle Floyd's chair and picked up her Bible. One of Caleb's notes had mentioned a psalm, and she thought perhaps the comforting words the Psalms always provided might soothe her spirit more than frenetic activity. Besides, it was Caleb who had suggested she read it. If only she hadn't thrown that note away—

The note.

Whispering a soft prayer of gratitude for the guidance, Rae hurried to her music room. She had stacked most of the music into neat piles. She rummaged frantically, scattering everything all over the floor again. Where was it? Had she trashed it without thought in her cleaning frenzy? An explosive sigh of relief escaped when she at last unearthed the scrap of paper, stuffed haphazardly inside the cover of the Brahms sonata where she'd first discovered it.

She studied the meaningless jumble of symbols for a long time, but all she could tell for certain was that they were lines of computer code. Rae's only experience with computers had been a class she had taken at Juilliard that taught a person how to compose music on-screen. One day she hoped to have the funds to purchase a computer, possibly a laptop, to use with her piano students, but until this wretched business with IOS was over...

An alarming possibility crashed into her brain. The folded piece of paper might be just that, a worthless scrap of paper some customer had forgotten to remove, used to mark a piece. On the other hand, perhaps one of those women who had worn the matching necklaces had accidentally *dropped* that folded slip of paper into the music while they searched through the bins. If so, and IOS needed the information, it was no wonder they had been hounding Rae so mercilessly!

If they found the paper in her living quarters, obviously moved, her life wouldn't be worth a used tea bag.

She had to alert someone immediately. Clutching the note, she scurried to the bedroom and hastily changed into clean slacks and a three-quarter-sleeve pullover while she determined what to do. Then she folded the note into quarters and stuffed it in her purse. No—too obvious. After a frowning moment, she dug it out and smoothed it into a slimmer shape, then put it deep inside the side seam pockets of her slacks.

She decided to turn it directly over to Caleb. Not only was he the acknowledged computer consultant expert, she could meet him in a more natural fashion to avoid alerting the already suspicious IOS watchdogs. He was supposed to be her boyfriend, after all. Besides, she couldn't very well stroll across the street and wave the paper at the agents on the second floor of the abandoned store.

She forced herself to walk at her normal pace to the garage. Her nose wrinkled at the heavy burned odor, but she didn't spare a glance at the damage as she climbed into her car. Too bad the undercover team had decided to abandon the room over her garage. It was an effort to back out of the driveway, then drive nonchalantly to a small shopping center several blocks down Colorado Avenue, when she knew she risked exposure not only for herself but the team assigned to shadow her. She pulled into a parking spot in front of the grocery store. Once inside, she hunted down a public phone in the back.

Nobody was within hearing distance. Palms damp, she called the number of the agents stationed across the street. "This is Rae Prescott," she announced in a low voice, speaking rapidly. "I need to get to Caleb Myers, fast. Can you tell me where he is?"

"Where are you calling from?" The voice was unfamiliar, the impersonal tone a warning.

Rae wanted to split his eardrums with a shrill scream. "I'm at a public phone," she said sharply. "And I think I might have found a clue." Her eyes cast furtive glances about the store. "I've got to get it to Caleb. He'll know what it means."

"Ms. Prescott, where *exactly* are you calling from? Give me the address, and we'll send someone along. You should have known better—''

"Look, there's no time for this. I appreciate what you're doing, but this information doesn't need to wait until you guys can concoct some fancy little plan so I can pass it to you." She glared at the phone. "Just tell me where Caleb is, and I'll take him the note myself! It will be far less suspicious that way—he's supposed to be my boyfriend, remember?"

"I don't think that would be a good idea, Ms. Prescott. Now, if you—"

"No," she interrupted. "Tell me where Caleb Myers is right now, or I'm going to stroll down the street and announce to everyone who walks by just what's going on on the second floor of the old hardware store." Of course she'd never do such a thing, but they wouldn't know that for sure, considering the reputation she'd earned with her powder-keg temper.

Sure enough, alarmed mutterings grew in the background, but Rae didn't care about their opinion of her right now. She *had* to get to Caleb, had to prove her innocence, and her best hope for accomplishing that lay with Caleb. By turning this note over to him, she would be demonstrating her willing cooperation and, she hoped, finally establishing her innocence once and for all.

"Listen, Ms. Prescott," the agent said in a more conciliatory tone. "Mr. Myers is in a meeting out at Falcon right now. He really can't be reached. If you—"

Falcon Air Force Station. "Thanks! Radio whoever is supposed to keep a tail on me that I'll be headed east on Colorado." She hung up in the middle of the agent's urgent protests, her mind racing.

Since she'd entered a grocery store, she better not leave empty-handed. Hurriedly Rae flung a selection of items in a cart, paying scant attention to either the items or the strange look the cashier gave her at the checkout.

Traffic was light this time of the afternoon, and she made it to the east side of town with no trouble. But a three-car accident at a busy intersection had snarled movement in all directions, and it took Rae ten minutes to finally maneuver past. She wondered if her watchdogs were keeping up, but refused to speculate on the vulture eyes of IOS.

The road to Falcon Air Force Station wound through fifteen

miles of almost treeless rolling prairie. Junkyards and occasional houses dotted the road at odd intervals. At one-thirty in the afternoon the road was relatively deserted. Rae spared a brief second to take her first deep breath. She patted her pocket, then almost panicked when she couldn't feel anything. Her fingers wormed beneath the seat belt, searching, and finally brushed against the paper. The loss of that note would have been a bit difficult to explain.

A huge black car roared up behind her, filling the rearview mirror. Rae glanced at her speedometer, which hovered a little above sixty. Her eyebrows lifted. Someone was in an even bigger hurry, and with an inward admonishment at such recklessness she pulled over so the car could pass.

The black car drew alongside her. Rae glimpsed the pale, sinister face staring straight at her, thin lips stretched tightly in a ruthless smile. A tiny shock stung a corner of Rae's brain, but the recognition came a split second too late. Even as she slammed on the brakes the other car swerved, banging against her car's front bumper.

Rae's hatchback hurtled into an out-of-control spin toward a wide, shallow ditch. The world spun violently, a cacophony of noise and speed and a white-hot pain bursting inside her skull. Then darkness.

Chapter Twenty

Faces... She sensed faces bending over her. Hands touching her. Rae tried to hit out, tried to squirm away but she couldn't see, couldn't move.

"Take it easy, Rae," a man's voice said. "Stay still, now—you've been hurt."

Something wet and sticky trickled down her forehead into her eyes. Again she tried to open them, but it was like prising the lid off a jar of three-year-old canned preserves. She was semi-conscious, but a deep-seated instinct told her that she had to fight, to resist even if they'd blindfolded her and tied her arms. She struggled to lift her arms to find out if she could move them and firm, restraining fingers closed around her wrist.

"Wait a minute," the calm voice ordered. "Wait until you're sentient. Try to move your limbs slowly."

Something soft was pressed against her forehead, and she was tilted very gently back until her head rested against the seat. Rae succeeding in opening her eyes and winced against the light. Pain and nausea rolled over her in a sluggish tide, but she concentrated on keeping her eyes open, blinking until her vision cleared enough to recognize the man leaning over her. Detective Evan MacArthur. His face was full of concern, and beads of perspiration had turned the deep chocolate skin a shimmering ebony in the bright afternoon sun.

"Hello," he said when he saw her eyes focus and register recognition. "Welcome back to the world. Try not to hit me again, okay?" His voice changed, flattened. "Ms. Prescott—Rae. Can you tell us what happened?"

Rae stared at him, mute. Something was telling her she mustn't talk. Couldn't tell him. Pain slashed through her skull. "An animal. I...um...I swerved. Lost control. Ran off the road," she managed to whisper.

"How's she doing?"

J.W. Ayers, his clever, good-looking face shadowed with worry, appeared behind Evan. The light gray eyes moved over Rae. "I radioed Falcon. Myers is on his way, but I don't think we better wait. She looks like she's in shock."

"Pulse is shallow, rapid—but I think I got the bleeding stopped on her temple. She might be concussed, but there's no broken bones, at least."

J.W. leaned forward suddenly, a frown deepening when Rae flinched. "Look at her throat. Does that look like something the shoulder strap would have done?"

Trembling, Rae shook her head, lifted feeble hands to push them away. "No," she protested, her voice alarmingly weak. "I'm fine. Just lost control." Her vision blurred, and the words suddenly seemed too large to escape her mouth. "Ran...off road," she repeated as the two faces swam in front of her, then began a slow slide down a long black tunnel. The voices faded in and out.

"She's scared of something."

"Yeah—whaddaya think?"

"I think we get her to the hospital and hope Myers can find out what it is. That guy could pry the pearl out of an oyster and have the oyster thank him."

"Maybe so, but I have a feeling we're gonna be in deep Dutch with both him and Grabowski but good for letting her get away from us."

"We're not responsible...Springs traffic...bad scene all the way around, man..."

The last pinprick of light vanished, and the men's voices were drowned out by angry bees swarming in Rae's head. She moaned an incoherent protest, then gave in to the bees.

* * *

The next time she regained consciousness she was lying on a gurney with a sheet covering her from the neck down. Antiseptic and ammonia smells stung her nose, and a continuous rumble of voices and scraping footsteps sounded somewhere beyond the light green curtain drawn around the cubicle where she lay.

Slowly, cautiously, Rae opened her eyes. Even more cautiously turned her head. And saw Caleb. He stood by the bed, strong and invincible. Caleb.

"Rae." He enclosed one of her hands in both of his, the touch warm, infinitely sustaining. "How are you feeling, sweetheart?"

"Caleb." She tried to smile, tried to speak, but all she could manage was a feeble whisper of his name. Tears welled, and he wiped them away with the backs of his hands.

"Easy, easy. You're okay, which is nothing short of a miracle and the blessings of seat belts."

"What..."

He understood instantly. "Your car's a total loss, but you really are all right. Bruised, slight concussion, and tomorrow all your bones will probably let you know about the battle you lost with a ditch." His voice roughened, and the fingers holding hers trembled. "But you're okay. Thank God you're okay."

Rae clung to his hand and tried not to think about the future.

The curtain billowed as Agent Ramirez, Detective Grabowski and a man Rae had never seen crowded around the gurney.

"Glad to see you're not seriously injured, Ms. Prescott," Tray Ramirez greeted her. He slid a black-eyed glance over Caleb. "Think you can you answer some questions for us?"

A harried nurse elbowed her way through the cluster of men. "Look, guys, I know you want some info, but the lady here doesn't need to be disturbed."

The man Rae didn't recognize took the nurse's arm, murmured something, then led her outside the curtain. Beneath the sheet, Rae's body had gone rigid, and she could feel the panic beating at the edges of her dazed stupor. Her gaze moved from each of the men, then fastened on Caleb. She didn't know what to do. *Lord? I don't know what to do.*

"Ms. Prescott," Ramirez persisted, his voice determined. "We know you were coming to Falcon to see Myers. We've listened to the tape."

If she closed her eyes, maybe she could fool them into thinking she'd passed out.

"She's hiding something," Grabowski said sharply. "You can see it in her face." He whirled. "Myers—"

"Back off. Give her a chance."

Rae's eyes jerked open, and she found Caleb was shielding her from the others with his body. He looked at Rae, and her heart began to throb in hard, hurtful thuds. She knew that look, knew with fatalistic dread that she didn't have the strength to withstand the implacable force of his will. Uncontrollable shivers rippled through her body. She didn't want him defending her, shielding her. Not now. Not when it could cost him his life.

"Rae, you have to tell me what happened. I know you found something that you wanted me to see. Is that what frightened you?" He leaned closer, searching her face, his gaze sharpening. "What did you find?" He let go of her hand and moved back, as if he knew she needed room. "It must have been pretty important, right?"

Rae stared at him dumbly.

"Ms. Prescott, have you been threatened again?" Detective Grabowski asked. "If so, you need to tell us immediately—unless chasing off toward Falcon with a supposed clue was another diversion?"

"Grabowski—"

The detective certainly knew which buttons to push. With a tremulous sigh Rae squeezed Caleb's hand. "It's all right." She wished her head didn't feel like a dozen jackhammers were drilling away, or that she felt so weak—it would be difficult to divert them. But she had to try and pray the diversion would work. She lifted her eyes to the detective and held his gaze without flinching. "I did find a clue. It looked like lines of computer code, and I wanted Caleb to see it because I knew he would know what it meant." She paused. "And I could also be sure of having the right motive attached to my actions."

"We searched your car, Rae," Tray inserted. "There was no sign of a note." He glanced from her to Caleb. "The contents of your purse were scattered all over the front seat and the floorboards. I guess the impact threw everything out, hmm? Possibly when the police arrived, the note could have blown out when they opened the door."

Grabowski growled something beneath his breath. Rae felt three sets of eyes burning holes in her, and she fought to hide her growing anxiety.

Caleb leaned over, and his fingers brushed droplets of perspiration from the unbandaged side of her head. "*Was* the note in your purse, Rae?" he asked quietly.

"No." With slow, awkward movements her free hand searched beneath the sheet, and her fingers brushed against the paper. The relief made her light-headed, and her eyes burned from fresh tears she was too proud to shed. The three men crowded around the bed, unable to hide their mounting tension. "I put it in my pocket." She withdrew the crumpled note and held it out to Caleb.

He unfolded it, and one eyebrow disappeared beneath the errant lock of hair that always fell over his forehead. "Well, well, well." Bending, he pressed a soft kiss on Rae's temple, winked at her, then turned to the other men. "Gentlemen, I think the case is about to break."

He handed the note to Tray Ramirez. "If I'm not mistaken, what Rae found is part of the commands from the Starseeker program."

He might as well have pulled out an M-16 and sprayed bullets in the ceiling.

"Are you sure, Myers?" Stunned, Grabowski looked from the note to Caleb, then at Rae. "Where did you find this, Ms. Prescott?"

"It was in a copy of a Brahms sonata," Rae said. She passed her tongue around suddenly dry lips. "The one in F minor. Opus five. I was just playing scores at random from some pieces I picked out after my store was vandalized." She kept her eyes on Caleb, praying that he believed her. "The note fell out. It didn't make sense at the time."

She tried to swallow, wishing she could have a drink of water. "I just picked up the Brahms, mostly because a corner of it had been sticking out. I was going to straighten it, then just pulled it out to play later."

"When did you realize it was more than just a random piece of scrap paper?" Tray asked.

His attitude toward her had softened, but Rae still had to force herself to look at him. A glimmer of compassion twinkled beneath the maddening blank-wall look all the agents seemed to have perfected. Rae swallowed convulsively, tears almost spilling over.

"Earlier...I was reading my Bible." She colored. "Caleb had mentioned a verse from Psalms in a note he sent me, and that was when I remembered the piece of paper—" she nodded toward the note "—and it occurred to me that it might have been part of a note rather than just a scrap some customer had used to mark a piece of music."

"Where's the music it fell out of? There may have been more notes, or writing on the music itself."

Rae felt her blush deepening into temper at Detective Grabowski's tone, which plainly indicated he still wasn't totally convinced of her innocence. "It's still on my piano," she replied, frost coating the words. "When I realized it might be a clue, I left the house immediately and called the agents from a public phone—I even remembered to buy groceries as camouflage—to find out where Caleb was. If I was planning a double cross or I was part of IOS, I would have destroyed the note, not tried to find Caleb."

"It would have been safer, and far more practical, to arrange to pass the note to one of our men immediately."

"I wanted to give it to someone I trust, who also trusts me," she answered testily. She tried to sit up, hating the vulnerability of lying prone while the obstinate detective towered above her. Pain lanced through her head, but she resisted Caleb's hands when they pressed against her shoulders. She glared at Grabowski. "Well? Would it destroy your reputation if you have to admit you were wrong about me?"

"Easy, Rae." Caleb leaned down again, so close his lips brushed her ear. "Your claws are showing, little cat," he murmured, so low the others couldn't hear.

"I'm willing to admit that your explanation and subsequent actions are plausible, given the circumstances at the time," Grabowski said, ignoring her comment. The ice blue eyes narrowed. "But I'm still waiting for you to tell us why you're frightened, and have been since the accident. According to my men, you tried to fight them off even before you were fully conscious. There have been several times these past few moments when you've been evasive." He crossed his arms. "How 'bout it, Ms.

Prescott? If you'll come clean about *everything,* most of my, um, nasty suspicions, shall we say, will be laid to rest."

Rae quit trying to sit up. Fists clenched, her mind scrabbled in tighter and tighter circles, and the pain in her head was almost impossible to ignore any longer. "Detective, I acted frightened because I'd just had the fright of my life. I could have died on that road. On top of that, I've been scared out of my skull most of the past two months. If you want to invest—if you think..."

She closed her eyes, but that only made her more dizzy. "May I have some water?" she asked weakly. "I...don't feel good."

"Quit stalling, Ms. Prescott. I'm still not satisfied."

"I'll ask the nurse if you can have some water," Caleb replied in a soft tone that sent prickles galloping down Rae's spine. "Grabowski. Tray. Let's talk outside." He gave Rae's arm a reassuring squeeze, and she listened to the rustling sound of the curtain as the three men filed quietly out.

When the clucking nurse appeared a moment later with a paper cup of water and a straw, Rae's hands were trembling so badly the nurse had to hold the cup and guide the straw to her lips.

"I should never have let that silver-tongued guy bamboozle me," the nurse said. "They've gone and upset you, haven't they?"

"No, it's not that. It's just all catching up with me." Rae took several more swallows, then asked the nurse to help her sit up. She had just gingerly swung her feet over the side of the bed when Caleb slipped into the cubicle.

Immediately the nurse bristled. "You're going to have to leave. She needs nothing but peace and quiet—"

"That's what I'm here to insure," Caleb interrupted with a lopsided smile that hushed the objections instantly. "I've talked to the doctor, and he assures me that it's perfectly safe to release Ms. Prescott. I'm taking her home."

He turned the potent force of that smile on Rae, and the lance of pain pierced her heart. *Lord, I don't want anything to happen to him.* Why did she have to love him so much?

Without quite knowing how it happened, less than ten minutes later Rae was comfortably ensconced in the seat of Caleb's government-loaned car, and Caleb was competently maneuvering through rush hour traffic. They didn't talk, and Rae sat in a sort of dumb lethargy, floating willy-nilly with the current she was powerless to control. Right now, she couldn't even summon up the energy to care.

A few minutes later her startled gaze flew across the seat to Caleb. "You missed the turn to my house," she protested, fighting to keep alarm out of her voice.

"I know." His reply was calm. "Lean back and rest, sweetheart. We're just going up the road a little ways." The car stopped at a traffic light, and he turned toward her, the light amber eyes deepening to the mesmerizing gold of a tiger's. "Then you and I are going to talk."

Lethargy vanished in a breathless whoosh. Rae's throat tightened, and her heart began to race. He was going to interrogate her, of course. And if she weakened, allowed his powerful charisma and her love to sway her, she would be responsible for his certain death. Yet if she somehow managed to maintain her silence...she might be responsible for her own.

Chapter Twenty-One

Bright afternoon sunbeams shot over the top of Pikes Peak into the valley below, reflecting off the incredible red sandstone slab-like formations of Garden of the Gods. Caleb turned onto the road leading into the park and drove along the winding lanes until he found a deserted spot to pull over.

When he opened the car door, he took a surreptitious couple of deep breaths and rotated his neck as he crossed to open Rae's door. The next moments just might possibly be the most significant of his entire thirty-two years, and he'd rather be facing a roomful of hungry tigers. The odds of survival were far stronger. His timing, unfortunately, was lousy, but events over the past several hours had forced his hand.

Mom, do you feel the earth moving along with me, all the way back in Georgia?

He helped Rae out, then kept his arm around her as they began walking. She was stiff, her eyes dark and turbulent as a captured doe's. Caleb dredged up a smile, wondering what had happened to his legendary detachment in tense situations. Right now he felt about as laid-back and in control as a bowl of Jell-O balanced on the edge of a rumbling volcano. Too bad he was the Jell-O—and Rae the volcano. *Hey, Lord? Since this was Your doing, how about dosing me up with courage, if I can't have cool?*

"Where are we going?" Rae asked, the question tentative.

"Not far." She felt so fragile, a delicate bundle of bruises and bravado, and she had almost died. Caleb ground his back teeth together and kept walking. "I thought this would be a good place to talk." He shifted her to navigate around some jutting rock and scrub oak.

The road behind them disappeared. He swiftly surveyed the area, and when he neither saw nor heard any sign of other people, he carefully helped Rae sit on a patch of dry ground. After kicking aside a couple of stones and some twigs, he dropped down beside her.

"How's your head? That medicine the doc gave you kicking in yet?"

"Pretty well...it still hurts, but it's bearable." She looked around. "Uncle Floyd used to bring Tyler and me here for picnics. We loved to climb the rocks."

"I've been coming here a lot over the past months," Caleb admitted, lifting his face to the warmth of the sun. "It's fascinating—peaceful, but somehow larger than life. Sort of helps me put this whole tangled-up case in perspective." He gave a rueful laugh. "Plus a few other things in my life." Like how he knew for the first time that there *was* something far more important than his work and his nomadic life-style.

Rae glanced around indifferently. "What did you want to talk about?"

He turned to look directly at her, memorizing the determined jut of her chin, the long narrow nose, the splatter of freckles dusting her cheeks. Her eyes.

She was so transparent—and he was in love with her. Incredibly, he could feel sweat gathering on his forehead and hands. He fiddled with his watchband, wanting to play the macho role of caveman instead of this ignoble chess game that he was rapidly losing. "There's a couple of things I need to say, but I want to tell you what I've found out about your father first." Pain twisted his heart at Rae's expression. Then her head bent so all Caleb could see was the shining mass of hair, hastily arranged at the hospital into a sloppy chignon that was already slipping loose.

Before he could help himself, his hands lifted to pull out the pins.

"What are you—Caleb, stop!" She slapped at his hands but it was too late. Her hair waterfalled down her back, taking Caleb's breath away.

"Helps your headache, though, doesn't it?" He touched her bottom lip with his finger. "And I like it like this. You have beautiful hair."

"I...I really am going to cut it all off one of these days." She gnawed on the lip he had touched, looking so uncertain he wanted to cover her mouth with his and banish her feelings of insecurity forever.

"Caleb? My father?" The gray eyes were fogged with shame and worry. "What did you find out?"

Help me to do this right, Lord. "He's one of the IOS couriers," he admitted without dressing it up. Rae had been lied to enough. "He also plays the part of front man, committing grand larceny and a host of other schemes to provide extra funds." He had to touch her again, but only allowed himself to lay his hand over one cold little fist. "Your father is the one who stole the funds out of that bank account in Denver, Rae. I'm sorry."

"I know. I talked to my brother."

"Uh-huh. I suppose you got an earful, since I hadn't had a chance to explain after your store was vandalized."

"It was a shock," she confessed. "But nothing worse than what I've suspected for years. Uncle Floyd refused to talk about him at all, and when I'd question my brother he'd get this horrible scowl and just tell me to shut up. By the time I was fifteen, I figured I'd be fortunate if he wasn't wanted for murder." She looked at Caleb at last, her eyes swimming in tears. "I know it's not supposed to matter when I'm a Christian, Caleb. But it does."

With an inarticulate groan he turned, wrapping her in a close, protective embrace. "I'm sorry, so sorry." He kissed her hair, then pressed his cheek to the soft strands, carefully avoiding her bandaged forehead. "I can't identify with your shame, Rae—but I can share the burden."

He clasped her shoulders, then held her a little way from him. "You're stronger than you realize, you know. All you need to do is reset your thinking knob to a Christian station."

"That's bad, Myers."

"Made you smile, didn't it?" He began stroking her arms,

loving the strength he could feel in spite of the delicacy of her bones. "When you're in over your head—and you are, so you might as well admit it—that's the very time to call on God's help. Let Him provide some of the confidence you think you don't have. It's also time to call on the *human* help—that's me, by the way—for backup."

"I was trying to—and it landed me in a ditch." Her throat muscles swallowed convulsively. "I—it happened so fast, Caleb. And there was nothing I could do. Everything went out of control. And there was nothing I could do." Her fingers lifted to fiddle with the buttons on her blood-splattered shirt, then dropped to fumble nervously in her lap. "These past months have been like that out-of-control car spin. I'm strapped in, totally helpless to do anything to stop the spin." She looked at her hands and tried to smile. "It's a shame there's not a piano close by."

"Ah. Is that how you release tension, regain a little of the control you feel like you've lost? When you're sitting on that bench, *you're* the one in charge?"

She looked bemused. "I suppose. I've never really thought about it that way, but you're right. I do feel like I'm absolutely in control when I'm playing the piano, which is sort of ironic. One of my professors once told me the only time I ever looked relaxed, lost almost, was when I finally mastered a piece and knew where I was going with it."

"How'd you get involved with music, anyway?" He turned her so they were sitting comfortably side by side, his arm still holding her close. Some of that pinched, white look she tended to wear when they talked about her father had faded, though she was still far too pale. He tried for an encouraging smile.

"There was an old upright in the parlor. I used to bang on it. After Mom died, Uncle Floyd would hold me on his lap and pick out tunes. He told me it was the only way he could get me to smile." She looked toward one of the massive red formations, her gaze unfocused. "He got me started on lessons, and the teacher said I had a good ear. Uncle Floyd was delighted and decided I deserved only the best—partly because he was an indulgent, impractical old man, but probably partly out of guilt for the mess his brother had made of all our lives."

She sighed, stretched her hands out and wriggled her fingers. "As you know, I ended up at Juilliard with the promise of a fairly successful career after I won a couple of competitions. Uncle Floyd was so proud—relieved, too. Finally someone in the family was going to make something of themselves. But finances... Well, to put it bluntly, my uncle didn't have an iota of financial management sense. I had no idea until his heart attack. He refused to let me help, and by that time Tyler was long gone.''

''That was his choice, his responsibility, Rae. Don't carry that burden, as well.''

''I try, but you've seen the place. The Prescotts were some of the first to settle this region. Until this last generation, our family was one of the most highly respected in the state. But my father pretty much destroyed that reputation, and even Uncle Floyd was considered something of an eccentric. Tyler couldn't escape fast enough.'' For a moment she stared fixedly, and Caleb watched the pulse in the hollow of her throat fluttering like a captive bird. ''But I cared. I *care*,'' she said fiercely. ''Ultimately, saving the Prescott family home mattered more to me than a career. It's the only decent legacy I have left.''

''Don't you realize how much courage that took? Most people with your opportunity would have kissed the place off without looking back, just like your brother did. He ran, sweetheart—but you chose to fight.''

A measure of tranquillity softened her face. ''Thank you for that. I did a lot of praying back then.'' She cut him one lightning-swift glance. ''It's nice to be able to say that and know you understand. Anyway, I just felt Uncle Floyd deserved more. He took us in, gave us everything, tried his entire life to make us feel like a—a family, tried to make up for what our father and mother were.''

''I'd have to say, knowing you like I do, that Uncle Floyd did a magnificent job with his niece.''

Color bloomed, and Caleb was entranced. His hand lifted to flick one rose-tinted cheekbone. ''You don't have to try and make me feel better, but thanks, anyway,'' she said, ignoring his intimate gesture. ''I've never regretted my decision, and somehow I think God has provided adequate compensation in return.'' A light laugh tickled Caleb's ears, and the musical sound punched him—hard—straight in the heart. ''Even if sometimes my ears flinch when I hear 'Für Elise' butchered, or the choir massacres Mozart...the smile on eight-year-old Jennifer's face when she conquers the E major scale, or the way the sanctuary rings after the choir pulls off a really good rendition...well, I'm content.''

He couldn't restrain himself any longer, and cupped her face in his hands, caressing the fragile cheekbones with his thumbs while he drowned in the bottomless pools of her eyes. ''Y'know something, Rae Prescott? I think you're one special lady.''

Her eyelids drooped and her lips half parted. Caleb could feel her trembling. Control and nobility shot, he lowered his head and kissed her, and her unguarded response sliced through him like a flaming sword. He barely retained enough sense to remember her injured status as he carefully wrapped her in a close embrace.

''Sweetheart,'' he whispered eventually, kissing the translucent eyelids, the narrow nose, ''I should apologize, I know— we've got to stop this and talk.''

''Don't want to talk...''

The words were slurred, almost sultry, and Caleb smiled against her temple. ''Neither do I,'' he whispered. The corner of his mouth brushed the edge of the white bandage covering her forehead, jogging his conscience, and a scrap of discipline grudgingly returned. He pressed his hand to her cheek until she opened her eyes. ''Rae,'' he said, very gently, ''we *have* to talk. I'm afraid your life may be in danger because of the Starseeker case and your father's involvement with IOS. So far, they've been playing with you, waiting to see if you could be used. But finding that computer code changes everything.''

She stirred, then went very still. ''I know.''

''You obviously weren't meant to find it. But because you did, I don't think IOS is going to be playing with you anymore.'' He firmly removed her arms from his neck and set her against the boulder again, keeping his gaze on her face. ''Now will you tell me what really happened when your car went off the road? You didn't lose control trying to avoid an animal, did you?''

She shook her head in agonized denial. ''Caleb. Don't ask me. Please.''

It was all he could do not to sweep her in his arms, then spirit her off to the sanctuary of his parents' home half a continent away. In a deliberate, calming movement, he stretched out prone, propped on his elbows, and watched a pair of crows lazily circling above them. After several moments of increasingly uncomfortable silence in which Rae's hands began their familiar restless playing pattern, he finally spoke. "I can't protect you if you don't level with me."

"I don't care about me!" she burst out suddenly. "It's you. You!"

He picked up a piece of straw grass and twirled it idly. "What do you mean?"

"I can't tell you anything because of what might happen to you. They said—" She stopped abruptly.

"Who said?" he asked, rising lazily to his feet and regarding her steadily. "Who, Rae?" He leaned over and gripped her elbows, tugging her upright.

Instantly she pulled free, standing in front of him stiff and frozen, trapped, her gaze agonized. "I can't!" she moaned. "Caleb—they'll kill you."

"Do you think they'll stop with bruising your throat the next time—or just running you into a ditch?" When he saw that his educated guess hit home, a slow, burning rage he had never felt in his life gathered force deep inside. "Who was it, Rae?" he asked, his voice lethally soft.

Rae backed away, bumping into the boulder.

"They ran you off the road, didn't they?" He followed, crowding her. "Was it the same guys as the first time? They ran you off the road and then they threatened you—warned you to keep quiet?"

After another tension-crackling moment, Rae slumped in defeat. "One of them started to choke me when he couldn't find anything in my purse," she said in a flat, dead voice. "The other one made him quit. Then he said they'd kill you if I tried to identify them. He told me nobody ever double-crossed IOS, and if I tried, I'd lose more than a few lousy trinkets."

He had suspected as much from the moment he heard what happened, but hearing it was like tossing a lighted match onto the gasoline. He wrapped her in his arms and pressed her head against his chest, fighting to control the trembling rage.

"I heard the siren from J.W.'s and Evan's car about that time, but I guess I passed out," she told him, the words muffled against his shirt.

"Rae..."

Her arms snaked around his waist and clung. "If anything happened to you, I couldn't bear it," she mumbled in a desperate, broken voice. "I couldn't."

"How do you think I feel about you?" He lifted her head, gazed deeply into her eyes. "Rae, sweetheart—" the words burst free before he could stop them "—I'm in love with you." He felt as though his heart had swelled into his throat, choking off his breath. "I love you."

Incredulous, incandescent joy washed into Rae's face, and two tears finally spilled. Her hands slid from his neck to touch his mouth, his jaw. "Caleb. You love me...." She blinked several times, then musical laughter filled the air. "That's a miracle, because—because I love you, too! But I never thought—I never dreamed—" The words stopped on a breathless gasp.

Caleb lifted her and twirled her around, oblivious to her head and sore muscles, oblivious to everything but the explosion of joy that was rocketing through his body. Then his head lowered and captured her mouth in a passionate kiss that seared all the way to his toes.

"God sure has a funny sense of timing," he mused a long while later, when the first euphoric joy had calmed to a steady, brightly burning flame. "I've known since the first time I saw you that you were different, special—but I was on a case. I kept trying to ignore the feelings, kept fighting them off—telling God I didn't understand why you stuck in my mind like a puzzle I couldn't solve and would He kindly solve it for me. So He did, in a way my mother will be happy to hear. She's been nagging me for years to come home with a good woman."

Rae rubbed her face against his neck below his jaw. "For me, it was your eyes and your kindness. Desire and compassion...a potent and irresistible blend." She kissed the pulse throbbing in Caleb's throat and whispered, "Nobody ever looked at me, or treated me, quite the way you did—the way you do."

"And nobody *but* me better look and treat you like I do in the future."

"You mean nobody else can treat me with Christian compassion?"

He kissed her soundly again. "That's what you get for having a sassy mouth."

"I'll try and be sassy more often, then." Suddenly she

clutched his shirtfront and pressed her cheek against his chest. The laughter in him died when he heard her sniff. "I just can't believe you love me," she whispered. "I can't believe God would give me someone like you."

The light touch—he had to remember that she responded better to the light touch. "Well, you're stuck with me now, no matter what. And that works two ways, little cat's claw. My mom's been praying since I was in my late teens that God would provide my mate, my perfect helpmeet. I really wasn't ready, much less interested. In fact, I'd about decided God was going to teach me a lesson for not listening to my mother—or Him, so that even when I was ready to settle down, there wouldn't be anybody left. I can't believe God saved *you* for *me*."

He gently tried to prise her face out of his shirtfront, but Rae resisted so adamantly he gave up and contented himself with running his fingers through her silky waist-length hair. Eventually he felt her draw a deep, unsteady breath.

"I'm not perfect, Caleb," she reminded him in a stifled voice. "I have this temper, if you'll remember. And I'm absentminded and nonobservant except with music—it's my past, Caleb! When your parents find out about mine—"

"Shh. Hush." This time, he wouldn't allow her to hide any longer. "Look at me—no, sweetheart, *look* at me and listen. When you gave yourself to Christ, you gave away your past. All of it, including the pain and mistakes of your parents. And guess what—God is not the God of yesterday, hovering over you with a club to constantly remind you of the past. He's the great *I am*. Think about it, sweetheart—what if you woke up every morning and the day was as fresh and new as our love? No yesterdays, just the promise of today and the hope of tomorrow."

"No yesterdays," she repeated slowly, her nose and forehead wrinkling in concentration. "I'll still lose my temper every day, probably. I keep trying, but I still fail." Her fingers came up to press against his beard-roughened cheek. "But if I'm hearing you right, and remembering my Bible correctly, then for every morning I wake up, I'll have a fresh start for that day. I do love you, Caleb Myers."

"I love you. Don't ever forget either one." Caleb hugged her. "Now—before it gets dark and we get lost trying to find our way back to the car, I'm afraid we have to finish the unpleasant part of this conversation.'' He covered her hand with his. ''Because it's suddenly become even more important to see to your safety and continued well-being.''

''No more so than yours,'' Rae replied. She shivered, and he saw her wince, pain dimming the glow in her eyes.

The sun vanished behind Pikes Peak, throwing crimson streamers across the sky and the world into darkening shadows. Caleb took Rae's hand. ''Let's go get something to eat,'' he said, ''and we'll try to come up with a plan of action.''

Chapter Twenty-Two

Rae watched Caleb more than she watched the surroundings while they drove through town. A lopsided smile curving her lips probably looked besotted . She didn't care. She didn't care that her head throbbed, or that all her muscles and bones had joined the pain demonstration. *He loved her.* She didn't even care that, buried somewhere underneath the euphoria, terror waited. Caleb would be with her, guarding her not only with his life—but with his love.

Never mind that, at the end of the drive, he would slip into his professional persona and she would slip into hers. They had both shared that golden hour in Garden of the Gods.

"You'll have to wipe that expression off your face if you aren't prepared for the razzing of your life, regardless of circumstances."

"I know." Their hands touched, briefly clung. "I will. I wouldn't want you to be embarrassed. But you'll have to wipe the same expression from your face."

Caleb made a rude noise. "That tears it. My reputation is shot forever. No longer am I the impassive and fearless consultant, able to stare down enraged executives with a single look."

The terror bit deep, jolting in its suddenness. Caleb was knowingly putting his life on the line. *What if IOS succeeded in killing him?* "Caleb?"

He shot her a swift, bracing glance. "Having a reality attack?"

Mute, she nodded, her gaze devouring his face, the shaggy hair and day's growth of beard unable to disguise the strength of character that radiated from him. He drove with relaxed confidence, and although he instantly understood her fear, his eyes—never still—testified to his poised alertness of their surroundings. He might *look* relaxed, but it was deceptive.

Rae struggled to subdue her fear, because the last thing he needed was to have his concentration diluted. *But he's still just a man.* God had brought them together, filled their hearts with love. He wouldn't allow Caleb to die now, would He? "I'll be all right," she said, determined to at least sound as though she had everything under control.

Another jolt sizzled through her, but this time it was one of revelation. She *wasn't* in control. But God was. "Either trust the Conductor or don't play as though you're part of His orchestra," she whispered to herself. "Well, I'm afraid," she amended aloud, "and I'm *trying* to be all right."

"It's all right to be afraid, sweetheart." A long arm snaked along the seat so his hand could massage the back of her neck. "I'm afraid, too—I just know how to deal with it a little better. Sometimes, anyway. Hang on to your faith. God is right here, with both of us. *Whatever* happens, He's here. We just have to try not to think about some of those whatevers, all right?"

"I'm trying, Caleb. But I have to tell you, being a trusting Christian has to be the most difficult piece I've ever played."

The circuitous route Caleb deliberately followed carried them over most of Colorado Springs, but eventually they arrived at Peterson Air Force Base. Night had fallen, though streetlights allowed enough visibility to see much of the surroundings, and several large buildings were illuminated. Curious, Rae was sitting up straighter and looking around. When he asked, she confessed that she'd never been on a military base before, in spite of living in the area most of her life. And—in typical Rae fashion—she'd never really noticed the base's appearance before.

Caleb watched her with secret amusement. "Not exactly what you pictured?" he queried after a few minutes.

"No." She returned his grin sheepishly. "I guess I thought

it'd look more like East Germany and Russia during the Cold War era. You know, miles of barbed wire and marching men and guards with machine guns.''

"And the only guard you've seen so far is the gate guard, who smiled at you.''

"Well, at least the buildings look bland and undistinguished and—military.''

"Undistinguished or not, security at this base is tight. Don't be fooled into thinking that just anyone could stroll past that smiling guard or drive onto the grounds for a casual picnic.'' He was silent a moment. "It's not easy, being part of a volunteer military force during peacetime conditions. The past couple of months I've really come to appreciate the sacrifices these people make.'' He chuckled suddenly. "I also appreciate Admiral Vale arranging things so we could set up another field office here on the base.''

"Why is the location so important?''

His gaze rested on her. "Here on a military base I don't worry as much about walking you into an ambush.''

They pulled to a stop in front of a low building with few windows. Caleb glanced swiftly around and stole a kiss as he helped her out of the car. He paid for the indiscretion when Rae bonelessly snuggled against him, and he had to exert every ounce of discipline to keep the contact brief. They exchanged a secret smile, then he ushered her inside the building and down some depressing-looking corridors.

When they entered the room, Tray, Joe Delano and Chuck Livingston, two other FBI agents, looked up from a long table covered with charts, files, and at one end a computer and printer. The men's frowning faces lightened a little.

"Sit down, Ms. Prescott.'' Tray pulled out a chair. "You look a lot better than the last time I saw you.''

Fresh color blossomed in Rae's cheeks, and Caleb suppressed a laugh. He winked at Rae as she sat. "Fresh air'll do that for you, won't it?''

Tray studied them a moment, and Caleb could practically see him analyze, weigh and come up with the correct conclusion. Dancing lights twinkled in the backs of his black eyes, but he kept his mouth shut. When it was all over, Caleb promised himself to reward such discretion with at least a steak dinner.

Once everyone was seated, all levity vanished. Delano handed Caleb a folder, and as he rapidly read the contents his mouth tightened. "Rae," he asked, watching her carefully, "remember when you told the Springs detective—J.W., wasn't it?—about the two women who wore matching necklaces?"

Rae nodded.

"I know you were unable to provide a physical description, but would you try again? I'll help walk you through the process, all right?"

The other agents leaned forward. Caleb knew their collective intensity made Rae nervous, but it couldn't be helped. "Close your eyes," he instructed. "Picture yourself in Joyful Noise. The door opens, and one of those women enters. What do you see?"

Rae obeyed, but after a few moments of painful concentration she opened them again and spread her hands ruefully. "I think the young one was blonde—and I remember smelling cigarette smoke around the other one. But beyond that..."

Face expressionless, Chuck Livingston casually flipped over a black and white snapshot and slid it across the table. "What about that?" he asked. "Does that jog your memory at all?"

Rae picked up the picture and studied it. "The face is sort of familiar," she allowed slowly. "But I couldn't swear in court it was the same woman."

Her nose wrinkled, and Caleb found himself wanting to kiss the elegant tip. *I'm losing it.* He ruthlessly tamped down the unwanted emotions and glanced at Livingston. "When and where?" He gestured to the photo.

"Denver, outside the bank where Ms. Prescott's account is. The man has known IOS connections. The woman was followed to the Springs, where she met Fisher in a local restaurant."

"Did they exchange anything?"

Ramirez scowled. "We don't know. They were sitting at a booth, and we weren't able to snag a table that enabled us to monitor any transactions."

Rae was still studying the picture. Caleb's gaze slid over her bent head as he continued talking in a low voice with the other agents. Tray verified that the note Rae had found was, as Caleb suspected, two lines of the Starseeker commands. Archie Cohen, Tray added sourly, had raised unholy havoc when Tray refused to release the note into his custody.

"Wait a minute." Rae grabbed Caleb's arm. Her voice vibrated with shimmering excitement. "Look. See the bag she's carrying? The photo's black and white, and that's why I didn't notice at first, but the more I looked at it, the more I realized there was something familiar about it. The bag—it's from Joyful Noise. It has the big treble clef on it, just like my car."

Tray exclaimed softly, triumphantly, while Joe pounded the table, and Chuck reared back in the chair, relief and satisfaction erasing the deep lines of tension in his face. "We've got them," Tray announced. "We're gonna nail 'em."

Caleb waited until the needed celebration ran its course before he dashed cold water on the moment. Beneath the table, his hand sought Rae's. "You better believe we're going to nail them," he promised, and his tone sobered all three men instantly. "And gentlemen, we're going to nail them *before* they have another opportunity to wreak havoc in Ms. Prescott's life. Let me elaborate...."

Over the next week security was tightened around the Prescott mansion, and Rae was rarely out of Caleb's reach, except at night, when a policewoman disguised as a visiting relative from Oregon was parked in the parlor. For Caleb, the most difficult task was learning to live with the depth of his feelings. He felt as raw, as naked as a newly hatched bird, ricocheting between hovering over Rae and hounding the police, FBI and OSI. Tray finally took him aside.

"Reel it in, pal, or you're going to find yourself pulled off the case entirely," he warned. "This isn't the time to lose it, Cal. Where's that easygoing detachment and laser brain focus you wowed us with last winter?" He punched Caleb's shoulder. "We all share your concern over Rae, but your feelings are interfering with everyone's ability to protect her—including your own."

They were sitting in Rae's kitchen while one of the undercover agents monitored Rae and the store so Tray could update Caleb on the latest developments. Caleb propped his elbows on the table and worried his hair with his hands. "I know," he admitted. "Trust me, I'm not happy with my behavior, either." He looked across the table. "You married?"

"Two years in June."

"How would you feel if it was your wife staked out like the tethered goat?"

"I'd hate it as much as you hate having Rae in that position. But obsessing over it won't get the job done, and we both know it."

"Yeah." Caleb also knew his only hope lay in God's sovereign awareness of circumstances. But he couldn't share that with Tray. The time and circumstances were wrong. *Remember Who's doing the timing, allowing these circumstances, and stop acting like a mule eating loco weed.* On countless occasions he'd self-righteously reminded Rae that God was in control. Now he was in danger of forgetting that fundamental truth.

It wasn't easy, living your faith in a society to whom the Almighty God was little more than a swearword.

"I hear you, Tray," he promised the agent. "Don't worry. I hear you. Besides, I have a hunch things are just about to break wide open."

The following Friday evening, he and Rae were enjoying supper at Gibson Girl. Rae was sharing her ongoing surprise at the sympathetic response on the part of her customers to the vandalism. "And I never realized, until this past week, that half these people even thought of me as a *person,* instead of just part of the store fixtures. But almost all of the customers who have been in before made a point of telling me how sorry they were about all my treasures." She nibbled a flaky crescent roll. "Remember the little old lady who sold me the Broadway music? She stopped by yesterday. You were out at the time. Anyway, her great-granddaughter had told her what happened, so she came all the way over to give me an English ironstone cream pitcher her husband had brought home after World War Two. She wanted me to have it, she said, because...because she wanted me to remember that there were still people left who cherished both things and people."

"Thank God for little old ladies. They usually have a clearer eye than the rest of us," Caleb agreed as he lifted his napkin to tenderly wipe stray crumbs from the corner of Rae's mouth. "It's easy to lose your perspective when you become immersed in the evil deeds human beings inflict on the world. You forget the good that still exists. I was thinking about that several weeks ago, when I flew to California.''

Rae's head was bobbing in agreement. ''I know. Take my customers, for instance. I have this constant internal battle with myself now, trying not to imagine that everyone who enters the store is a criminal just because two female customers turned out to be part of an evil organization.'' She laughed. ''It's so absurd, when I think about it, trying to imagine one of my customers passing government secrets. There's this timid little man—he was in today, as a matter of fact.''

She dug into the spinach salad Karen had placed in front of her with a smile and sideways smirk at Caleb. ''He's shy and retiring—collects old and out-of-print classical sheet music, if you can believe it.'' Chewing, she grinned across the table. ''Can you imagine someone like *that* being involved with IOS?''

''Was he looking for anything special today?'' Caleb asked very casually, though all his senses had leaped to full alert

Rae shrugged, took another bite. ''Not really. He did ask me to keep my eye out for a particular edition of Mendelssohn. Come to think of it, I need to give him a call. Some woman called just before the store closed—she wants to sell a bunch of music from an estate sale.''

Caleb leaned forward, his mind racing. After a moment Rae blushed, and he realized he'd been staring at her without speaking.

''Do I have dressing on my nose now, instead of crumbs on my chin?'' she asked, swiping at her nose with her napkin.

''Your nose is covered only by freckles,'' he murmured absently. ''Sweetheart, do you think there's a chance that Mendelssohn might be in the music the woman wants to sell?''

''I know it is.'' Her voice was innocently triumphant, electrifying every nerve ending in Caleb's body. ''I asked her, so she searched right then while I waited and actually found it. I thought it was really great, and told her I had a customer who was going to be very happy. Isn't that a marvelous coincidence? I've been waiting all afternoon to tell you about it.''

''I—'' Caleb spoke very softly ''—don't believe in coincidence.''

Rae dropped her fork. It clattered on the plate unnoticed as she gaped at him across the table. ''Caleb?''

His eyes swiftly scanned the nearby diners. "When did this woman say she would bring all the music to your store?"

"This Saturday." Rae bit her lip. Suddenly the gray eyes were dark, filled with uncertainty. "It wasn't a coincidence, was it?"

Caleb shook his head. "No, sweetheart. It wasn't a coincidence."

"But that means Mr. Fisher..." Her voice trailed away, and she shook her head in denial. "Caleb, he's so *timid.* He can't be involved."

Right now Caleb could have casually dangled Fisher over a cliff. He might even have dropped him. "Your timid Mr. Fisher is one of the programmers who designed Starseeker. And he's also the one who's been selling the technology to IOS, a piece at a time. You can bet the ranch he's nervous, probably even scared. But he's shrewd, greedy—and after revenge."

Rae shoved her salad aside. "Was Mr. Fisher the one who left that note in my music? The note with all the computer codes I gave to you?"

Caleb nodded. His hand reached across and patted hers, unsurprised to find it trembling. "We've suspected Fisher for months, but I didn't tell you because I was afraid you wouldn't be able to act normal around him." He squeezed gently. "You're too honest. And I hate to have to tell you, but you'll never win an Oscar for your acting skills."

"Apparently Mr. Fisher suffers no such qualms." Though Caleb easily read the gathering temper in her, he was relieved that she was learning to keep it under wraps. She'd even picked up enough these past months to glance around and lower her voice before she spoke. "Caleb—the music. He's using the music, isn't he?"

He nodded, pleased and alarmed at the same time. "Tray and I suspected as much last week, after you told me where you found the computer code. Hoffman—he's FBI, out of Denver—and Grabowski agree with us. We've been racking our brains trying to think of a way to prove it, come up with a way to catch them in the act without further endangering you."

"Isn't all this evidence enough?"

"'Fraid not. We have to catch Fisher and his IOS contact in the act of passing the information to have any real hope of a conviction."

Restless, feeling the urgency racing through his bloodstream, he stood, pulling Rae with him. "Come on. Let's borrow Karen's apartment. I don't like talking in here. Will she mind?"

"Not at all." Rae favored him with a very dry look. "But if you're thinking of stashing me someplace while you face the line of fire alone, you might as well save your energy. We're in this together—and that's the way we'll stay."

Chapter Twenty-Three

Up in the apartment, Caleb motioned Rae to a chair. He was, she knew by now, in what she dubbed his secret agent mode, though when she'd teased him about it he'd given her a thoroughly disgusted look. "I'm a *consultant,* not a secret agent," he'd growled. Rae cheerfully agreed and let it go. She sat obediently in the chair while he made sure Karen's phone and the apartment were free of any uninvited bugs. But when he placed a call to Tray, she wondered if he thought of himself merely as a consultant.

When this nightmare was all over, they were going to have a serious discussion about semantics and self-perception versus reality.

"I think Rae stumbled onto the system." Caleb spoke to Tray in his normal low, easygoing voice, but she detected the underlying excitement, and in spite of her determination to stay unruffled, she had to sit on her hands to keep from playing a Bach fugue on the chair arm. "Yeah, I'm serious," Caleb was insisting. "I think this is it. Fisher asked her to be on the lookout for a particular piece of music, and several hours later Rae took a call from some woman conveniently wanting to sell a pile of old music." He listened, his free hand twirling the lock of hair that always fell over his forehead. "Mmm. I agree...especially when one of the pieces just happened to be the copy Fisher's after."

He glanced at Rae. Smiled reassuringly. Rae wasn't fooled, but even if she couldn't act, she could return a falsely reassuring smile. Caleb shook his head and turned his back on her. "I know, I know. All we have to do is catch 'em passing the info, and pray it's condemnatory enough for a conviction. Like I said, Tray, if my hunch is correct, this will be the one. Things have gotten too hot, especially after Rae botched things by finding the computer code. What? Where?"

Rae's heart leaped into prestissimo at the exclamation. She rose and hurried over, and Caleb's arm enfolded her, gripping her shoulders in an almost painful vise.

His brows scrunched together. "That makes it even more likely they're winding it up and IOS will hand over the big pay-off. What? Next Saturday. Yeah, I know. I don't, either." He raked a hand through his hair. "It's risky, but I think you're going to have to do what I suggested last week and put a team on the second story, over Joyful Noise."

"Caleb, no. IOS will see them—" She clamped her lips together, then relaxed against him, her hand lifting to lightly stroke the hand gripping her shoulder. She could feel his muscles, iron hard, poised on the brink of violence.

"Don't hand me that. I want to catch them—*all* of them—as much as you do. But I will *not* allow Rae to be placed in that kind of danger. She's a civilian, Tray."

"Now you wait just a minute, Caleb Myers. It's not your—"

He laid firm fingers over her mouth, cutting off the words. "Tray, we'll discuss it later, at our usual time. You can get hold of the others—you might give Grabowski and the Springs intelligence unit a call, as well. Right. I'll see you in a couple of hours." He hung up.

"I won't let you wrap me up in protection like a baby in a blanket," Rae announced belligerently, and pinched the hard muscles below his ribs. "I'm an adult, and I love you. But you can't—"

"Watch me." With a swiftness that left her speechless he hefted her into his arms like a sack of groceries and stalked across the room, ignoring Rae's instinctive struggle. He deposited her at one end of Karen's Victorian fainting couch, then leaned over her, trapping her with his palms braced on either side of her head. "Listen to me, you little tigress. I *love* you

I've never felt like this before, so whether you like it or not, I'll do anything I think is necessary to keep you safe, even if you end up hating me for it. Ya got that?''

His mouth covered hers in a possessive kiss, but beneath the implacable male protective instincts, Rae sensed his turbulent fear. The same fear for her safety that plagued her about *his*. Instinctively she softened, capturing his head between her hands and trying to tell him without words that she understood.

Abruptly he broke the kiss and straightened, cramming his hands in his pockets.

Bewildered, off balance, Rae searched his face.

"Rae, sweetheart, your father was spotted in a bar down on Platte last night."

Numbness cascaded in a river of ice, coating her from head to toe. "What are you saying?" she asked, her voice carefully stripped of feeling. *No. Please, Lord. I don't know if I can stand what I'm going to hear. Help me....*

Caleb studied her a long, unsmiling moment, then expelled his breath in an explosive sigh. "Remember what I told you? That we think he's a courier for IOS? That means he acts like a mailman, picking up deliveries from one location and delivering them to another. If he's here, it's either to pick up the Starseeker technology or to bring in the rest of the money IOS is paying Fisher. Maybe both."

She crammed her fists over her mouth to keep from screaming a denial and closed her eyes. Caleb dropped down beside her, and gratefully she leaned against him. He dropped another kiss on the tip of her nose. "Rae, I'd like to put you on a plane and send you to my folks in Georgia until this is over. I don't suppose you'd consider it? They have a beautiful old place, and all my sisters would visit—everyone will slather you in southern hospitality. You can see my boat...."

Rae kissed him to block the desperate flow of words. "No way," she breathed against his lips after a long time. Even though her eyes were wet, she pulled her head away because she wanted him to see the determination in her face. It more than matched his. "No way will I leave you here alone, with everyone out for your head, because my absence will blow the Starseeker case to smithereens. Because of my father I'm involved up to my neck, whether we like it or not."

She took a deep breath. "He's using me—and my store—as though I was less to him than a faceless drug pusher or some homeless bum he passes by on the street, and it's time I faced that." Even as she spoke the words, she could almost feel the shift deep inside, like ice floes breaking up after an endless frozen winter. Like she used to feel whenever she'd finally *understood*, all the way to her soul, what a composer had felt when he wrote the music she was trying to master.

A tentative confidence stirred, gathering force with each word. Awed, Rae savored the feeling and offered up a grateful prayer. "I'm seeing it through to the end, Caleb—whatever that may be."

"I don't want you to be hurt." His voice was rough, almost hoarse.

"I don't want *you* to be hurt." She threw herself against him. "And we'll both take every precaution, be as careful as your training and my determination allow. But Caleb? Our safety ultimately isn't up to us. Is it?"

His hands clenched in her hair, then he tugged her head back and kissed her again with a tender violence that Rae met—and matched.

It was difficult, she learned over the next few days, to live a normal life when there were two armed men stashed upstairs, figuratively looking over Rae's shoulder and breathing down her neck. Even when she knew they were there to protect her and nail a group of traitors, she found it almost impossible to relax.

For the first time since she could remember, playing the piano didn't help. She had never minded an audience when she was performing onstage, because she was far too disciplined and her love for music had always enabled her to overcome any stage-fright. But now, after months of living in goldfish-bowl circumstances, she found that she simply couldn't lose herself at the piano like she used to because she was too aware of those unseen eyes on the second floor.

Without the release of music, she felt lost, restless, in spite of her deepening spiritual maturity. Caleb had been summoned to Chicago by Polaris Corporation, over his strong objections, so Rae didn't have the comfort of his presence, either. She chatted with her customers during store hours, and Lucy, the phlegmatic police matron, in the evenings. But the days crept by, each hour suffocating in its slowness. Paperwork, household chores, even reading her Bible...nothing recaptured that brief moment of affirmation God had showered over her that evening with Caleb in Karen's apartment. And she yearned for more moments like that even as she accepted that part of faith was waiting patiently between those moments.

It was as though she was being tested, her growing faith perfected within the painful fire of divine silence, and denial of every prop upon which she had based her existence.

Unfortunately, her temper began to simmer, bubbling beneath the tissue-thin serene persona she fought to project to the world. More than once she had to fight an overwhelming compulsion to dash outside and scream at the top of her lungs. Maybe kick a tree or the foot-high wall surrounding the mansion. Something immature but infinitely satisfying.

By Friday afternoon she couldn't even pray beyond a constant plea for God to keep her from shattering into a million pieces like her lost treasures. At least Caleb would be back this evening. Lucy had told her so an hour earlier, the placid voice calm, round face expressionless as always. Every afternoon the policewoman, in her guise as Rae's relative, went for her daily "walk," window-shopping in Old Colorado—and maintaining contact with all three agencies—the police, the FBI and OSI. Rae had reached the conclusion days earlier that her personality was definitely *not* designed for undercover work. Her expression would give her away every time, just as Caleb had told her.

It was a gray day, chilly for the first week in May. Instead of sunny skies and mild temperatures, winds with a wintry bite whipped around corners, plunging temperatures into the forties. Sullen clouds slogged over the mountaintops, and the smell of rain hovered in the air.

At a little after three, the store bell jangled, the wind almost tearing the heavy oak door out of Mr. Fisher's hands as he entered the shop. Wisps of mousy hair were tangled all over his balding head. His nose and ears were pink with cold.

"Not much of a spring day out there," he greeted Rae.

"No, it's not," she returned, avoiding eye contact. Her smile felt like more of a baring of teeth. For days, she had mentally rehearsed her behavior for the next time she saw this man and given herself countless silent lectures on controlling her temper. On allowing *God* to control her temper.

Mr. Fisher rubbed his hands together, darting surreptitious looks around the store. "So—how's business been lately? Had, ah, any more excitement around here?" The darting eyes bounced off the healing cut on her forehead.

"The destruction of the entire collection of priceless birthday gifts my uncle gave me over a span of two decades is enough excitement for several lifetimes." Not to mention a paltry thing like abduction, threats, being run off the road... Rae looked him straight in the eye. "Most of those objects were irreplaceable. It's almost more than I can bear, unlocking the door to the store every morning now." *Zip your lip, Rae, before you lose it.*

"Oh." Mr. Fisher looked slightly sick, his sallow complexion emphasizing the sharp bones of his face, the prominent Adam's apple above his expensive silk shirt. He glanced toward the bare shelves, just visible through the doorway. "I heard about—I mean a friend of mine who came..." He floundered to a halt. "You, uh, you say my Mendelssohn will be in tomorrow?"

"Yes." Rae pretended to look for something under the counter so he couldn't see her face until she regained her composure. She genuinely hadn't realized what a formidable task undercover cops and agents faced, having to hide their feelings all the time. No wonder they all wore those impenetrable masks of indifference.

"What are you doing down there?" Mr. Fisher asked sharply, and Rae's head jerked up with a snap, her hand flailing.

Music, store sacks and her ledger cascaded to the floor in an untidy heap. Rae pressed her fists against her temples and ducked to tackle the mess before she tackled Mr. Fisher.

"I'm sorry." He stood on the other side of the counter, all but dancing on nervous feet. "Here, I'll come around and help pick—"

"No!" Rae interjected, much too sharply. She tried to soften the word with a reassuring smile. "It was my fault. I'll take care of it. You go look around." When he didn't leave, she clenched her hands, casting about in desperation for something else to say. "Was...was there another piece of music in particular you were looking for, like the Mendelssohn?"

His complexion turned pasty white, and behind the thick glasses his eyes blinked rapidly. "Why do you ask?"

His agitation was spreading to Rae. *Maybe he was so nervous because IOS had warned him or they were hiding outside in the bushes. Maybe he somehow knew she'd found the code.* "Well, you collect old music," she stammered, standing up, wiping her perspiring hands on her slacks. "I—I just wondered if you'd heard that I had something else. Musically, I mean. You...it's just that you don't usually come in on Fridays, and I wondered..." She stopped, filled with self-disgust.

Mr. Fisher was backing away, looking as if he expected one of the IOS thugs to jump out at him like they had Rae. "I just remembered—I have an appointment. I'll come back another time. Tomorrow. Right now obviously isn't a good time for you."

He whirled and fled, shoes clattering on the warped oak flooring, fingers scrambling to tug open the door. Cold tentacles of wind slithered across the room in his wake, rustling papers and blowing strands of hair from her face. Rae despised herself, but she ground her teeth and bent to pick up the mess on the floor. If the past six months of painstaking investigation collapsed, she had no one to blame but herself.

A little before five the phone rang. It was the woman who planned to bring in all the music from the estate sale, and she told Rae she wouldn't be able to come in after all.

"There must be some way we can work it out," Rae burst out across the woman's goodbye noises. "Mr. Fi—I mean, my customer will be so disappointed." Heart pounding, she frantically cast about for a more persuasive argument.

"I'm sorry," the cool voice on the other end was saying. "Tell your customer maybe another time."

"Wait—where do you live? I'm—I'm more than willing to come pick the music up." If Caleb had been there he would have ripped the phone from the wall and hurled it across the room. She could only imagine the reaction of all the other listening ears.

There was nothing but dead silence from the other end of the phone.

Rae's hand was slippery with sweat, heart slamming against her rib cage. "I really wouldn't mind," she pressed, praying for a calm, professional voice. "I did promise I would have the Mendelssohn on Saturday, and I hate to go back on my word."

"Just a minute."

The phone was covered, and Rae could hear nothing but the somber ticking of the mantel clock over the fireplace. That and her own erratic breathing.

"You'd have to be here at four o'clock. Can you arrange to close your store early?"

Rae wiped her palm on her slacks. "Where do you live?"

"If you can't be here by four o'clock, your customer will just have to be...disappointed. I have an engagement elsewhere."

The woman was obviously not going to provide directions until Rae agreed to the time. "I can be there by four," she answered slowly, reluctantly. *Caleb, forgive me.*

There was another crackling pause, then the woman issued a set of sharp directions, and the fear rolled over Rae in a crescendo as she listened and wrote the instructions on a store bag, her slippery hands ice cold.

"If you're not there by four," the curt voice added, "you'll have made the trip for nothing. I have to leave no later than five after."

"I'll be there."

Chapter Twenty-Four

"I don't care if you plan to bring in the National Guard. It's too dangerous. She's bait for a trap. You know it. I know it." Caleb snagged Rae's eyes in a brief, searing glance. "Even Ms. Prescott knows she's been set up."

The conference room at Peterson throbbed with tension. Not only were Caleb, the FBI and Detective Grabowski present, but a deputy investigator, Sergeant Benthall from the El Paso County sheriff's office, was there, as well. Throughout the night Sergeant Benthall and Tray had been coordinating the deployment of people, studying maps and photographs—and planning.

And throughout the night Caleb had brought to bear every persuasive power, every bribe, threat or plea, argued logically and finally, for the first time in his life, he'd raised his voice, almost yelling. The episode still smarted, not only over the crack in his indomitable calm, but because it hadn't worked. Nothing had dissuaded the men with whom the final decision rested from involving Rae.

Strictly speaking, *nobody* wanted to. She was a civilian, an innocent bystander, and though Caleb's protests were the most vehement, he was not alone in his reluctance.

Detective Grabowski said it best. "Only exigent circumstances allow this," he finally admitted. "I can't think of another case

with these unique circumstances, but as of this moment I don't
see that we have any better options."

Dennis Hoffman crossed and recrossed his legs. Long and
lanky, he looked more like the center for a basketball team than
an FBI agent. Right now, he looked like an aggravated, *tired*
center. "He's right, Myers. This is our best, possibly our *only*
chance to nail at least some of the IOS kingpins, and you know
it." He leveled a look at Rae. "Even Ms. Prescott knows it. At
least give her credit for being willing to—"

"I don't want to hear another word about sacrifice and the
nobility of her motives."

Caleb stalked to the other end of the room, breathing deeply,
fingers twitching. The back of his neck burned, and he knew that
every person in the room was gawking at him. The realization
irritated him like a bad case of poison ivy. Did they think he was
some blasted android, some character like Data from *Star Trek:
The Next Generation,* a nonhuman devoid of feelings? A man
could change, couldn't he? Hadn't anyone in this blasted
room—outside of Tray—ever been in love? Caleb's concern for
the woman he loved was neither illogical nor unreasonable.

Pivoting on his heel, he stalked to the waiting group.

Rae wrapped her fingers around the chipped ceramic mug one
of the agents had scrounged for her. "Caleb, there isn't another
way. Besides, it's my fault Fisher spooked, so it's up to me to
make amends."

Caleb didn't look at her. She'd said words to that effect in a
dozen different ways in the past ninety minutes. And he couldn't
change her mind, any more than he'd been able to change Grabowski's or Tray's. Even Jackson Overstreet had reluctantly concluded Rae's participation in the setup was necessary.

Caleb did something then he'd never dreamed he was capable
of. He picked up an ashtray full of cigarette butts and hurled it
across the conference room. It slammed against the wall, rending
the shocked silence with the sound of shattering glass. Then—
focusing his gaze on Hoffman and Grabowski—he slammed his
palms on the table with such force the table and everything on
its surface jumped. Both men instinctively shoved their chairs
back.

"Rae's a *civilian*," he enunciated with lethal softness. "Regardless of her feelings to the contrary—which are due in large

part to carefully orchestrated emotional blackmail by everyone in this room—she is *not* responsible for fouling up the case. Hoffman—'' he leaned across the table, spitting the words with the stinging precision of a bullwhip ''—you've been especially adept at playing on her guilt. Don't do it again. Ever.'' His gaze lifted to rake across the group. ''Now, why don't we all concentrate our mental faculties on coming up with an alternative plan.''

Frozen into silence, the men in the room stared at each other uneasily. Caleb rose to his full height and allowed himself to look at Rae for the first time in ten minutes. Without speaking, she carefully put her mug of lukewarm tea aside and rose. A needle of pain stabbed beneath his skin. She moved as though approaching a cornered wild animal. Did she think he would direct the force of his anger at *her?* Unmoving, he watched her approach.

She walked all the way to him and laid tentative fingers on his bunched shoulder muscles. ''Caleb, you can't put the blame on Agent Hoffman or anybody else. I volunteered. I choose to do this of my own free will. It was my decision alone. Mine.''

Surprised—and relieved—Caleb felt his tension loosen, and in vague wonder sensed a trembling begin inside his body. Adrenaline. He shook his head, refusing to soften his stance. ''Why won't you listen to me, instead of everyone else? You've done enough, Rae. You've had enough done to you. I want you out of it. Now.''

''Caleb,'' Rae said with underlying steel, ''you don't have the right to give me that order.''

Her eyes pleaded, love burning openly for the others to see, though he knew she wouldn't bring their relationship into the open for fear of compromising whatever authority he still enjoyed. Ha. Lately, his authority was a joke, thanks to the grave, gray-eyed woman who had stolen both his heart and his common sense.

''I'm going to be wired,'' she reminded him, ''and there will be undercover cops and agents positioned all over the place.'' Incredibly, her mouth flickered in a half-humorous smile. ''About like fleas on a stray dog, from what Sergeant Benthall tells me. I'll be fine, Caleb.'' Her fingers brushed the back of his hand. ''You're just going to have to trust me. I'll be fine.''

''We don't *know* that.'' He glowered at her, unreasonably aggravated that *she* was all calm and collected while he stood there breathing like an enraged bull...and acting like one. Still... "There are so many variables, so many things that you haven't got the training, much less the experience and temperament, to anticipate. In spite of all the bells and whistles and gadgets, there's just too much that could happen that will be beyond our control."

"Then," Rae murmured in a voice only Caleb could hear, "we'll just have to depend on the One who is always in control, won't we?"

He took the gentle counsel like a roundhouse to the gut, and all of a sudden his shoulders slumped. Dropping into the chair, he closed his eyes, wondering if this was how Jonah must have felt inside that whale. His hand reached to press against his temple. After a minute, he looked at Hoffman. "I'm sorry, Dennis," he apologized quietly. "I had no right to behave as I did. I still think I'm right, but—" he glanced at Rae "—so is Rae. She's made her decision, so all I can do now is respect it and try to help her—and all of you—any way I can."

A collective sigh of relief rippled around the room.

"Don't worry about it." Hoffman waved aside the apology. "We're all concerned about Ms. Prescott. But unless she keeps the four o'clock appointment, the Starseeker case is dead in the water. We can't prove Fisher left the program inside a piece of sheet music, and we don't have a positive ID on the woman who seems to be controlling him. Without Rae, the whole case wouldn't stand a chance of making it into court."

Caleb looked at Rae at last. "I know," he answered, his gaze asking forgiveness, betraying fear, admitting defeat. "God help me, I know."

Rae drove south on I-25 toward Pueblo. To her right, rolling hills and water-chiseled ravines covered with scrub and a few trees provided training grounds for Fort Carson. To her left, a winding ribbon of cottonwoods lined Fountain Creek. On that side the terrain was flat, with few hills. Few places to hide.

Beneath the loose knit top she had carefully selected, Velcro held in place a thick belt with its tiny, sophisticated transmitter. The stiff, scratchy contraption tugged Rae's skin, but she ignored the discomfort, choosing to focus instead on the task awaiting her. Caleb had counseled her, over and over, to keep her mind only on what she was *going* to do and what she *could* do—not on the things she couldn't change. His last bit of advice had been the most difficult to heed—avoiding the deadly what-if syndrome.

Her hands were gripped too tightly around the wheel of the rental car she was driving. She relaxed her fingers, one at a time, in a disciplinary tactic she'd learned at school years earlier. The knot lodged just above her breast loosened marginally, allowing her to take a relaxing breath.

"Try not to worry," Sergeant Benthall had told her. *"We'll already have everyone in place long before you show."* He had smiled at her, gold-capped tooth flashing, but the dark brown eyes remained watchful, flat.

Almost ten miles now. The exit should be coming up soon.

"Just be as natural as possible, Ms. Prescott. If the woman gives you a stack of music, thank her and leave. If she dreams up some excuse for not having it, smile and thank her, no matter how implausible the excuse. Then leave." That had been Tray Ramirez, looking serious and grim, his suit jacket tossed aside to reveal the ominous belt rig with the ugly butt of his gun protruding.

Through all the last-minute instructions, Rae had managed to keep her face calm, and even if it hadn't been an Academy Award performance, her relatively collected behavior had won an approving gleam from Detective Grabowski. Inside, of course, she was more terrified than she'd ever been in her life, including the car accident. That, at least, had happened so fast there had been little time for terror.

There it was—the exit the woman had told her to take. Rae flicked on the blinker and headed down the ramp. Perspiration rolled between her shoulder blades, dribbled down her temples. At the intersection, she turned left, crossed over the freeway, then turned onto a dirt road paralleling I-25.

A dust-colored car was tucked in the shadows beneath the overpass, almost indiscernible. The quivering pent-up breath escaped in an explosive puff of relief. Rae swiped at her face, then tried to sing. Her voice warbled into a croak when she belatedly remembered how law enforcement officials would be picking up the sound of her voice. Grimacing, she hushed, playing Grieg on the steering wheel while she searched for landmarks.

There. A dirt road winding east toward Fountain Creek, with smatterings of cottonwoods on either side. She crossed the railroad tracks, dust billowing behind her in a choking cloud. Yesterday's rain had never materialized, and the morning had dawned, in typical Colorado fashion, warm and sunny. Perfect May day.

Rae didn't see any other cars and was almost as panicked as she was relieved, because if *she* spotted them, IOS almost certainly would. There were few places to conceal men and cars in this relatively flat area, which was probably why this out-of-the-way rendezvous had been selected. Clever bunch of criminals. Paranoid, evil, lower-than-a-snake's-belly contemptible...criminals.

The vitriolic spate of name-calling helped, though Rae didn't feel the slightest inclination to lose her temper. *"Rae, just remember to keep your temper—stay cool."* In the thick silence of the car, she could almost hear Caleb's voice speaking in her ear, his golden eyes bathing her in loving concern. *"They might suspect you of all sorts of schemes—but they don't know for sure, so they'll wait for your behavior to clue them how to react."*

"I'll remember," she whispered, not caring if the sensitive microphone picked up her words. If Caleb was listening, he would know to whom she had spoken.

"I'll be praying every second you're out there, not only for your safety, but for God's loving Presence to fill your spirit, instead of fear." Rae swallowed. The hard lump was swelling again. She remembered how Caleb had looked just before she had climbed into the car, remembered his parting words, which he'd whispered in her ear as he fastened the seat belt for her.

"Don't forget all those guardian angels that will be surrounding you, since I can't." And then, *"I love you. Please. You have to come back to me."*

A hairpin curve in the narrow, winding road forced her concentration to the matter at hand. Rae slowed, drove carefully around the bend between a stand of cottonwoods and oaks. Off to the right, almost hidden in trees, nestled a run-down house with a For Sale sign leaning drunkenly in the front yard.

"I'm coming up on the house," she murmured. Officer Helen

Dix, who had helped position the belt and explain how it worked, had promised that Rae's voice and any others within twenty feet would be picked up. Miles away, in an innocent-looking van, every word would be faithfully recorded.

Rae turned into the front yard—there wasn't a driveway—and the stubborn lump in her throat ballooned to the size of Pikes Peak. Her hand hovered over the key. She breathed a last prayer and killed the engine. It was time for the curtain to rise, and Rae Prescott needed to give the performance of her life. *For* her life.

The house looked deserted. Sagging front porch, dingy, peeling paint, screen door with the screen ripped halfway out—the place fairly screamed, "This is a setup!"

Rae squared her shoulders and lifted her chin, keeping her gaze on the two windows. They stared back like two blank eyes covered with black patches. *All righty, Rae. Dive in.* With icy fingers that barely felt the rough wood, she dragged open the screen and knocked on the front door.

It was yanked open so suddenly Rae's hand hovered in the air, poised mid-knock. "Hello," she croaked, then cleared her throat and smiled. "I'm Rae Prescott, here for the music?" *There. Much better. Friendly, but professional. You can do this, Rae.*

Suddenly, through the roaring in her ears and the suffocating pounding of her heart, Rae felt an inexplicable sense of calm wash over her. It was incredible, amazing...miraculous. She clung to the feeling with every ounce of her being. She might have delivered herself into a den of lions, but power and confidence were flooding her veins in wave after wave. She had never felt this kind of power before, even when she was playing—and winning—in all those piano competitions so many years ago.

The power of God.

She stared into the face of a tall, dark-haired, dark-eyed woman, and she wanted to tell the woman to give it up—she couldn't win this particular battle, no matter what she did to Rae. Then her eyes fell to the necklace draped around the woman's neck, and she dropped with a resounding thud into the realm of foolish mortals.

"The necklace!" she exclaimed with unforgivable stupidity.

Chapter Twenty-Five

T he woman's eyes narrowed to slits, and her breath escaped in a hiss. "I knew it." She clamped surprisingly strong fingers around Rae's wrist and tugged her into the room. "All right, you two-timing little schemer, what's your game? Where's the note you stole out of the Brahms?"

Hot color flooded Rae's face. She wrenched her arm free and stepped back. "I don't know what you're talking about. I came here to pick up some—"

"Shut up!" The woman reached forward with a ring-laden hand, her eyes smoldering. "Don't waste your breath. No one cuts in on my turf, do you hear? *No one.* It's been tried before—and it's too bad you were stupid enough to try and pull a double-crossing stunt on me."

"I haven't—"

"I told you to shut up." The glittering eyes raked over her. "You're pathetic. A weak, pathetic wimp. What possessed you to think someone like you could steal Starseeker for yourself? Did you actually think your two-bit innocent act would fool me?"

"I'm not acting!" Goaded, Rae snapped, her tone so furious the woman quit her ranting. "I recognized your necklace—it's beautiful, and I think I told you so the first time I noticed it." In a bold move born of desperation, she attacked, unleashing the temper Caleb had warned her over and over to keep under control. "What's your problem, anyway? I've driven all the way out here—at *your* convenience—to pick up some music, and in the process I make a harmless comment on your necklace. I'm sorry if that somehow offended you. If you'll give me the music, I'll get out of your hair and out of your life. If I weren't trying to accommodate a valuable customer, I wouldn't even bother at all."

The woman stood motionless, studying Rae as if she were an unfamiliar insect crawling across the floor, which she couldn't decide whether to step on or ignore. Finally she spoke without taking her eyes off Rae, raising her voice slightly. "I think she's lying, Jim baby. Why don't you come on out and see what kind of reaction we get?"

There was silence, then the sound of footsteps scraping hollowly across a bare floor in another room. When Mr. Fisher's stoop-shouldered form shuffled into view, Rae didn't even try to suppress her astonishment. "Mr. Fisher!" she squawked. There. That should have been loud enough for every official in that twenty-mile radius to hear.

Mr. Fisher looked at Rae in sheepish apology. He was practically quaking in fear. "I'm sorry, Ms. Prescott. I never meant—''

"You shut up, too!" the woman hissed. "We've got to find out how much she knows before we clean house and...disappear." Her mouth curled in an unpleasant sneer. One ringed finger stroked her cheek with the most exquisitely manicured nails Rae had ever seen. "So, Ms. Prescott, just tell me what you know. I can be reasonable, given enough incentive."

"Larissa, wait a minute." Mr. Fisher's face turned a sickly green. Behind the glasses his eyes were liquid with fear. "You promised that no one would get hurt. I brought the rest of the noncontaminated program. Let's just leave her and go."

"Jim baby, you're beginning to get on my nerves. And your blubbering mouth—" she advanced on the hapless man "—is way too indiscreet."

Good word, Rae decided, realizing that a discreet exit for *her* would be in order. She edged backward one careful step at a time.

Mr. Fisher glanced at her, then hurriedly away—but it was too late. Larissa snapped around. "Don't even try it."

Hmm. The latent menace of the order was unnerving, but Larissa's bulldozing arrogance enraged Rae. She had always despised bullies, especially female ones. They were so crass. "Are you going to run me down? Shall we engage in a catfight? I don't think so—that would be beneath my dignity."

Incredibly, Larissa colored. The nut brown eyes glared, but Rae could see the woman's struggle to bring her temper under control. In a macabre moment of recognition, Rae identified with Larissa's struggle. "Why don't you try to explain what's going on," she persisted. "If I understood, perhaps I could help sort it out." At what point, she wondered, did bluffing become stupidity? "Since it apparently involves Joyful Noise, I'd say I have a right to know."

"I knew I shouldn't have given in to Jim's whining. If we'd moved the drop as I suggested, all this could have been avoided." Larissa glanced out the curtainless window, fingers drumming on the dusty ledge.

"The store was perfect—nobody should have suspected," Fisher mumbled.

Larissa was right, Rae thought. The man *did* whine.

"The store wasn't perfect for anyone but you." Larissa strolled to Mr. Fisher, spearing him with a barbed look of contempt. "You had to feel safe. You wanted—*insisted* on—that store, so what happens now is all on your shoulders. Remember that." She turned to Rae. "I've told you once that your two-bit innocent act wasn't fooling me. You're wasting your time."

Rae affected an indifferent shrug. "All right, then. I know you must be doing something illegal, and I don't appreciate your using Joyful Noise. But if—"

Larissa's face changed. "Don't threaten me, honey. If it hadn't been for your old man, you'd have been out of the picture weeks ago." She watched Rae, then laughed an ugly laugh. "That hits you where it hurts, doesn't it? Your father thought you might be a useful tool, and I suppose for a while he was right. Your father," she repeated. "How does it feel, knowing your own father doesn't care this much—" she snapped her fingers under Rae's nose "—about his own daughter?"

"Larissa, don't," Mr. Fisher pleaded, glancing uneasily at Rae's face.

"If I hadn't been so suspicious that he might be using you to pull a double cross on me, those two visitors at your house would have done a lot more than just threaten you." Larissa moved behind Rae to block the only door. "Give it up, honey. Just tell me how much you *do* know."

"Why don't you tell me what the two of you—or however many of you are in your little club—have been passing back and forth in my sheet music?" Rae countered, dropping the pretense of ignorance. Larissa's calculated barbs hurt, but not nearly as much as they would have a week ago. Besides, Rae had something far more important to concentrate on right now—her life.

Mr. Fisher's face had turned an ugly shade of mottled red. "You've known, all this time, haven't you? You've *known*. Ms. Prescott, I thought you were nice—I even felt sorry for you because—" He stopped, shooting Larissa an uneasy, sullen look.

Rae regarded him incredulously. "You use my store to steal a top-secret government project, jeopardize national security, and you stand by doing nothing while evil thugs destroy my property. You taunt me about my father, throw his indifference toward me in my face—and *you're* upset with *me?*"

"You don't understand."

"I understand more than I like. I understand the truth, which is more than I can say for you. You don't care a thing about me, Mr. Fisher. You only care that you've been caught with your hands in the cookie jar. But if you think I'll close my eyes to what you're doing, you're in for a disappointment."

"I doubt that," Larissa murmured behind her.

Rae's pulse skittered, but she kept her gaze glued to Mr. Fisher, recognizing the weakest link of the chain binding her in this decrepit prison. "What you're doing is worse than illegal, Mr. Fisher—it's treason. I hope they hang you."

"I don't care about the country—it's corrupt anyway. The government deserves to be compromised—and so does that smug, pompous Overstreet!"

"Fisher—"

He ignored Larissa. "Sitting on his millions, taking all the credit—well, not this time. It's my turn now. This time *I'll* have the money, the prestige. *I* will." He turned to Larissa, his eyes pleading. "Won't I, honey? Just like you promised? I've brought the last of the program with me, like I said I would. Your boss won't have any reason to doubt now. Let's just leave Ms. Prescott and go."

Larissa gave an unladylike snort. "That's right, Jim baby. Leave her here to blab everything to the feds. They've been sniffing around you for a month now, trying to pin some evidence on you."

Fisher swallowed hard. "I don't want anybody hurt."

"You'll look real spiffy in a prison suit."

Desperation flooded his face. He looked like a trapped animal, wild-eyed, searching for a bolt hole. Rae didn't move, afraid to tip Larissa over the edge. Against her waist, the scratchy Velcro belt dug into her skin, a welcome reminder that every word in the room was being monitored. Unfortunately, if Larissa pulled a gun, not a single one of the authorities would be able to crash through the door in time. *Pray harder, then.*

"You won't have to watch," Larissa was saying acidly. "Jules and Romo will take care of it. All you have to do is deliver her to the address I give you." Her voice rose impatiently. "Oh, quit looking like such a rabbit! Did you honestly think we'd leave behind any tale-telling mouths? That's not how it works, baby."

She took a step toward Rae. "We can either do this the easy way, or I knock you out." She studied Rae, and her mouth curved in a little smile. "It's a shame, really. You've got a lot of moxie, for a wide-eyed innocent. But that's the way it is, right, Ms. Prescott? Now—I have a brown belt in karate and none of your dainty Christian scruples, so what's it going to be?"

In a physical confrontation, they would inevitably discover the transmitter. Rae's only hope of rescue lay beneath the folds of her sweater, so she held up her hands in a mock gesture of surrender. "I've been beat up on enough," she admitted.

"I always did admire someone who gives in gracefully," Larissa murmured, stepping closer. "There's a rope in that closet," she told Fisher. "Fetch it for me like a good boy, in case she decides to change her mind."

"Ms. Prescott, she means to have you killed!" Mr. Fisher exclaimed hoarsely.

"I didn't think she wanted to play jump rope," Rae managed

to retort. Her mouth was dry, and she began to sink into the choking quicksand of terror she had kept at bay. She tried not to shiver as her arms were wrenched behind her back. Rough strands of rope were wound around her wrists, then her ankles, the coarseness biting into tender skin. Rae bit her lip, focusing on the window and the world beyond. Somewhere out there were a lot of men and women. They would rescue her before it was too late.

Caleb would rescue her.

And if he couldn't, God was with her. He would always be with her, even when Caleb wasn't. She smiled at Larissa. "You think I've given in gracefully," she said. "But you know what I just realized? You're wrong on a number of levels."

"I have to give you credit for stubbornness. Don't make me revise my opinion by this blind persistence in trying to bluff me."

"I'm not bluffing. You're the one who's blind, because you've been wrong ever since the first time you came in my store. In fact, it's because you were wrong that you're in a whole lot more trouble now than you're willing to admit."

Larissa's hand shot out and fastened in Rae's hair, yanking her head painfully. "What are you talking about?"

Her eyes watered from the burning pain in her scalp, but Rae gave look for look. "You don't know the first thing about music," she managed to say between clenched teeth. "You proved your ignorance when you asked for the 'Ode to Joy' from Beethoven's Fifth Symphony."

She heard Mr. Fisher inhale sharply.

"The 'Ode to Joy' is from Beethoven's *Ninth*, Larissa Whoever-you-are," Rae finished, then gasped when the other woman gave her hair another vicious tug. "You were wrong about the music—and you're wrong about me."

"How could you be so stupid!" Mr. Fisher raged. "This whole thing is your fault! Yours! *That's* why the code wasn't in the music that time you kept insisting the mistake was mine. *That's* why you had to send those two goons to try and intimidate the girl and ended up with the police as well as the feds on our tails. That's—"

"Shut up!" Larissa shoved Rae at the raging man, almost causing both Fisher and Rae to fall. "Just take the sanctimonious little nun to this address and get out of here. I'll take the program.''

Mr. Fisher cast her a frantic look, staggering beneath the dead weight of Rae's trussed-up body. ''My money! What about my money?''

''It will be deposited in your account *after* my people run a test on the whole program.'' Her voice dripped acid. ''So you better take care of her, and you better do it exactly like I've told you—or you won't be around to spend your money, Jim baby.''

Her gaze clashed with Rae's. ''Say your prayers, honey. Regardless of which stupid symphony that song came from, I guarantee you there won't be any odes to joy where you'll be going.''

This time Rae's smile wasn't forced at all. ''Wrong again, Larissa. You're wrong again.''

Chapter Twenty-Six

"**W**e have to pull her now." Fear coiled in Caleb's stomach, a timber rattler poised to strike. "You heard what Fisher said. They're going to kill her."

The stark words hovered inside the murky confines of the cream-colored van, where he, Tray and one of Benthall's men had been listening to the grim performance a few hundred yards away. He exchanged glances with Tray. With one accord the two men snatched binoculars, then jumped out the back doors. Crouched, alert, they crabbed their way to the front of the van, then belly-crawled along the ground to a position where they could see the house.

"We have to get her out now," Caleb insisted again. Outwardly he was still, his voice a bare rustle of sound. But his insides were molten lava, every nerve ending screaming for action.

Tray didn't move from his prone position. His eyes were glued to the binoculars. "Be cool a little longer, man. You know we can't make our move yet. If this Larissa had planned to ice her, she would have done so by now. It's under control, Cal—Rae's gonna be all right. She's one gutsy woman, your lady."

"I know." Slowly the death grip on his binoculars eased, and Caleb relaxed infinitesimally. "Thanks, Tray."

"Sure. It's going down this time, Myers. Thanks to Rae, we

have a fighting chance of nabbing more than just Fisher and the woman.'' He shifted slightly. ''You stick with Fisher, okay? That way, when he transfers Rae, you can move in with the others.''

''Yeah.'' A pebble was gouging a hole in his hip, but Caleb barely noticed. He'd stick with Fisher all right, but more vitally, he'd stick with Rae. His heart had quit beating when she lit into Larissa as though they were two kids on the school playground. He forced his muscles to relax again. ''When this is all over, I'm going to haul her to Georgia by her hair and stash her in my boat.''

He saw the corner of the FBI man's mouth lift. ''I'd say she's done pretty good for a rank novice. You heard her—we should be able to get a conviction on attempted murder as well as theft of classified technology, thanks to Rae's presence of mind. She's got a lot of class, Cal.''

Caleb was proud of her, too, but he also knew Rae better than Tray did. She might sound calm, in control, like he did. But the terror lurking in the backs of her eyes could take over at any time. If it did—once again, he stopped the thought, jamming the binoculars against his eyes with enough force to bruise his bones.

It was impossible to relax, especially since they could no longer hear what was going on inside the house. Lying belly-down in the dirt beside Tray, sweat dribbling down his forehead, Caleb struggled to keep his hands steady on his binoculars. He wasn't used to field surveillance, since the bulk of his work took place in the high-tech jungles of multistory office buildings, following paper trails. He kept himself in top physical condition through workouts and jogging, not—as Rae fancifully liked to accuse him—from living the hazardous life of some super spook.

What would happen if he didn't have the skill or the necessary instincts to save her?

You're playing the what-if game, aren't you, Caleb? Let it go, and trust.

He almost jackknifed onto his back, so clearly had he heard the words. His pulse was racing, and he risked a sideways glance at Tray, but the agent hadn't moved a muscle. After a while his pulse returned to near normal, and Caleb realized that a sort of pervasive peace had stolen over him, renewing his confidence. His spirit had soared on the wings of an eagle. A slow, almost invisible smile began and barely tickled the edges of his mouth. He was okay.

The door of the ramshackle house opened. "They're leaving," Tray muttered.

Statue-still, both men watched as Fisher and a tall, dark-haired woman manhandled Rae outside, across the barren, stubbled yard. Her arms were bound behind her back, and the rope passed to her feet, hobbling her so that she was limited to baby steps. Once her knees gave way and she almost pitched face-forward to the ground.

Caleb jerked, his teeth snapping together with an audible click. The powerful binoculars focused directly on Rae as close as if he were standing right in front of her. Pain bleached her face, and he watched her bite her bottom lip. But her eyes...under any other circumstances, Caleb would have grinned. Dark, stormy, yet almost serene, she conveyed the heroic acceptance of a martyr. Caleb could tell from the bonelessness of her body, however, that she was creating as much trouble through passive resistance as she could manage, using her captivity with the only means left open to her.

They finally reached the blue sedan Rae had driven, and Fisher opened the back door. Caleb saw Rae's lips move as she offered some final comment. The black-haired woman, Larissa, looked murderous, and all of a sudden her hand snapped up and she slapped Rae across the face.

Caleb half rose, muscles bunched and ready, but Tray's hand pushed him down, his voice brusquely reminding him of the need to stay concealed. "She's all right—just a stinging cheek, Cal."

Caleb nodded. "Sorry." The dispassionate, almost exalted state of perfect detachment and utter confidence continued to pour into him. With the clarity of an avenging angel, he watched. And waited.

Rae was inside the car, across the back seat. Fisher climbed into the driver's seat, and Larissa slammed the door behind him. She leaned in the open window, obviously issuing final instructions, then turned and strode rapidly toward a shed almost hidden behind a stand of willow oaks.

Fisher started the engine, then gunned the car down the dirt lane, a billowing cloud of dust marking his route. Tray whipped out his hand unit, speaking rapidly. "Suspect headed west in victim's car—two-toned blue ninety-five Taurus. License plate Kilo, Uniform, Hotel, three-seven-seven. Male suspect driving.''

A wicked-looking black Lexus pulled out of the shed, with Larissa behind the wheel. She roared down the dirt road in the opposite direction.

Caleb and Tray scrambled to their feet, Tray reeling off the info on the Lexus. Hands dangling in poised suspension, Caleb watched the two departing cars with the calm eyes of a patient predator.

''They're far enough away. Let's get moving!'' Tray snapped beside him. ''We've got tails on them both, so get hold of yourself. You can either come with us in the van, or—'' The words were cut off as their gazes met. Tray shivered. ''Okay. You've gotten hold of yourself. Try not to annihilate the rest of us in the process.''

''I'm only here to protect Rae. Instant retribution would be nice, but that isn't up to me.'' He smiled. ''Too bad.''

They tore off down the gully at a dead run. The fleeing cars had shrunk to miniature toys, weaving with drunken haste toward I-25. In their wake, the rolling cloud of dust wafted gently toward the two running men.

''Offhand, I'd say your reputation has been understated,'' Tray observed between breaths as they sprinted down the wash to the spot where they'd left their cars. ''I hope you don't ever decide to come after me, man. The scene yesterday at Peterson was an eye-opener, but this—'' They dodged a cluster of tumbleweeds. ''Is this what you're always like when you're about to solve a case?''

''Nope. This is what I'm like when I'm protecting the woman I aim to marry.'' He marveled at the words, spoken aloud for the first time, and wondered again at his incredibly poor timing. On the other hand, he couldn't very well tell Tray that the reason for the restoration of his fabled detachment was that God had spoken to him.

About a hundred yards south, they joined the other agents, Benthall's men and the Springs police. ''Did you copy everything?'' Tray asked them.

Dennis Hoffman nodded. ''Fisher's headed toward the Springs. Benthall's unit will pick 'em up when they hit the freeway. The Lexus is headed south—I've got another car on her tail." He allowed satisfaction to coat his voice. "I think we got 'em."

"Until Rae Prescott is safe, nothing is finished," Caleb observed mildly. He tossed his binoculars to Tray.

Dennis peered at his face and grimaced. "You got it, Myers. I'm with you, a hundred percent."

Tray slapped Hoffman's back. "It's cool, man. Fortunately, he's not after us anymore."

"I'm going after Rae," Caleb concurred. "I want to be there when Fisher tries to...dump her."

"Stay out of it, Myers," Benthall warned. "Your part in this is over. It's our business now."

Caleb looked at him. "I don't think so," he replied gently.

He didn't waste time on words, but sprinted toward his car, hidden in the cottonwoods growing thickly along the creek. Behind him came Benthall's furious voice, followed by Tray's matter-of-fact retort. "Get out of his way and let him help," he heard the FBI agent counsel. "He's the best ace in the hole we've got."

That wasn't likely, but Caleb didn't waste time patting himself on the back because Tray thought he was something special. Besides, he knew better. He was calm, in control, all right. But locked deep inside, bound by divine intervention, he was as scared as he'd ever been in his entire life.

He reached the car, yanked open the door and threw himself behind the wheel. After turning the ignition with a savage twist, Caleb gunned down the rutted path that led to the dirt road. Impervious to the damage he was inflicting on the car's undersides, he aimed the hood like a rifle, rocketing over the rough ground in a screaming, teeth-rattling ride.

He rounded a curve, topped the rise—and there was Rae's car, gathering speed as it headed up the entrance ramp to I-25. Caleb watched in grim satisfaction as the undercover cops stationed beneath the overpass pulled out, climbed the embankment and pursued Fisher at a discreet distance.

Caleb rammed his foot on the accelerator. Then he was under the railroad bridge, with the freeway just in front of him. The engine whined, tires squealing as he roared up the ramp at seventy miles an hour. An eighteen-wheeler was approaching in the near lane, but Caleb shot in front of the cab with room to spare. He ignored the warning blast of the truck's airhorn.

Traffic was heavy. He dodged cars with the icy calm of a jet fighter pilot, keeping the speedometer needle hovering near ninety as he wove from lane to lane, simultaneously surveying the road ahead. When the traffic piled up, he finally—reluctantly—eased back on the accelerator. This was no time to have an accident, nor did he have the right to endanger innocent people, regardless of the circumstances.

Scenery passed in one continuous blur, while time stretched, elasticized seconds that seemed to last hours. Two minutes slipped by, then six. The icy calm wavered—he gripped the wheel tighter, forcing himself not to raise his speed. Rae's car was being closely monitored. Fisher wouldn't be able to lose the squad cars, who would be in active pursuit once he hit the city limits. Restlessly his eyes searched the road. He grabbed the radio. "One-X-fifty-one to One-X-fifty. Request position of suspect vehicle."

"One-X-fifty. Vehicle entering city limits. Maintain positions."

He was too far back. Cautiously the car gathered speed, creeping past seventy-five. Almost ten minutes passed. Caleb topped a hill just in time to see the Taurus exit at Nevada.

He noted with abstract astonishment that he was sweating like a racehorse, even though his mind was clear, calm as the balmy spring day, and he was confident of God's sustaining presence here—and with Rae.

Without warning a vivid memory flashed across his brain: Rae lying unconscious on the narrow emergency room bed, her face waxen except for her bloodied forehead. She had looked...dead.

Caleb jerked, and the car swerved. He wrestled the car under control, but it felt like an eternity before he wrestled the painful memory away and regained control of his mind. When the exit approached, he was quoting the Twenty-Third Psalm in lightning fast repetitions—an effective spiritual painkiller. He took the ramp too fast, screeching to a standstill at the bottom behind a bright red four-wheel-drive vehicle. Up the heavily traveled street, the car with Rae in it turned right and disappeared.

Caleb grabbed the radio again. "One-X-fifty-one to One-X-forty-seven. Request immediate intercept." Protocol be hanged. He wanted Fisher picked up *now*. Which patrol units were covering this sector? McArthur and Ayers, he knew, were the detectives on site, and they drove an innocuous gray sedan. So where were they?

He was forced to wait to turn onto Nevada while an endless stream of cars chugged past, all with the speed of a dying snail.

The radio crackled. "One-X-forty-seven. Suspect turning right on—" Static garbled the transmission, but not before Caleb caught a bitten-off exclamation.

He finally pulled into the street, but by the time he made it to the corner where Fisher had turned, it was too late. The detectives' car was pulled to the curb, and Caleb slammed to a halt behind them, then sprinted to the car. "What happened? Where's Fisher?"

"Get in with us. Tell you on the way." Evan slapped a fist-size portable siren bubble in place while J.W. spoke rapidly into the radio. Caleb barely had time to slam the door before they tore off in pursuit of Rae's car.

"Fisher did an illegal U-turn, practically got wiped out by a truck." MacArthur threw the words over his shoulder, his face grim, savage. "They stopped in front of that alley, another car pulled up, and a guy jumped out. He grabbed Miss Prescott, tossed her in the back of the car and took off."

"They're headed west on Colorado," J.W. added. He spoke into the radio again. "Responding code three—we're westbound on the avenue and attempting to intercept suspect vehicle. Request code one and assistance." He twisted his head and caught Caleb's eye. "She'll be okay," he promised, trying with little success to sound confident. "There's at least four units responding, not to mention the feds and OSI."

Caleb nodded grimly. He watched the stores and cars and people without seeing them while his fingers fiddled with his watchband. Calm...control. It was still there, allowing him to sit quietly, but the detachment was nowhere to be found.

At this moment, he was utterly powerless—but God wasn't.

He had lost all control of the situation—but God hadn't.

He didn't know if Rae would be alive or dead the next time he saw her—but God did know.

Over the past endless hours that knowledge had sustained and fueled Caleb, keeping him sane. He would carry the memory of

that audible voice to his grave, along with the awesome power
that had coursed through him then. But right now the voice was
silent, and Caleb's knowledge offered cold comfort when his
heart was bracing itself to be destroyed.

Chapter Twenty-Seven

❧

Terror circled Rae like a pack of frenzied pit bulldogs. She could tell from the sounds of traffic that they had entered a city—was it the Springs or Pueblo? Were the good guys keeping up? *Where was Caleb?* Clamping her teeth together, she worked to free herself in spite of maniacal driving that was tossing and bouncing her all over the back seat. She was afraid to reason with Mr. Fisher—much less plead—for fear the distraction would precipitate a serious accident.

Good, Rae. You're worried about being involved in a car accident when this guy's driving you to your execution?

She unclenched her teeth and took a deep breath. "Hey! Mr. Fisher! You don't need to do this!" she yelled over the seat. "Please...while there's still time. Stop the car, toss me out. Don't do this!"

Mr. Fisher ignored her.

Rae shouted louder, talking nonstop as fast as she could, not caring what she said or sounded like. Her only intent was to distract.

Suddenly the car slammed to a halt, almost throwing her onto the floor. Rae squirmed, struggling to reposition her trussed body closer to the back of the seat. Without warning Mr. Fisher was looming over her. His face was slippery, flattened out, like melting wax. Behind the ugly glasses his eyes were fixed, glittering.

"Shut up!" he screamed. "Just shut up! I have to do this! I don't have any choice!"

He turned, and the car shot forward. Outside, brakes shrieked. A horn blasted angrily.

You always have a choice, Rae thought, wondering if she should keep shouting. Well, what did she have to lose? "You always have a choice!" she yelled, furiously sawing at her wrists. "You always—"

Once again the car turned abruptly, this time so violently she was flung first against the seat, then onto the floor when they slammed to a halt. The door was yanked open. Hard, urgent hands grabbed her, hauled her out. Fear and anger exploded. Rae twisted and squirmed, opened her mouth to scream. The attempt ended in a choked gasp when she was flung into the back of another car and her head struck a glancing blow on the door handle.

"Get moving," a dead-fish voice ordered. "The little chip head's brought company."

Rae knew that voice. Shaken, stunned into immobility, she lay across the seat. *Lord...Lord—help me.* She knew that voice. She would hear it in her sleep the rest of her life.

He turned to gaze over the seat. "You don't learn, do you, Ms. Prescott?" he asked, then smiled. He'd smiled like that the day he had run her off the road, then throttled her. All the time his hands were squeezing, squeezing, he'd been smiling.

If I throw up now, I'll just die, Rae thought, swallowing convulsively. A hysterical giggle crowded into her throat. She *was* going to die. Surely she would have been rescued by now if the cops—if Caleb—had been able to keep up. No. *No!* She didn't want to die—wasn't ready to die. Not like this. Not like—

"Cops on our tail." Panic coated the driver's rough voice. "Where'd they come from? What'll I do?"

"Lose them," her nemesis ordered without inflection, his head jerking around, away from Rae.

Relief flooded through her. For several precious seconds all she could do was lie on the seat, blinking back tears of gratitude while her fear-knotted muscles slackened and began to tremble. Then, buoyed by a resurgence of hope and fresh determination, she once again set about the task of freeing herself. She could do it. She *would* do it. She just had to concentrate, ignore the pain, the fear. Focus. "You'll never make it to the top if you don't focus," her piano coach used to remind her, over and over.

The apostle Paul had promised she could do all things through Christ. Paul had been in prison, and God released the chains. Maybe... *Focus, Rae. Do what you can, and let God take care of the rest.*

"They're getting closer!"

"Turn on Thirtieth. Take the road into Garden of the Gods. We'll lose them and dump her there."

So. They had brought her home. Home to die. *No! Don't think it. Focus!*

She had five minutes, maybe less.

Blood trickled, dripping between her fingers onto the seat. Her wrists burned, throbbed. Pain shot into her shoulders, insistent, weakening her will. *Renew my strength, Lord.*

Caleb, I love you. Where are you?

Outside the window, huge red monoliths rose in Rae's blurring vision. Garden of the Gods. The mountainous boulders protruded from the gray-green earth like dorsal plates on a gigantic stegosaurus. Jurassic Park. She was going to be eaten by a dinosaur. *Stop it, Rae! Focus!*

The car swerved into the park entrance on two wheels, throwing Rae across the seat.

"Be careful, you fool!"

Rae's little finger slipped free of the rope. Her heart jerked once, then tripped over itself when the man turned to stare into her face with his dead pits of eyes.

"Say goodbye, Ms. Prescott." He shifted his body, preparing to reach over the seat.

Rae froze, eyes locked to his. She shook her head, heart hammering, unable to speak.

The car fishtailed wildly. Cursing, the man grabbed the seat to keep from being thrown against the driver. The two men began arguing, a furious exchange of curses and forceful gestures as Rae's killer was forced to give terse directions to the panicking driver. *He wasn't looking at her right now.*

Rae waited a fraction of a second, then tugged on the ropes in a burst of desperate strength. Her ring finger slipped past, then her thumb. Tears poured down her cheeks, blinding her. She scrubbed her face against the rough fabric of the seat as she gave one hard tug. Her right hand flopped free, dropping uselessly behind her like the hand of a—of a corpse.

Sirens keened in the distance, drawing closer, promising help. No time. They wouldn't be there in time. She was going to—

Focus, Rae! Rae...you can do this. It's all right. Focus...and fear not.

The control poured over her in a cataract of warmth and power. Urgency still flooded her, but her mind had somehow grown clear, detached from the terror. She felt as though she had just stepped onto the stage at Carnegie Hall, and yet somehow the feeling was different. Rae kept her gaze on the two men, while behind her back she worked her fingers, ignoring the pain because she needed to use them. *Play an F-sharp scale, Prescott, that'll limber those fingers. Count while you're doing it, to keep the rhythm. Count seconds. Five, ten...*

"They're practically on our tail—we gotta dump her now!"

"Take that side road—" No longer cold and flat, his voice rapped out the words, control slipping. "There—there, you fool! We'll lose them and dump her at the bottom of— Hey! What the—"

Rae attacked like an enraged Doberman, teeth bared, eyes trained on nothing but its prey. She hurled herself toward the driver, hands clawing his face, scratching at his eyes. Even as he automatically lifted his hands, Rae was grabbing the steering wheel. She wrenched it to the right as hard as she could.

The driver was screaming in her ear. Hands tore at her wrists, her waist as the world disintegrated into a kaleidoscope of whirling sound and color. Swerving like a drunken rocket, the car crashed against a guardrail, spun halfway around, then pitched headfirst down a scrub-choked ravine.

I love you, Caleb. Love you—

She drifted to earth slowly. The roller-coaster motion had stopped. All the yelling and screaming had stopped. *Dead—or dreaming?* Had to be one or the other, because in the midst of the overpowering silence and stillness, she could hear Caleb's voice right next to her ear.

He was talking to someone. The words... She needed to listen so she could understand. Wait—was that her name? But he sounded upset, choked. As though he was...crying? Why? *God? Am I dead?*

"No, you're not dead, Rae. Thank You, Lord, dear God—no, sweetheart, you're not dead...."

Oh. Caleb was telling her she wasn't dead. Rae tried to move, tried to force her uncooperative eyelids to open.

"Rae, it's all right. It's over. You're all right. Please wake up and talk to me, sweetheart. Rae, I love you...."

Like a curtain lifting, strength and full consciousness returned. Rae opened her eyes, blinking in the bright afternoon sunlight. Caleb! She was alive—and Caleb was here. His face, white and gaunt, rimmed with dust and lines of fatigue and worry, had never looked more beautiful.

A smile tickled the corners of her mouth, spread irresistibly. *She was alive!* And the man she loved with all her heart was alive, as well—and holding her as though he would never let go of her. "You're late again. What took you so long?" she tried to tease, but the words emerged in more of a hoarse croak.

Tortured eyes widened, searching her face. He stared at her for almost a full minute without speaking, his pale cheeks hollowed, mouth a compressed white line. Gradually the gauntness faded, and lights began to twinkle in his eyes. A smile crept across his face. Finally he began to laugh. Then he hugged her and buried his face in her neck. "Rae, sweetheart. Thank You, Lord. Thank You," he whispered in her ear, the phrases blurred, running together in a rhapsody of relief.

After a long time he lifted his head and covered her face with kisses. "I got here as soon as I could," he murmured, laughter in the words as he tenderly mimicked the ones he had spoken months earlier. A lifetime ago. "Guess my timing wasn't much better than when I was on the second story of the hardware store across the street, was it?"

Rae's giddy smile wavered, almost turning upside down. "But you're here. You're here, Caleb. I love you."

"Myers! Hey, Myers! The ambulance is on its way." Tray Ramirez slid down the embankment, skidded to a halt next to them.. "How is she? Cal—how's Rae?"

Rae shifted her gaze to the other man. The imperturbable agent sounded almost as shaken as Caleb looked. "Believe it or not, I think I'm fine."

"It was a miracle," Caleb concurred. "No broken bones. She's conscious—talking." Rae saw with astonishment that his eyes were wet. "She should have been—"

"Well, I have a few injuries to complain about," Rae hastily inserted. Her eyes were stinging. "Nothing that a little more Merthiolate won't heal, though." She lifted a raw and bloodied wrist to flick the lock of hair on Caleb's brow with unsteady fingers. "But since Caleb's so good at patching me up, I won't need an ambulance. And I *sure* don't need a hospital."

"Well, I'm taking you there anyway. *I* need to be sure," Caleb said.

The plea in his eyes belied the dictatorial statement. Rae didn't argue. She glanced at Tray. "What about—"

Caleb put his hand to her cheek. "I'll tell you all about it later, okay?"

"Everything's cool, Rae," Tray put in. "Don't worry about a thing." He looked at Caleb. "Take her by the hospital, hero. I'll keep everyone's attention elsewhere. You can bring her in tomorrow for the debriefing."

All of a sudden Rae became aware of the activity churning all around them. Lights flashing, radios crackling, movement. Voices talking in subdued, efficient tones. The emergency was over, danger neutralized. *It was over.* Rae looked into Caleb's eyes, and abruptly the world fell away into a deep indigo twilight. She was alone and safe. Safe in the arms of a man who loved her. *Loved* her.

Safe, as well, in the arms of a loving Father who loved her. *Loved her.*

Her heart began to swell in a symphony of music. She knew, deep inside, that the melody playing in her heart was music that would last a lifetime no matter *what* happened in that lifetime. God's music, she had learned, was like that. Better even than Mozart. Better than Caleb's laughter, though she would always be especially grateful for the joyful sound of it. *Thank You.*

She looked at him and smiled. "Will you do something for me...right now?"

"What is it, sweetheart?" He held her closer. "What do you need? You hurting somewhere?"

"Not exactly." She squirmed, grimacing. "Just that...can you *please* take this wretched Velcro thing off my waist before we leave? It's driving me crazy, irritating my skin.'' Heart full, Rae watched laughter fill his face again. Then she added, her voice breaking a little, ''I don't mind telling the police and the FBI and the OSI...the *whole world* how much I love you. But I've had enough eavesdropping in my affairs for a while.''

''I think that might be easily arranged, Ms. Prescott.''

He deftly removed the equipment, then lifted Rae into his arms and stood. She tried to peek over his shoulder, to see the car.

''Caleb, what about—''

''Tomorrow, sweetheart. I'll fill you in on everything tomorrow.'' He tightened his grip, then began picking his way along the scrub- and rock-choked ravine. The path was difficult, the climb steep—but his arms never relaxed their protective hold. And his feet never stumbled.

Rae closed her eyes, laid her head on his shoulder—and relinquished control.

Chapter Twenty-Eight

They drove to Peterson the next morning through an unrelenting downpour, but Rae wouldn't have cared if the weather had dumped a six-foot blizzard of snow. For the first time in months—in her life—she had slept like a baby all night long. Surveillance was being maintained awhile longer, as a precaution, and Caleb had refused to leave until Lucy was competently ensconced in the parlor for the night.

Didn't matter to Rae. Eventually the surveillance teams would leave, as would Lucy. Even Caleb might leave. Come bedtime, Rae would still be able to lie down in perfect peace. She knew, with a more profound assurance than she had ever known, that she would *always* be watched over.

But not by *human* eyes and ears.

Snugly fastened in her seat belt next to Caleb, she savored the delicious sensation of being alive. Of being...free. "I've learned some things about myself," she announced when Caleb stopped at a red light. Rain pounded the windshield, turning the city to a colorful tear-streaked Monet painting.

"What things?" Caleb asked, slanting her a possessive glance. His hand slid across to brush her gauze-covered wrist.

Rae held her bandaged wrists up, studying them while she talked. "For one thing, I learned I really *don't* have to be in control for things to work out all right." She smiled a little heepishly. "All these years I've tried to be such an obedient Christian. I thought I was—well, *helping* God by taking charge of my life. He gave me a will, a brain, all that stuff."

"Yeah," Caleb agreed. "All that stuff. And then?"

"You charged into my life."

"Literally," he added helpfully, chuckling when she swatted his arm.

The light changed to green. Rae sat back with a contented sigh, eyes half-closed, listening to the swishing tires, the rhythmic clack of the windshield wipers and the incessant drumming of the rain. "I learned," she murmured dreamily, "that life is more rewarding when I leave the driving to the Lord." Another quiet chuckle from Caleb. "You know, you taught me the true nature of God's unconditional love—you really never cared who and what my parents were, did you?"

"Nope. I cared that *you* were burdened. But God's presence in your life, in your heart, was obvious to me from almost the beginning. All I wanted to do was to prove your innocence in the Starseeker case. After I learned about your father, I wanted to prove your innocence to *you.*"

"I'm never going to see my father, am I?"

He hesitated, then answered gently. "Probably not, sweetheart. He's gone to ground again and might not surface for another five years. If he'd wanted to see you, meet you—he would have done so by now."

Rae closed her eyes. When Caleb squeezed her shoulder, she sighed, turning her cheek to rub the back of his hand. "Thank you for being honest. I—it helps. I suppose there's always going to be a hurt little girl inside of me somewhere, wishing my father had loved me. That my mother— Well, never mind. I'm trying hard to let God's love change those feelings instead of trying to work through them by myself and—" she gave a rueful laugh "—continuing to fail."

"I know. If it helps, you're not the only one who's had to learn a few hard lessons." They stopped for another red light, and he removed his hand. "God has a way of blasting us out of our securities and comfortable preconceptions so we *will* depend completely on Him, doesn't He?"

"I would have preferred a gentler method than IOS."

"Mmm. But if it hadn't been IOS, you might never have come to terms with your father."

For a while they were both silent. Rae had a feeling, from the lines pulling either side of Caleb's mouth, that his thoughts had tumbled briefly to the nightmare of the past twenty-four hours. "I guess we seldom appreciate how precious the life we have is, until we realize— Caleb?" She stopped, gnawing on her lip.

"What is it, sweetheart? Don't you know by now you can tell or ask me anything?"

"You might think I'm...ascribing wishful thinking, or hallucinating—I don't know. It's something that happened when I was in the back of that car, tied up." She saw his hands clench on the wheel, and a muscle jumped in his cheek. "I'm sorry," she recanted, contrite. "It's nothing. I shouldn't have reminded you— us."

"Don't be silly." He glanced at her, then turned into a parking lot and stopped the car, set the brake. "What happened, Rae? Tell me now, before we get to the base. I need to know." He reached out, touched her cheek with his fingers. "I need to know," he repeated.

She searched his face, seeing the love shining nakedly, and with a little laugh threw up her hands. "I heard God speak to me," she admitted in a rush. "In the car. I was about to panic and I heard— Caleb? What? Why are you looking at me like that?" She grabbed his arm. "Caleb, I warned you that—"

He crushed her against his chest, stifling her words. Against her ear his heart thundered like the rainstorm, and he was holding her so tightly she could barely breathe. "Caleb, you're going to suffocate me." The crushing hold instantly softened, but he wouldn't free her. His hand came up to cradle her head, and then he began to speak, the words low, so full of emotion goose bumps sprang up all over Rae's skin.

"If we're crazy, then we'll have to be crazy together. Fools for Christ," he whispered. "God...spoke to me, too. It's amazing, isn't it? We talk it, believe it...but until something like this happens and we *experience* the absolute reality of His presence—it's just blind faith. But then..."

"I once was blind, but now I see. Amazing grace."

"Do you know a song for everything?"

"Just about." She burrowed comfortably against him. "Deal with it, Myers. I'm a musician."

"Mmm. I have a feeling—" He stopped, and Rae felt a chuckle build strength until it tickled her ears in a puff of laughter. "Yep. I have a lot more feeling than I ever realized." He tugged her head up and kissed her. "Thank God for feelings, even if my reputation's just been permanently revised, updated. Reprogrammed."

"Do you know a computer analogy for everything, Myers?"

"Just about." He kissed her again. "Deal with it, Prescott. I'm a computer security consultant."

"Are you *sure* you're not a secret agent?"

He groaned, set her away and started the car. "I'm sure of a lot of things, Ms. Prescott." He pulled onto the road. "I'm sure that I love you. I'm sure—now, especially—that God really does have perfect timing to go along with His perfect love. Perfectly demonstrated by the miraculous changes that have occurred in both our lives."

"Caleb Myers..."

"I'm sure that Admiral Vale will rip a strip off *both* our skins if we're late for the debriefing."

"I'm sure I'm going to commit an act of violence to your person if you don't stop teasing me." She shook her fist mock-threateningly at him. "Tell me that you're just a consultant. Now."

"I love a tough woman. What happens if I don't tell you what you want to hear?"

Her heart leaped in a not-quite-comfortable somersault. He *was* teasing her, wasn't he? "I'll throw a real-live temper tantrum? Take out an ad in every major U.S. newspaper highlighting everything I know about you?" Her voice faltered. "Caleb?"

They turned into the road leading to Peterson Air Force Base. Caleb stopped to show the gate guard his ID, then they were on their way. Caleb didn't speak until they reached Admiral Vale's office and parked the car. He pocketed the key, unfastened his seat belt, then reached over and unfastened Rae's. "Come here, sweetheart," he ordered, very sternly.

Rae's mouth went dry, her euphoria faltering. He looked so serious all of a sudden, even though his eyes were still smiling and the corner of his mouth kept trying to curve upward. Even though they had made no vows to each other, no commitment beyond admissions of mutual love... She prayed her deepening faith would help her survive—never knowing. "You are, aren't you?" she whispered, her voice tremulous.

His head tilted, and his eyes narrowed. "Do you honestly think I might have lied to you?" he asked, taking her shoulders and turning her until their gazes were only inches apart. "Little idiot," he murmured lovingly after a long moment where she forgot to breathe. "I can see I have my work cut out for me the next half-century or so."

"I— *What?*" She gaped at him, dizzy and more breathless than ever. "What did you say?"

"Hmm. I think what's more important is what I meant, isn't it?" His fingers went to her chin and held it still. "I love you. You love me. We both love the Lord. I want to be part of your life forever. In my book, Rae Prescott, that means marriage. What does it mean to you?"

"I—I...you want to marry me?" Her voice rose to a squeak.

Incredibly, an expression of wonder filled his face, followed by wry amusement. "Yeah, I do. Another miracle, of sorts. I can't think of anything more I want out of life, Rae Prescott, than to marry you."

"But—my father... The Prescott family isn't... I mean..."

He stopped the halting words with a tender kiss. "Then my offer is the perfect solution to the problem you seem to have with your name." The amber eyes glowed even brighter. "Change it to Myers." He glanced swiftly at his watch, and the wry amusement deepened. "It's a good thing Christ will be the head of our family. I think I might have discovered an ongoing problem with my sense of timing concerning you."

"I think I could learn to live with that," Rae managed to say, all of a sudden floating higher than a weather balloon. "If you can live with my faults, I can live with yours."

"Is that a yes?"

Lids drooping, she slanted him a provocative look. "I'll tell you," she promised sweetly, "*after* you tell me what your job *really* is."

He gave a shout of laughter, pulled her close and bent to whisper in her ear. Then, hand in hand, they went inside for the debriefing.

* * *

Admiral Vale's office was crowded. Rae recognized most of the people. Tray Ramirez, Detective Grabowski, J.W. and Evan, Agent Hoffman. Caleb introduced her to the others—the FBI Denver section chief, the civilian contractor who headed the Starseeker program out at Falcon, Admiral Vale.

Overwhelmed, a little intimidated, Rae let the contractor, a nervous medium-size man with cowlicks all over his hair, shake her hand until she was afraid he would squeeze it off.

Admiral Vale clapped her shoulder with so much force only Caleb's swift reflexes kept her from pitching into a wastepaper basket.

"Young lady," he boomed, pointing a striped candy stick at her, "The U.S. Space Command, the Air Force—and our country—owe you an aircraft carrier-size thanks."

"I didn't do anything," Rae protested. "It was Caleb who pulled all the pieces together and figured it all out."

Everyone grinned indulgently at her. Rae gave up and sat gingerly in a chair J.W. held for her. Assorted bumps and bruises were singing an anvil chorus this morning, but she wasn't about to complain. She was alive, relatively sound—a miracle in anyone's terms.

"Can someone finally tell me the details?" she asked, her gaze moving shyly over the room. "I want to know. I think I *need* to know. For...closure?"

"Fill 'er in, Ramirez!" Admiral Vale ordered with a wicked grin. He winked at Rae. "Young woman, don't tell *anyone* a word of what you hear in this room, or I'll have to have you shot at dawn."

Rae swallowed a gasp of laughter, her gaze flying to Caleb.

"I've already threatened her with that one," he said, enlightening Admiral Vale. He dropped into the chair next to Rae's. "Sorry 'bout that, sir."

"Feel free to quote me anytime, son," the admiral quipped before leveling an unnervingly intense gaze upon Rae. "I reckon I won't worry over the matter as long as you're as staunch in your faith as Myers here is. Proceed, Mr. Ramirez."

Tray gave Rae an encouraging look. "Anything in particular you'd like to know first?"

"Mr. Fisher," Rae said without hesitation. "Is he... He's not—"

"He's alive and in custody," Tray promised. "We caught him at the airport—he's agreed to turn state's evidence. Larissa Holman, the woman who engineered your attempted murder, was his contact with IOS. Fisher was an easy enough mark for her to lure in, then trap. She used a combination of flattery and the promise of money followed by the inevitable blackmail and threats."

"A black widow spider," she observed with a shudder. The men exchanged quick grins, which Rae bore good-naturedly. "Did you catch her?"

Ramirez hesitated, glanced at Caleb, who nodded. Rae tensed, clenching her hands in her lap, and felt Caleb's close over hers.

"She's dead," Tray revealed flatly. "Car spun out of control in a high-speed chase down the freeway. She tried to exit where there wasn't one. Car flipped six times. She wasn't wearing a seat belt."

"Oh." Rae looked at the table. Larissa had been committing reprehensible acts of evil, but that was a terrible way to die.

"Rotten luck," Dennis Hoffman put in, then added callously, "means a dead end to tracking down IOS."

"Um...what about the other two men?" Rae asked after a moment. "The ones Larissa hired to— Well, what happened to those guys?"

"Grabowski's men were there first." Tray nodded to the detective, and he met Rae's carefully bland expression with a sour smile.

"They won't be going anywhere for a while," he assured her. "The one called Romo has a broken collarbone and a concussion. Jules broke both legs and a couple of ribs. Amazing, truth be told, that all three of you weren't killed, considering what that car looks like." He peered at Rae. "Did Myers tell you that Jules, the driver, is the reason you're relatively unscathed? You were pinned between him and the seat. His body protected you from the front, and the car seat from the rear."

Rae stared at him, then at Caleb. "How...ironic," she managed to say eventually. "Does he know?"

The detective shrugged. "Doubt it. They were both still unconscious when the ambulance took 'em off. If you like, I'll be sure to pass the information along, right after they're informed that they're to be tried for attempted murder."

"Among other things," Caleb murmured. He squeezed Rae's cold fingers.

"Were they from IOS?"

"Probably." Tray Ramirez took up the narrative again. "Neither one of them is talking right now. We'll find out, though. And—" this with a quick grin to Caleb "—within reason, we'll see that you're apprised. Fair enough, Myers?"

"Fair enough," Rae said tartly before Caleb could speak, and everyone laughed.

Agent Hoffman slid a piece of sheet music across the table. "You might be interested in that, Ms. Prescott."

It was the Mendelssohn. Rae freed her hands, then slowly flipped the cover open. A single sheet of paper with a few terse sentences typed across the middle covered the first page of music. "Your time has run out," Rae read aloud. "We require the rest of the program within seventy-two hours. Otherwise, no additional funds will be deposited in your account. Your association will be terminated. Permanently." Rae carefully laid the ominous paper down. She wanted to wash her hands all of a sudden. "Charming." She suppressed a shudder. "Was it meant for Mr. Fisher?"

Caleb nodded. "Sent him right over the edge. He'd been passing the Starseeker program a few lines at a time, remember?"

"I remember."

"IOS apparently got impatient," Tray continued. "Larissa Holman sensed everything closing in. She leaned on Fisher. So when he came into Joyful Noise the other day and *you* were so nervous, he was petrified that everything was about to go up in smoke."

"Everything did," Grabowski put in, very dryly. "Thanks to the courage of a woman who took a lot of abuse from a lot of different sources the past few months." He stretched his arm across the table. "Mostly from me. I'm eating my words, Ms. Prescott. And may I say that I'm relieved to have to do so?"

Coloring, Rae shook his hand. "You had cause. If it helps any, I've come to understand the difficulties *you* have to face, being constantly surrounded by liars and murderers and the like. Human beings at their worst. I was looking at my potential customers more as potential criminals myself!"

The magnanimous gesture had been difficult for her to make.

Then the harsh lines in Detective Grabowski's face softened, and for a fleeting moment gratitude and respect gleamed out of his eyes. It was enough. Rae ducked her head, her blush intensifying. But there was one more thing she had to do. A ghost she had to lay to rest once and for all.

Rae looked at Agent Ramirez. "Caleb has helped me understand that I'm not responsible for my father's actions. But I would like you to know that I'm sorry about all the trouble he's caused." She paused, struggling to keep her voice even. "If I have helped your investigation, I'm glad. I hope...I hope you'll be able to view the Prescott name in a *little* more charitable light."

The men looked uncomfortable, awkward. Tray cleared his throat. "I don't think that will be a problem."

In a graceful move Caleb rose to his feet, then tugged Rae to stand beside him. "Perhaps," he volunteered with a sideways smile at Rae, "this is as good a time as any to make an official announcement of another kind."

"Caleb!" Rae said out of the side of her mouth. "What are you *doing?* Timing. You need to think of your execrable timing..." She began to sputter as his grin widened. He turned her so that her back was to the room. His hands rested on her shoulders. "What about waiting on the Lord? What about God's perfect timing? What about letting God control your actions? Your—"

"What Rae's trying to confess in her own charming manner—" Caleb's honey-smooth, commanding voice easily overrode hers "—is that she likes *my* name a lot better than Prescott. Since I'm an honorable fellow, I offered to share it with her. On a permanent basis, of course." He kissed her indignation into blissful silence.

Laughter and good-natured heckling filled the room. Someone produced cups and a couple of cans of soft drinks. Amid congratulations, hugs and teasing kisses, Rae toasted her new fiancé—and spilled half the drink in her lap.

"Might as well get used to it." She giggled as Caleb resignedly helped mop up the mess. Rae dabbed the front of her blouse and skirt with paper towels, too happy to care about her habitual clumsiness.

"When's the big day?" Tray asked, a huge grin on his face.

"Haven't a clue," Rae began, at the same time Caleb announced, "As soon as possible."

She pressed a kiss to the corner of his mouth. "I *do* know what our processional's going to be," she informed the others. "Beethoven. The 'Ode to Joy.'"

"The one from his Fifth Symphony?" Caleb inquired teasingly.

"I thought the 'Ode to Joy' was from Beethoven's Ninth," Admiral Vale commented, his booming voice perplexed.

Fresh laughter erupted from everyone, and Rae threw her arms around Caleb. "Who cares?" She smiled at the circle of indulgent masculine faces. "We'll have them both!"

* * * * *

Dear Reader,

I started out writing *NIGHT MUSIC* as entertaining romantic suspense—which incidentally, I hope it proves to be! But somewhere along the way, Rae and Caleb took over, the struggles they face against the conspiracies of evil men broadened, until they were struggling with themselves and their faith as well. It's incredible to me how much God really does care about we fumbling, fallible humans. Even those who insist, like Rae, that He can "take care of the big things. I take care of my life."

Because Rae is a professional musician (and the author is sort of an amateur musician), song pervades *NIGHT MUSIC*, from Psalms to Beethoven and a whole lot in between. Caleb points Rae to Psalm 32:7…she plays a piano selection based on Psalm 27. Then there's Beethoven's *Ode To Joy*, which figures prominently in the plot.

Yet sometimes, even a writer who loves words has to concede that…there are no words to adequately convey the depth of God's unconditional love. But when I listen to a stirring rendition of Mozart's *Ein Kleine Nachtmusik*…or old hymns played on a hammered dulcimer and Autoharp, well…I feel God's loving presence. Actually, perhaps my hope for *NIGHT MUSIC* can best be summed up in a homily I read once: God gave us music, that we might pray without words.

May whatever songs you sing bring you closer to the joy of His presence.

Colossians 3:17

Sara Mitchell

P.S.
Beethoven's *Ode to Joy* is featured prominently in this story—by design. Twenty-seven years ago my husband and I chose it for our wedding processional!

WELCOME TO *Love Inspired* ™

A brand-new series of contemporary inspirational love stories.

Join men and women as they learn valuable lessons about facing the challenges of today's world and about life, love and faith.

Look for the following February 1998
Love Inspired™ titles:

A Groom of Her Own
by Irene Hannon

The Marriage Wish
by Dee Henderson

The Reluctant Bride
by Kathryn Alexander

Available in retail outlets
in January 1998.

LIFT YOUR SPIRITS AND GLADDEN YOUR HEART with *Love Inspired* ™!

Steeple
Hill™

LI298

This February,
Love Inspired
brings you three
heartwarming stories
celebrating the joys of marriage.

Irene Hannon
invites you to be a guest
at the wedding in the second book
of her VOWS series.
A GROOM OF HER OWN

Dee Henderson
offers a wonderful story about a
solitary man whose one and only
birthday wish is for a wife.
THE MARRIAGE WISH

Kathryn Alexander
brings two lonely people together
in an unforgettable story
about forgiveness.
THE RELUCTANT BRIDE

Celebrate the wonder of love
and family this month—
and every month—in

Love Inspired

Take 3 inspirational love stories FREE!
PLUS get a FREE surprise gift!

Special Limited-time Offer

Mail to Steeple Hill Reader Service™
3010 Walden Avenue
P.O. Box 1867
Buffalo, N.Y. 14240-1867

YES! Please send me 3 free Love Inspired™ novels and my free surprise gift. Then send me 3 brand-new novels every month, which I will receive months before they appear in bookstores. Bill me at the low price of $3.19 each plus 25¢ delivery and applicable sales tax, if any*. That's the complete price and a saving of over 10% off the cover prices—quite a bargain! I understand that accepting the books and gift places me under no obligation ever to buy any books. I can always return a shipment and cancel at any time. Even if I never buy another book from Steeple Hill, the 3 free books and the surprise gift are mine to keep forever.

103 IEN CFAG

Name	(PLEASE PRINT)	
Address		Apt. No.
City	State	Zip

This offer is limited to one order per household and not valid to present Love Inspired™ subscribers. *Terms and prices are subject to change without notice. Sales tax applicable in New York.

ULI-198   ©1997 Steeple Hill

Welcome to *Love Inspired*™

A brand-new series of contemporary inspirational love stories.

Join men and women as they learn valuable lessons about facing the challenges of today's world and about life, love and faith.

Look for the following April 1998 Love Inspired™ titles:

DECIDEDLY MARRIED
by Carole Gift Page

A HOPEFUL HEART
by Lois Richer

HOMECOMING
by Carolyne Aarsen

Available in retail outlets in March 1998.

LIFT YOUR SPIRITS AND GLADDEN YOUR HEART
with *Love Inspired!*™

Steeple
Hill™

LI498

Continuing in February from

 *Love Inspired*

VOWS

a series by
Irene Hannon

Don't miss this deeply emotional series
about three close friends....

*Each has a secret hidden in their past.
Each will experience the love of their own special
man. But will they be able to conquer the shadows
that still haunt them...and look to the
future with renewed faith?*

The series began in October with...
HOME FOR THE HOLIDAYS

And continues in February with...
A GROOM OF HER OWN

Samantha Reynolds had finally found love.
Reverend Brad Matthews offered her a chance to
make a new life for herself, and build her trust in
the Lord. But would Samantha ever be able to reveal
the tragedy in her past...without losing the man
she adored?

And look for the third book in the series...
A FAMILY TO CALL HER OWN, available in May
from *Love Inspired*

IVOWS2

Welcome to *Love Inspired* ™

A brand-new series of contemporary inspirational love stories.

Join men and women as they learn valuable lessons about facing the challenges of today's world and about life, love and faith.

Look for the following March 1998 Love Inspired™ titles:

CHILD OF HER HEART
by Irene Brand

A FATHER'S LOVE
by Cheryl Wolverton

WITH BABY IN MIND
by Arlene James

Available in retail outlets in February 1998.

LIFT YOUR SPIRITS AND GLADDEN YOUR HEART
with *Love Inspired!* ™

Steeple
Hill™

LI398

Beginning in January from
Love Inspired...

FAITH, HOPE & CHARITY

a new series by

LOIS RICHER

Meet Faith, Hope and Charity—three close friends who find joy in doing the Lord's work...and playing matchmaker to members of their families.

Delight in the wonderful romances that befall the unsuspecting townsfolk of this small North Dakota town.

Enjoy the surprise as these matchmaking ladies find romance is in store for each of them as well!

Don't miss any of the heartwarming and emotional stories.

FAITHFULLY YOURS
January '98

A HOPEFUL HEART
April '98

SWEET CHARITY
July '98

♥™ *Love Inspired*™

IFHC1

The lives and loves of the residents of Duncan, Oklahoma, continue to warm readers' hearts in this series from *Love Inspired*...

by
Arlene James

EVERYDAY MIRACLES

Every day brings new challenges for young Reverend Bolton Charles and his congregation. But together they are sure to gain the strength to overcome all obstacles—and find love along the way!

You've enjoyed these wonderful stories:

THE PERFECT WEDDING
(September 1997)

AN OLD-FASHIONED LOVE
(November 1997)

Now Reverend Bolton Charles gets a second chance at happiness in:

A WIFE WORTH WAITING FOR
(January 1998)

And a couple who marry for the sake of a child find unexpected love in:

WITH BABY IN MIND
(March 1998)

Love Inspired

IEM98-2